A Day at the Beach

Books by Helen Schulman

P.S.

THE REVISIONIST

OUT OF TIME

NOT A FREE SHOW

WANTING A CHILD
(COEDITED WITH JILL BIALOSKY)

A DAY AT THE BEACH

A DAY
at the
BEACH

Helen
Schulman

Houghton Mifflin Company

BOSTON   NEW YORK

2007

Visit our Web site: www.houghtonmifflinbooks.com.

Library of Congress Cataloging-in-Publication Data
Schulman, Helen.
A day at the beach / Helen Schulman.
p. cm.
ISBN-13: 978-0-618-74654-5
ISBN-10: 0-618-74654-4
1. September 11 Terrorist Attacks, 2001 — Fiction.
2. New York (N.Y.) — Fiction. 3. Hamptons (N.Y.) — Fiction.
I. Title.
PS3569.C5385D39 2007
813'.54—dc22   2006023704

Book design by Melissa Lotfy

PRINTED IN THE UNITED STATES OF AMERICA

QUM 10 9 8 7 6 5 4 3 2

To Zoe and Isaac,
and to Bruce, my centerpiece

A Day at the Beach

S HE YAWNED.
It was 8:30 A.M. The Falktopfs were sitting in the kitchen of their apartment in a pool of cool sunshine; it streamed in sideways through the old warehouse windows. Gerhard, Suzannah's husband, was already fuming on the phone with his lawyer, and the light, for some reason—perhaps because it was softened by a scrim of industrial grime—flattered his face as he seethed into the receiver, making fifty-five-year-old Gerhard look much younger than he was. That or he wore his rage well. He seemed surprisingly handsome for someone that unhappy, Suzannah thought. He'd been on the phone just about an hour, but he'd been fuming since he'd woken at five.

"*I* was up at five." Gerhard's words curled out from between his teeth right into the handset. He was trying to contain his anger. She was proud of him for this, so Suzannah lightly laid her hand on the back of his neck, on her way over to the counter to pour more coffee. At the sense of her touch, Gerhard looked up from beneath his thick silver brows, pursing his lips and sending her a silent, distracted kiss.

5:00 A.M. For once, Gerhard had been up before Nikolai. Usually it was Suzannah who got up with the kid, allowing

Gerhard to sleep in. To what? A nice, crisp, productive 6:30. But this morning Gerhard had been up before daybreak, rattling around their bedroom, turning on his bedside lamp, rereading yesterday's paper, because 5:00 was too early for *this* angry phone call, too early even for the arrival of the morning edition of the *Times*. In the tumbling juncture between sleep and wakefulness, Suzannah had half-listened as he'd walked over to her desk and rummaged noisily through her stuff, looking for — what? Unpaid bills? Something juicier? Perhaps he was nervous about this day for the same reasons she was.

No. It had fast become disappointingly clear that the reason that Gerhard was up at daybreak on this fall morning was that he was once again on the hunt for some notepaper so he could resume the endless cycle of writing and crumpling his searing, accusatory letters, and sighing so loudly as he performed this fruitless task that Suzannah had been forced to open her eyes and lie quietly in bed: Gerhard's audience.

Gerhard did not want to talk, at least not to her, not then — let's face it, he'd already talked her ears off. Shingshang, he wanted to talk to. His lawyer. Suzannah understood this. Gerhard had wanted only not-to-be-awake-and-alone in the apartment. He'd required existential, nonparticipatory company. Silent support. This much was obvious. They'd been married thirteen years.

So once the precious little sleep that was allotted to her — in spare, nightly dollops, it felt, since Nikolai's birth — had been stolen, Suzannah had stared silently at the flaking pale, pale lavender ceiling, a calming, dopey hue, wondering idly if they'd ever have enough money to replaster, until the thundering hooves of Nikolai's little feet were heard at a quarter to six as he barreled down the hall from his room. It was when Nikolai dove into their bed headfirst that she felt free to exercise her voice.

"Good morning, angel potpie," she said to Nikolai.

Nikolai. Gerhard and Suzannah Falktopf, a German by birth married to a Polish Jew from the Bronx, had conspired to award their lone offspring a Russian given name, not as some bizarre historical joke—ha ha ha, Suzannah often felt inclined to add —but solely because they liked the sound of it. *Ni-ko-lai.* It had a lilt and lift to it, the first and third syllables were practically winged; it was the secret, "true" name of a butterfly, Suzannah had often thought privately, all those charmed months when she was pregnant and dreaming about the baby within, already head-over-heels in love with him.

He proceeded to rest in child's pose—head down, butt up—on their bed. Suzannah patted his rump, which, packaged in a pull-up and pajamas, was the size and consistency of a small life preserver. On the bulletin board above her desk, Suzannah had tacked up a cartoon she'd torn from *The New Yorker* several weeks earlier. It was a drawing of a baby in a diaper standing in front of a three-way mirror, craning his head to see his own derrière. The caption read: "Does my butt look fat?" It had resided on the fridge for a nanosecond before Gerhard tore it down. Cutesy, unframed, ripped not snipped—it offended his sensibilities. Suzannah's desk and its environs were off-limits to such aesthetic demands—thank God.

Gerhard had been up since 5:00, proclaiming at 6:45 to his wife and child with a smirk that as far as he and farmers everywhere were concerned, the business day had just officially commenced. There was a boyishness to Gerhard, even now, a Dennis the Menace quality—and the image of Gerhard as a farmer had forced Suzannah to smile and hand the phone over to him, against her better judgment. She'd had such high hopes for this day. Gerhard all riled up was not the way to start. But clearly, Suzannah had no choice in the matter.

He had only managed to reach Shingshang, his lawyer, on his cell phone around 7:30-ish. By that time, Suzannah was sure, he'd risked a major case of carpal tunnel syndrome—Gerhard abhorred speed-dial; for all his pragmatism he was, peculiarly, a technophobe — so there must have been something oddly satisfying about punching in again and again those same eleven digits or he simply wouldn't have continued doing so.

To save herself from the Chinese water torture of the sound of Gerhard's fingers on the keypad (was it racist to say "Chinese" water torture? Suzannah wondered; was it racist even just to think the phrase when talking to oneself?) Suzannah herded her family into the kitchen for breakfast, which she fixed. Celine, the gorgeous twenty-one-year-old French African au pair, all endless legs and arms gift-wrapped in satiny skin the deep purple-black of an eggplant, didn't "do" food really. She would most likely sleep in until noon, tucked away in the little back bedroom that pre-kid used to be the Falktopfs' storage closet.

Le petit déjeuner. Puffed O's and organic milk for the baby. "Luckies," as in Charms, for Gerhard. With a splash of one percent. Plus fresh raspberries airlifted in from some country where the migrant farmer who'd picked them was probably paid slave wages and had little or no sanitation, no proper place to pee — Suzannah didn't like to think about it. She had arranged their bowls, soft-boiled a couple of duck eggs for Gerhard — the yolks were more orange and more viscous than chicken eggs; he liked them that way — and set them upright in two little silver egg cups with matching demi-spoons in the hope that these tiny, exacting pleasures would provide him some modicum of comfort. Push come to shove, Gerhard favored intensity. Fassbinder, Lever House, *A Love Supreme*, Lichtenstein, sea salt.

The duck eggs were sold at the Union Square Farmers' Market, Quattro Farms, as were the artisanal loaves of bread that Suzannah cut into dunking strips. It was the small things that mattered, her mother always said, between a man and a woman. A little extra effort could keep a husband happy. Gerhard would decapitate the eggs with one smooth motion of his

4

knife and then chop up the yolk and white very finely within the shell with the demi-spoon, sprinkling in enough salt to make a paste before dipping in the long, thin fingers of bread. Suzannah made Gerhard his espresso doppio long, as was his preference, from the Capresso C3000 she'd maxed out her Amex on for his last birthday. Suzannah preferred an IV of caffeine, herself. All morning. French press. At home, she had her coffee black, no sugar. Out in the world, she liked her leche frothy.

Gerhard had reached his lawyer right after the first egg slid down. The second sat fat and white and shiny, its shell intact, smug in its elegant cup. Suzannah assumed it was now cool to the touch.

"Say, Shingshang, are you sleeping on the job?"

Gerhard's tone as he spoke into the phone was jokey, either mocking or self-mocking—which? At this point, who had the energy to parse it out? The day hadn't even begun yet. Even as week after week she was growing almost used to Gerhard's constant seething, Suzannah found it increasingly too painful to bear. She turned her attention to Nikolai, who was playing trains and humming that high buzzing hum of his in the corner by the range and the fridge, lost in his own private Shining Time. She took a sip of her coffee in the pretty ceramic cup from the service Gerhard had brought back after the company's last tour—was it Portugal? She and Nikolai had stayed home. The colors of the flowers were so vibrant, reds and greens, and there was a tangle of blue vines winding around the cup's stubby but surprisingly graceful form—it squatted on its own little puddle of a saucer as if it were sitting in *grande plié*. Upon examination now, the stenciling on the enamel appeared as a veined, living entity, the flowers' black pupils nearly dilating, making her wince. The cup was an uncharacteristically folk-arty gift from Gerhard, who preferred sleek, modern lines, and so it had aroused some nonspecific suspicions in Suzannah at the time

5

(six months ago it must have been) because there was something warm and fuzzy about it; as presents go it was affectionate.

Passionate, Gerhard was; affectionate, not.

Now placing the cup down carefully on the countertop so as not to crack it, Suzannah wondered idly if Gerhard had somehow sensed the trouble to come and was preparing her for it by giving her this gift; the act itself was both needy and demonstrative. Neither adjective, to Suzannah's knowledge, had ever been used to describe her husband before. Each piece of pottery had come swathed in tissue paper, like a lily on a lily pad, sitting on its own petaled plate, and Gerhard had petted her arm as she'd unwrapped them. Hmmm.

None of that mattered now, the trouble had come and neither husband nor wife had been prepared for it; Gerhard had lost the company, *his* dance company, and then what? This defeat, *this* robbery, was rapidly becoming part of the fabric of their lives, a stain, a stain on the immaculate, allergic-to-failure, incredibly resilient, and crafty Gerhard. But they'd go on, wouldn't they? He'd figure it out; he'd always figured things out for them before. Up until now, Gerhard had managed it all — the company, her career, their home — he'd managed it all for both of them. They'd survive; she was sure of it. It had already been five and a half weeks . . .

Perhaps human beings can get used to anything, Suzannah mused, once the shock of the new is over, even a grinding, painful reality can come to feel normal. Sooner or later, she hoped, Gerhard's mood would improve, he'd take positive action, and they could move on, to what, something new and yet to be invented. Why not? That's what life was. An unstoppable force if you bothered to pass the baton. Gerhard would grieve. He'd either win back the company or get a settlement, or start something new. Be a competitor? Retire? Not Gerhard.

It was much too early to tell.

Suzannah leaned back on the barstool. She looked over at her husband, still yammering away on the phone. Gerhard, a guest choreographer? A gun for hire? Thinking of the paltry commissions, now with Manhattan preschool tuition to pay for, gave her vertigo. Today was Nikolai's very first day of school. Back in March, seven preschools had turned him down. Seven sets of applications, seven application fees, seven school tours, seven parent and child interviews. (Just dragging Gerhard out of the studio in the middle of the day had felt like a full-time job!) It was Shingshang who pulled the strings. One of his clients was on the Board of Directors of St. Luke's. On June 13th, she'd gotten the phone call that had allowed Suzannah, finally, after so many months, to breathe. St. Luke's was willing to take Nikolai for the fall, provided that he start out at half a day, three mornings a week. It was even okay with them that he was still in diapers.

And now finally, today was the day: an hour-long meet-and-greet with Nikolai's preschool teachers that was scheduled for 10:00 A.M. Once Suzannah attended to herself, then dressed Nikolai, she'd have to pry Gerhard away from both the telephone receiver and his malaise so that he could shower and dress and they could make a unified and concerned, yet witty, impression. Successful downtown, arty parents who put their child first. Faded black jeans, great glasses, self-deprecating humor that somehow elevated their status, a lot of "good job, bud"s directed volubly at Nikolai. That type of stuff. On the walk over, she'd do her best to cheerfully remind Gerhard of the particulars of his role.

Suzannah had been sweating this day all summer—that is, since she'd almost immediately moved on from the relief of Nikolai's acceptance—at once both apprehensive and thrilled about the prospect of her one and only beginning a life out of her reach and sight. Could it be that in a group of his peers, with warm and loving teachers bringing out the best in him (after the hell of that grueling application process), her confidence in her kid would be restored?

From her perch at the breakfast bar, Suzannah watched Nikolai closely. He was playing Thomas the Tank Engine versus the Naughty Diesel, and humming. Lots of boys played with trains. Nothing unusual about that.

Once the nervous-making school visit was behind them, they'd get a cookie and a coffee, and if they still couldn't jolly Gerhard up, they could dump him! Nikolai and Suzannah would be free to restart their day. Alone together—no longer under scrutiny—they'd end up in the playground for sure; she'd arranged for a little lunch date with Zack F. and Zak H. and their mothers by the sprinklers, but first Suzannah and her boy would head to the local public school to cast their ballot for mayor. She still wasn't so sure . . . was it the billionaire or the asshole who deserved her vote? Suzannah was excited to take Nikolai into the little draped booth—let him decide! She was looking forward to explaining the process: "In this country, we elect our leaders," when of course this old saw was no longer entirely true, the last presidential election having proven that axiom antiquated. It was reassuring to go over the day this way in her head. She wanted so much for it to be memorable.

It was time to get going. Over the breakfast bar, she gave Gerhard the high sign that she wanted to go down the hall to bathe. Could he watch the kid?

"*Per favore*, Gerhardy."

Gerhard nodded his head over the receiver. He was nodding his head yes. So Suzannah slipped off the chrome stool, quietly, not wanting to disturb Nikolai, for he was still playing intently, and she was hoping to sneak away from the open-air kitchen—"the module," as she'd long ago termed it—without Nikolai noting her absence. Nikolai had this thing about having Suzannah in the room; he liked to be with her—which was perfectly normal at his age, Suzannah would explain, with a bemused and studied nonchalance, to visitors or new babysitters, when Nikolai clung to her knees, caterwauling, his little face broken, wet with tears, slimy with mucus, whenever she tried to leave the house. Nikolai's aching, naked need for her was both revelatory and a royal pain in the ass.

House arrest was to motherhood what vulnerability was to romantic love. The downside. Bring on the SAT analogies, thought Suzannah. She was thirty-six and out of the studio — she could pass those stupid tests now!

Suzannah pulled down her sleeping T-shirt — it barely covered her bikini bottoms — and began to tiptoe away from the module and through the wreckage of her apartment. Foam blocks, finger-paints, books and shoes and toy trains and cars. Who cared about the disarray (except Gerhard!), the exposed pipes, the painted but still crumbling walls — it was a perfectly fine environment for a child. Did Nikolai even really need to go to school? Couldn't she provide everything he required here, at home, with her? He was barely four. Oh, those butterflies in her stomach. She wished it were not 8:30 in the morning and she could legitimately pour herself a gin and tonic!

Suzannah was just twenty-one when Gerhard first brought her back to this apartment. There were only two other inhabitants in the building at the time, a sculptor and a hat designer — the rest was factory and storage space. Back then she'd been taken with the building's rough-edged, industrial charm. Childless, unmarried Gerhard had collected art: stuff produced by his set designers, his friends' work, things he picked up at open studios. (Art long ago sold to bail out the company. He'd even unloaded his favorite — a Robert Ryman, white, white, white! — a few years before, although they were still clinging to the lone Agnes Martin, which hung in Gerhard's office, because of how goddamned beautiful it was.) Between the cement floors and the ratty hallways and all that art, Suzannah had been intimidated. As soon as Gerhard handed her a drink, Suzannah had tossed back the cocktail and immediately felt drunk, and then she'd tossed back her hair, which had hung halfway down her back in inky black ringlets—"Zoozie's pre-Raphaelite stage," Gerhard said a little acidly, whenever they looked at the old photos—and she'd sputtered out: "This isn't a room, it's a module."

Even now, the memory made her cringe. The comment was so clumsy and adolescent—but the kitchen, a walled-off island (Gerhard built it himself) did have a free-floating modular quality. Very *Lost In Space.*

It was Gerhard who had encouraged Suzannah to cut off her hair. She reached up her right palm now to touch it—it was piled up in a little ponytail on top of her head. His indispensable movement theory put into domestic practice. Remove the indispensable movement, music, performer, gesture from a dance he was choreographing, and he would know the true strength and weight of his piece in progress.

"If you don't cut it off," said Gerhard at the time, "eventually it will be all anybody sees. You will be reduced to a head of hair."

Suzannah had listened to him—she always listened to him—and immediately went out and got a crewcut. On Astor Place. The punks and motorcycle guys and the Wall Streeters all staring open-mouthed as Tony the barber took the clippers to her scalp, Suzannah's black mane falling to the linoleum in long ropes. It had surprised her, once she'd dared to look in the mirror, how oddly small her head was, surfacing from beneath the heavy drapery of those tresses, her eyes and ears large and twitching like a baby fawn's. It had been, honestly, a little like birth. An emergence of sorts. For years after, that was the way Suzannah wore her hair. Gerhard Falktopf had ordained it. A short little black lawn. Like a lesbian. Until Nikolai, when everything loosened up, her curls included, because they had to. But sometimes, even now, in this very moment, while actively trying to avoid her anticipation and fears about preschool, (how ridiculous, Suzannah told herself, it's *preschool*!) when she was anxious, she'd run her fingers through her phantom hair, expecting, well, more of it.

Gerhard Falktopf.

Suzannah turned back to look at the handsome gray-haired man who was now sputtering and fuming on the telephone in the module; the man who had nodded yes, he would watch the kid, their kid; the man who against all odds had become her husband. She'd been in love with him since forever it seemed; she was in love with him since even before she'd met him. And in the beginning, she'd thought about him not simply as Gerhard but only as the compound: Gerhard Falktopf. *The* Gerhard Falktopf. For years to come, Suzannah referred to him this way not just in her own mind but also in conversation, initially as a point of deference, with downcast eyes: "Yes, I'm working/seeing/living with Gerhard Falktopf," because she could hardly believe it herself. Little Suzannah Sucher from Riverdale, the Bronx—all those red brick cookie-cutter buildings, the apartments a warren of small, rectangular rooms, coveted luxury manifested in a neighbor's white terrace too tiny for a table *and* chairs—dancing, dating, sharing the same toothpaste with the great Gerhard Falktopf. Later, after years of seeing Gerhard lying on the couch in his underwear, hearing his morning fart blurting like a trumpet when he entered into the bathroom to pee —intimacy breeding contempt of course, *who'd a thunk it!* — she used his proper and surnames in conjunction in an effort to charm.

"Gerhard Falktopf had to jerk off in this little closet at the doctors; they supplied the magazines. FYI: There are pictures of buxom twins in dirndl minis at Cornell Hospital. They saw us coming."

She'd tried so hard to be amusing about their infertility. To keep it light, in an attempt to sneak all the cost and effort by him.

"It has become painfully obvious to me," Gerhard would remark dryly, over a glass of wine at some stupid fundraiser or other, "that *I* am the child I am destined to raise."

Ironic then that he'd managed to impregnate just about every woman he'd ever dated, except for Suzannah, and then convinced one after the other to get an abortion. The problem with conceiving had been hers, hers alone. All those years of dieting, living on air . . . now barrenness and, more likely than not, osteoporosis down the road. Ironic again, that Suzannah had wanted children so desperately she'd practically forced him into that hospital closet at gunpoint.

"Get it up, Gerhard," she'd gibe, her hands in a stick-'em-up position, in an effort to entertain him, but the truth was she might have left him if he hadn't. Who would have been his muse then?

Now Suzannah opened the door to the linen closet to get a towel for her shower. Gerhard had stacked them by color (darker hues on the bottom, lighter on top) and by size — this was so, so Gerhard. Suzannah would have thrown them on any old shelf haphazardly — it was a wonder that the two of them managed to stay married. She rose onto her toes, causing a nice, popping stretch to percolate up her spine, and brought down two bathsheets, one for her body and one for her missing hair, and a washcloth, all the color of picholine olives (Gerhard again). With the stack of towels in her arms, Suzannah closed the door to the closet with her foot, causing one side of her panty, as always, to creep annoyingly up her butt. So she balanced the towels in one hand and with the other slipped a thumb in the elastic to free it, snapping the leg back into place.

"You're snoring, Shingshang, I can hear you." Gerhard's phone voice was now definitively mocking; she could hear him all the way down the hall. "Hee-haw, hee-haw," Gerhard snorted into the receiver.

"People like Shingshang don't sleep," Suzannah muttered. It

was true; they didn't need sleep. They wheeled and dealt till all hours then went to dinner, to parties, to dinner parties. They worked at home throughout the night, sitting up in club chairs next to their marital beds, reviewing documents and channel-surfing the foreign markets while some wife's streaked hair fanned out behind her slumbering head. Had he been giving his still-sleeping IVF-induced twins, Owen and Olivia, or was it Sammy and Pammy? — Suzannah could never remember, the children had been named either something alliterative or something rhymey — a pat on the head, silently wishing them a good first day of school, when Gerhard began dialing? (Patti Shingshang and Suzannah had at one point shared the same infertility specialist. They'd stumbled upon this salient and embarrassing fact at a Christmas gala, recognizing one another, even without the tears, from the Park Avenue waiting room.)

Was Shingshang already in the Lexus, negotiating downtown Greenwich, swigging his extra-oxygenated water, turning on the phone, opening up for business, by the time Gerhard's forefinger had reddened and calloused from hitting the touch-tone dial pad? Of course he was. He had been putting off dealing with Gerhard, and clients like him, for as long as possible. Gerhard, with his German accent intensifying inside his fury, Gerhard with his little italicized "I" — "*I* have been up since five" — as if he were the only person in pain here. Gerhard presenting his insomnia as irrefutable evidence of the damage that was done him, compensational damage as it were.

Although there must be some money in this, Suzannah thought. There has got to be money in this.

Suzannah stepped down the hall to the open door of the bathroom.

Gerhard's nod had said yes when Suzannah had asked him to watch the kid. Mostly he left the boy up to her, but here in the midst of his ranting, Gerhard was willing to allow Suzannah a stolen private moment, a shower, where she could be alone, the water pounding down her back, her neck, her hands rising up toward the hot spray in the prayer pose, reaching for the showerhead, the escalating temperature traveling into her body through the tributaries of her fingers—she could almost taste the heat, the privacy. Ordinarily, Nikolai cleaved to her. He even put his face on her lap when she was on the toilet to pee. It was a rare waking second without Nikolai there to fill it.

Gerhard, her husband, was willing to grant her the extravagance of solitude. For this, for a moment, he had her undying love.

But halfway into the bathroom, Suzannah found herself turning on her heels and rushing back toward the module, she felt the need to clarify the gesture, the way she might return from halfway down the block to her apartment just to make sure that she'd really turned off the stove; had Gerhard meant yes? Who could tell, Gerhard was seething so. He was nodding over the receiver in that rhythmical way, as if in prayer, as if he were davening; it was almost comical. Gerhard davening. He could have been nodding yes, or davening, or rocking to the rhythm of his own anger. Perhaps too much time had elapsed since she'd first asked him; perhaps Gerhard had forgotten her request? Nikolai could not be left unattended. Who knew what he'd do? Stick a fork in a light socket, swallow something hallucinatory; he'd committed both of these suicidal acts before, using Suzannah's mother's silver and the hash brownies Gerhard had baked as a gift for a rival choreographer. That had come up with Ipecac. Her little boy, daring her. Suzannah craved clarity in matters relating to Nikolai.

Nikolai must have sensed his opening when Suzannah peeked back into the module, for suddenly he was screeching, that high, horrific screech—"like an air-raid siren," Gerhard said whenever Nikolai let forth, Gerhard's fingers rising to his ears. It was unbearable. Nikolai was screeching and holding out his arms to her, and a quick glance at Gerhard verified that the sound was enough to push him over the edge—her husband's face was crimson and his head looked like it was about to shoot off his neck. So Suzannah gestured to the boy, "Come, come, cookie-puss, come, come, darling," and he ran screeching to her, his handsome little face a red, wrinkled miniature of his father's.

She squatted low and hugged Nikolai hard, her hands compressing his shoulder joints, her knees his hip bones, as some busybody mother from the playground had demonstrated on her own impossibly demented child, until Nikolai calmed down enough to grab onto the back of Suzannah's nightshirt, fistfuls of it, and follow her down the hall. He followed Suzannah so closely that his little head kept bumping into her bottom, his tears wetting the back of her panties; by the time they arrived at the bathroom Gerhard had installed himself, the cotton had soaked through and stuck to the skin of her butt.

He would not disentangle from his mother, Nikolai Samuel Falktopf, Suzannah Sucher's one and only, her sweet boy. He followed her like a little kite tail. So Suzannah had no choice but to include him in her morning ablutions once she entered the blue-tiled bathroom and reached into the shower stall, coaxing the temperature exactly as it should be, not too hot, not too cold, but baby-bear just right, once she'd adjusted the various showerheads by employing a wrench they left in the bathroom for just this purpose—they'd run out of money mid-renovation, and eventually the old handle had broken off. Because they were dancers, and the shower was deemed by Gerhard and his wily accountant to be therapeutic, they'd embarked on the project as a tax write-off. Like the 150 square feet of "office space," cordoned off the living room by a small Shoji screen, home to the Agnes Martin. Thank God, Gerhard had come to New York when he did, circa thirty-five years ago, when industrial footage was still cheap, when he bartered master classes for contracting work, when some male dancers still earned their keep by carpentry instead of modeling, or worse.

By the time Suzannah moved in, three other women had already moved in and out, and the whole apartment had been converted into livable space. In this real estate market you could probably term it a loft. They had a shower where the jets shot water from all sides, massaging the muscles, allowing a dancer to pretend that the physical pain that was part and parcel to the profession and omnipresent in every other moment of waking life had actually ceased, and that he or she were cured, or better yet, young again.

The landlord was dying to get them out. If he ever succeeded, Suzannah was unsure what would become of them. In debt as they were, there was no hope of obtaining a mortgage. They'd gotten this far on smoke and mirrors, the generosity of their patrons, talent, energy, Gerhard's charisma, the wingspan of her youthful *à la seconde*. What would middle age and the loss of the company do to that equation?

Suzannah stripped Nikolai of his pajamas — Nikolai, who was calm now and blinking prettily, his eyes as clear and empty as if the storm that just passed had washed the morning sky — and undid the diaper. From habit she admired the sculptural beauty of his thighs, so cut, like an Angel Corella or Baryshnikov in his prime, his small, high rump, his graceful little penis; he could have been carved from marble. She beheld his physical beauty the way someone with a beachside home might look daily upon the ocean: a constant marveling at its powers, but a marveling that became part of one's routine. Breakfast, a slow walk down the drive to collect the morning papers, awe.

Once Nikolai was properly disrobed and she herself had shed her T-shirt, peeled off and stepped out of her panties, Suzannah entered the shower. Then she brought the kid in with her, stepping into the jet stream first. Her theory: if anyone were to be scalded, by all rights it should be the mother. Just in case the temperature of the water rose of its own volition. This was suddenly the nexus of Suzannah's fears. She was afraid of water growing inexplicably hot because it wanted to. But it didn't. Mother and son were safely ensconced behind the Plexiglas shower door, the temperature uniform and just fine, the water cascading out and down, surrounding them.

♂

DOWNSTAIRS, Gerhard Falktopf was on the phone with his lawyer. He'd been talking with him for about an hour. Gerhard had made the commute with his attorney from Connecticut on the cell phone, accompanying Shingshang on the Merritt and down the West Side Highway, taking note as Shingshang left the keys to his car with some parking attendant at a garage, waiting impatiently as Shingshang said hello to an acquaintance in an elevator. Shingshang had a breakfast meeting, but he wasn't about to cut off Gerhard Falktopf until the decaf two percent latte was plunked down in front of him and/or his appointment had arrived. That's what he said to Gerhard, he said: "You've got me till the latte." It was his endurance and focus that made Shingshang so beloved by his clients. That, and the durability of their time-honored partnership: Shingshang had been representing Gerhard since Gerhard first incorporated. He was an animal, Shingshang, but he was also a balletomane. In that one ardent chamber of his scheming heart, he was at risk, vulnerable to Gerhard's gifts. He also kept putting his hand over the receiver, while Gerhard was talking to him. Which was infuriating.

"Shingshang! Shingshang! Flirting with your waitress is not a legitimate billable hour!" The receiver gave off only the muffled sounds of a gagged prisoner. Who knew what secrets and lies Shingshang was putting forth past the shield of his palm?

Gerhard was enraged. He was ready to hang up.

But he did not.

He was an angry man. But he was not a fool.

For one, there was the pro bono, "consignmenty" (Suzannah's term) nature of their alliance, an alliance that was not, and had never before been, documented by any formal agreement, nothing on paper, both Gerhard and Shingshang preferring it that way—Shingshang out of some sheer slippery snakelike intelligence, Gerhard supposed, Gerhard because he mistrusted anything that required the bind of his signature.

"I am formerly German," Gerhard would say with a flip of a hand, as if to brush aside any question of his compliance.

Culpability was not exactly his thing, which his wife liked to attest was another product of his discarded roots. He was German and not-German, said Suzannah, whenever such depictions most suited him, which was, Suzannah insisted, a kind of chilly practicality that was wholly German in its essence.

What husband and wife could agree upon was that Gerhard had been in New York such a sustained period of time—since he was seventeen—that the city itself had become his only country. It no longer seemed possible that he could live elsewhere. Why should he? Why, when there was the stimulation of a metropolis full of artists and the deep pockets of those who appreciated them. The restaurants, dim sum, bookstores, the Museum of Modern Art, the fact that he could walk out his door and go hear live jazz every night of the week, stylish women, fashion, transvestites, the subway, Film Forum, and now good coffee; before, that had been the sticking point, all that melted brown crayon water in those blue-and-white take-out Greek coffee shop cups—gone gone gone, replaced by espresso, drinkable but imperfect, on every corner, a perfect demitasse attainable only at San Ambroeus on the Upper East Side, worth the trip. Still, of course, the nation of his birth had forever leached into Gerhard's blood.

He'd left Germany in '63, right after Hoechst Pharmaceuticals, his father's employer, built the Jahrhunderthalle, an exhibition hall, in the small town just outside Frankfurt where Gerhard had grown up, Höchst en Main. The city might as well have been a thousand miles away—Gerhard's childhood couldn't have been more crabbed and routine; he was motherless and deprived, and ran the basic hamster wheel of school and chores for boys his age until he rebelled. The Jahrhunderthalle was pure public relations penance for Hoechst's prior use of slave labor, Gerhard asserted, even after his father, a chemist and a company man, slapped him across the face for the impudence of his remarks. Gerhard had been flirting with the life of a career criminal—rejoicing in the success of a couple of minor break-ins—when his father forced him to grace the hall with his presence at a performance of the Hamburg Ballet as an expression of familial allegiance to Hoechst Pharmaceuticals.

Papa used his belt when Gerhard expressed his desire to become what he'd just witnessed, "a human bird in flight," as he'd told *Dance* magazine in 1981, for his first profile. The belt episode was exactly what Gerhard was after, a reason to sever his relationship with his father. Gerhard left Germany with money he stole from a metal strongbox in his father's desk drawer. In New York, Gerhard first took open classes at ABT, working the front desk in exchange for tuition, and sleeping most nights in the male changing room, and then quickly he found himself on fellowship and living in a dormitory with six other aspiring danseurs. They never spoke again, Gerhard and his father. Indeed Gerhard hardly ever thought of his father, except to wonder idly, from time to time, if a) he were dead, and b) if not, did he still live in that same ugly little apartment Gerhard had so despised?

Had he ever learned of what had become of his son? Did Papa know of his success? Gerhard had to admit, he'd wondered. Especially when presented with the six Bessies of his career, his Isadora Duncan Award, the Dance Spirit Medal of

Honor, etc., etc. Gerhard supposed there would be no reason that his father would have kept up with the American avant-garde dance scene, a tiny arena Gerhard had to admit, even for the cognoscenti. Papa's specialty at Hoechst Pharmaceuticals had been fertilizers.

All that remained for Gerhard of his previous life was his accent—that is, when it served or pleased him—and his arrogance. It was this arrogance that kept him from signing contracts, from formalizing agreements. Hence the wiggly nature of his association with his attorney. There were many years when Shingshang was recompensed solely with tickets and invitations to cool parties.

But with this newest wrinkle—the fact that Gerhard had been ousted as director from his own company, *his own company*, by some evil and wealthy idiots who over the years had finagled their way onto the board for status' sake, as a fashion statement—the relationship with Shingshang grew more and more complex. Gerhard had been too busy working, choreographing modern masterpieces and running the whole complex enterprise, to vet them fully, these newer board members—the character of their souls, their artistic sensibilities and sensitivities, whether they were assholes or not. At some point Elspeth, his major patron, had started overseeing bookings and funding, which left Gerhard with rehearsals, schedules, personalities; just the dancers alone with their schedules and personalities were enough to fill up every minute of every hour. Elspeth had insisted, and rightly so Gerhard supposed at the time, that the company needed the money.

So he'd added them on, one by one, Grubberman and Spicer and Huntwall, the bankers and the traders with their nouveau Gatsbyesque gestures and extravagances and their Botoxed wives, under Elspeth's prodding, until traitorously she'd up and died in her sleep last April at the precipitous age of sixty-nine. Sixty-nine and without a will. All that money and no will. At present, her various children from her various marriages were suing the shit out of each other, tying up the capital in probate. Elspeth's unmitigated devotion to the company was recognized only by the youngest of them anyway, Angus, and he a feckless cokehead, eternally in and out of rehab. Not a lot of hope for monetary support from that corner . . . Well, the point being that a financial agreement between Gerhard and Shingshang had never even been verbally ratified.

Gerhard wasn't quite sure how and when Shingshang expected remuneration for his time — which now, for the first stretch in all their years together, was proving quite considerable. Before he'd basically consulted Shingshang on insurance, liability, taxes, the lease on a studio, a cancelled tour, that sort of thing. Plainly, Gerhard wasn't certain if all of this present action gab gab gab and strategizing was on contingency and what that would mean for him ultimately. Percentage-wise. (Suzannah had asked him this and he'd waved her off, but the question stuck, as well as the phraseology: "percentage-wise.") He wasn't quite sure if Shingshang would expect payment whether they persevered or not. He wasn't sure if Shingshang expected payment via Gerhard's beloved Agnes Martin, which was all he had on hand, right at the moment, to pay him off with. That, and the lease on his apartment. He could sell the lease back to the landlord, but then where would they live? His personal debt, now so tied into the company's, was, if he bothered to think about it — and Gerhard had spent a considerable amount of time bothering to not-think about it — pretty staggering. For so long the company had been such an extension of Gerhard's very self that he had not paused before writing checks to benefit either one of them. Of course, there had always been Elspeth to back them up.

Gerhard didn't want to rock the boat by hanging up on Shingshang, although playing the diva had only enhanced Gerhard's standing with Shingshang in the past.

Things had changed. And were changing still as Gerhard waited for Shingshang to return his attentions to him. The whole world was changing while Gerhard waited.

"An egg-white omelet, fresh orange, no, fresh grapefruit, do you hand-squeeze your juice?" Shingshang was ordering breakfast.

"Earth to Shingshang," said Gerhard. He sipped his espresso, which had cooled, and placed the cup down on the counter. "Do I or do I not have any hope of regaining control of my company?"

There was a pause, which Gerhard did not like. When Shingshang spoke, he spoke in a tone that Gerhard also was not keen on. It was soft, and the speech itself seemed stripped down to its quintessence. Shingshang was simplifying for Gerhard Falktopf—no one simplified for Gerhard!—and he was delivering the simplified news with a gentleness that belied the noxiousness of its contents.

"Gerhard," said Shingshang, "these jokers are playing harder ball than I anticipated. At this point, the most salient issue is maintaining the rights to your dances. The dances have to be fixed, that is, notated or filmed with the proper copyright notices, and they haven't all been videotaped, have they? *Day at the Beach*, has it even premiered?"

Shingshang was playing stupid; that or he'd stopped paying attention, which was a terrible sign, a sign of treachery, of fleeting affections.

"What are you talking about?" said Gerhard. "I don't own my own work?"

He slid off the stool at the counter and then, for no apparent reason at all, sat back down again. He hadn't shaved yet, and so he stroked his stubbled jaw. This grounded him, the stroking kept him aware of his body, his beingness, the sandpaper of his face kept Gerhard from railing, at Shingshang, at the world, although when he looked down at his feet in their sheepskin slippers, he saw the rogue nerve in his left leg was pulsing wildly. Nothing mattered more to Gerhard than *Day at the Beach*.

"You know it hasn't premiered, Shingshang. They cut my balls off before the premiere, they cut my balls off before I could even finish orchestrating the last three movements. You know that, Shingshang. Do not insult me."

Gerhard had started working on the damn thing almost two years before. He'd been listening a lot to the Beatles back then; his girlfriend Yuki played them incessantly in her East Village apartment. She'd bop around in an old Kiss T-shirt and striped panties, her glossy black hair cut short and bleached white within an inch of her roots — she was young and adorable, adorable! — and after watching her romp that way (she was a classically trained ballerina; she'd studied at Ana's School of Dance in Tokyo and then the Royal Ballet of London, but she moved like a puppy dog) he'd decided to reassess the music in terms of gesture, transference, that is, how it would transmogrify into action, as Suzanne Farrell said, "sound in movement, space in sound." Gerhard had been concentrating on *Rubber Soul*, which seemed unmistakably to have been a turning point, not only for the band — the lyrics more introspective, complex, and nuanced than those that had come before — but also for rock in general, the first album released as truly whole, without padding, a hinge in the culture, a pivot between before and after, which interested Gerhard. The axis. What came between ante and post. The breach in a continuum. He liked those.

Gerhard initially made some halfhearted attempts at devising a piece to "I'm Looking Through You," when, while doing research, he came across an article about *Pet Sounds*, the Beach Boys' lively retort to the Beatles album. Gerhard loved this story; he himself thrived on the galvanizing effects of competition. This had always worked for him, with Twyla and Maguy, Meredith Monk, and always Cunningham, Cunningham — in Gerhard's own mind, Merce was his totem, his idol,

23

the one to surpass, to best, the father to topple—the competition, it spurred him on.

As a German, theoretically immune to the powers of sun and surf, as a man whose own lost adolescence solidified around him like amber, locking him into a perpetual state of erupting energy and sexual arousal, the Beach Boys spoke to the self that had been denied him. They were seemingly happy-go-lucky, but surprisingly mysterious and deep; on the surface Gerhard was the opposite. Suzannah liked to joke that the band spoke to his "inner teen."

Pet Sounds had been a revelation for Gerhard. It was the ideal blend of high and low art forms. Like Gerhard, Brian Wilson, the Beach Boys' main songwriter and producer, embraced both —like Wilson, Gerhard was an exacting Pop Artist. His dances required masterful technique and a strong sense of composition, and indeed, more often than not, his classically trained female dancers were on point. Frequently his work had a mesmerizing, intellectual quality, but he could veer dramatically into sudden outbursts of color, the texture and sexiness, the exuberance of popular culture. He loved the life of the street, the zeitgeist, and so many of his movements emanated from athletics, from social dancing, even from the exaggerated comic gestures of cartoon characters. His pal, the photographer Thomas Struth, had once said over dinner, "Art is a means of locating yourself in your time," and Gerhard agreed with him, going one step further. Art was a means of locating yourself in your true time, the time that you were meant to live in, not perhaps the time and place where you were born. The Beach Boys were perfect for the chilly, "formerly German" Gerhard. They spoke to his secret self, the history of his skeleton.

Pet Sounds had led him to *Smile,* the famous lost album of rock, Brian Wilson's unfinished masterwork. Gerhard had become so mesmerized by the bootlegs he'd found on the Internet, he'd even choreographed to it in the same halting and repetitive manner as Wilson had composed, absorbing Wilson's

24

method of invention into his own process, working in an increasingly disjointed approach. More assembly than linear progression. Wilson hadn't really recorded songs but rather multiple snippets of music, which he then stitched together into glorious arias. The complexity of this process led to the involvedness and density of "Good Vibrations"; it lent it its celestial quality. This is what Gerhard aspired to in his own work.

"A teenage symphony to God," Brian Wilson had called *Smile*, before he'd completely and totally lost his mind. (Too many drugs.)

Gerhard would complete this quest for him. Before he died, Gerhard, who had so little faith, Gerhard the atheist would make something sacred.

He had been in the process of stitching his own choreographed phrases together, which was both time-consuming and costly — he'd needed the dancers to work with, he'd needed the physical space, he'd needed the musicians, the sound and light technicians, he'd needed it all, Gerhard — he was working his way through such enterprising and audacious tracts as "Vegetables" and "Mrs. O'Leary's Cow" when they'd shut him down. "Good Vibrations," the jewel in the crown, was only partially "discovered" at this point. He'd had the first three movements down, the rest in pieces, but it was going to be tremendous.

It was going to be the greatest modern ballet of his generation — he knew this in his bones! — *Day at the Beach*, with "Good Vibrations" as the finale. A supreme symphonic work. Gerhard was sure he could pull it off.

The board had demanded an open studio. *After* they saw the books. It had been a mistake, a doozy, to workshop in front of those Philistines and Shylocks — at that point in time, Gerhard had to be honest with himself, *Day at the Beach* did somewhat resemble a dismantled radio. To the untrained eye. The parts were brilliant . . . indisputably. What Gerhard needed now was to make it whole.

Gerhard took a deep breath and spoke into the phone to

Shingshang. "Are you saying that I don't own my own work?" he repeated himself.

At first there was no response. Just a damning silence. Gerhard could not even hear Shingshang breathe. The vacuous hush, a break in this distressing conversation, possessed some of the inherent defeat and reprieve of nothingness.

Did Shingshang have his hand up the waitress's skirt? Had he gone to the men's room and left the phone precipitously on the sink? Was he pausing, heaven forbid, because he needed to find the right words to answer Gerhard, when a simple "Of course you own your work" would surely suffice and was exactly what Gerhard needed to hear?

This was a delicate moment of negotiation in their performance. Gerhard knew the wisest choice was not to rush him.

There were dishes in the sink. A whole mound of them. It annoyed Gerhard when Suzannah forgot to rinse and stack them in the dishwasher.

He could wash those dishes. He could wash those dishes while Shingshang found his voice.

Just then Shingshang spoke.

"Look, you have to bear with me a little here. I didn't expect these guys to be such shits . . . and, well, the intellectual property laws as related to dance are fairly murky. Usually dances aren't copyrighted, you know, the way a piece of literature might be, you've kept up with the Graham business . . ."

"Martha let her ego get the best of her; she was too wrapped up in her own vagina. Ron's a user, a sycophant . . ."

"Gerhard, the problem is that you created some of those dances as an employee of the company, you had a salary, they withheld your taxes. They did withhold your taxes, didn't they?" said Shingshang. And then, ostensibly to the waitress, "Pink grapefruit? What a color. Matches your pretty pink cheeks."

"They withheld my taxes, sure," said Gerhard.

If they hadn't withheld them, they wouldn't have received them! Gerhard couldn't be bothered with taxes, and Suzannah, Suzannah was hopeless when it came to money. The whole endeavor — earning it, spending it, saving it — frightened her.

There was a fly buzzing around the cereal bowl. A fly! A transporter of germs and disease. Gerhard slid down off the stool once more and made his way to the sink.

"Well, if they want to be total assholes they could employ a work-for-hire doctrine . . . Sweetheart, the juice is great but I still need my latte." Shingshang was drifting off.

This was too much. Gerhard shouted into the receiver.

"Shingshang!"

He was on the receiving end of Shingshang's palm again, and all he could manage to detect were the high and low tones of Shingshang's teasing patter.

"Shingshang, I'm going to hang up!"

No response.

Gerhard grabbed a roll of paper towels and smashed the fly to smithereens.

If Gerhard hung up on Shingshang it could be hours before he might catch up with him again. It could be days. Gerhard didn't have time for this now, for the cat and mouse of lawyer and client, for the competitive gamesmanship of who was busier and therefore more sought after, who would deign to take whose call. He and Shingshang had so long enjoyed such posturing and finagling, but Gerhard did not have the time for this kind of diversion any longer, now that he had so much goddamned time on his hands. He had so much goddamned time on his hands Gerhard did not always know what to do with himself.

He scraped up the remains of the fly off of the marble countertop with a bread knife. He deposited the vestiges of its body on a paper towel, a fresh one, not the sheet colored by the bloodstain of the initial assault. The ruins of the insect looked like a spot of jam, with one small hint of wing remaining, lacy and skeletal, that's all, to suggest that it had recently been a creature, a creature that was alive. Just moments before, this jam had been a fly. Gerhard threw both towels out. He carefully placed the roll back in its holder. Rinsed the knife and put it in the dishwasher. Reached under the sink and got some Lysol spray and disinfected the marble.

Shingshang spoke into the phone. "Gerhard, my call waiting is going apeshit. I'll call you back, in five minutes I'll call you."

"Shingshang . . ."

The line went dead.

Gerhard stared at the dead receiver. He put the receiver down on the newly disinfected marble.

Now what? What to do with his time, while he waited?

The dishes. He could rinse and stack them and turn the dishwasher on to sterilize.

It was pathetic, really, how much time Gerhard had on his hands. Now, when he wasn't talking to Shingshang or some stray loyal board member or chewing the ear off some sympathetic friend—how Gerhard clung to and then resented his sympathetic friends; they sucked him in, got him all naked and vulnerable, and then used this defenselessness against him in order to feel better about themselves; schadenfreude is what it was, Gerhard thought, and it was no accident that the word was German—it was hard to know exactly what to do with himself. Sometimes he found himself a little like Nikolai, toddling after Suzannah. She had been his greatest inspiration—he'd choreographed all his best work expressly for her—and now, as his wife and the mother of his son, there were days that just being in her presence was the only thing that brought him solace. The great Gerhard Falktopf, with nowhere to go and nothing to do and so much time on his hands, trotting after his wife like a loyal little terrier.

He'd follow her around the house and out into the street, or sometimes he'd catch up with her midmorning, after his round of European calls were over, on the park bench as she yawned her way through a double latte and the monotony of a play date. With his mornings free, he who had worked like a madman most of his life now had nothing much better to do than to wander over to the playground and read the newspaper silently by her side, feeling hulking and out of place in this peculiar chit-chatting coterie of mothers. Or when he really felt like a nuisance, a third wheel—they were an island of two, Suzannah and the kid; they had their rhythms and routines, so simple and so totally bereft of responsibility, on bad days how Gerhard envied her!—he'd sit at a café across the street and spy on her.

She was a thing of beauty, moving around the playground, laughing when she got in the way of a water pistol battle, blowing kisses to friends across the yard, running after Nikolai with one of Gerhard's own linen handkerchiefs to wipe his nose. His greatest dancer. Before the child, she'd been his lover.

Gerhard readied his workspace. Dishtowels, soap, Cascade for the dishwasher, rubber gloves. The phone now safely placed on the dry island of the cutting board, awaiting Shingshang's call back.

With Gerhard and Nikolai in tow—her "boys" as she called them—Suzannah would duckwalk her way into the playground, her gait slow and rhythmic, her head and neck still stretched impossibly high, looking every bit like the ballerina she was, gangly in street clothes, her dark eyes hidden behind her black sunglasses, her blue-black hair unbrushed, unwashed, cut short and curly and fashionably pulled back with some stretchy black headband *"shmata,"* a little like a swan waddling on shore—no matter how hard she tried to hide it, to cover her great gift up, *to be normal,* it was patently evident—and open the gates. She'd wave to whomever she was meeting there, a goofy youthful wave — a wave much younger than she was; she used her whole arm — and she'd shove Nikolai off toward the sandbox or the sprinkler. On the park bench, she was the picture of downtown maternal complacency, a yummy mummy, fit and attractive and strikingly casual, as if she had been born solely for the purpose of being a parent.

The liar.

Some days, when it seemed she was full of hope, she'd venture forth from her languid lounging on the blistered green paint of the wooden bench with an encouraging, "Nicky, man, how about some slide action?" She'd nudge him along with her palm on his rear, her knees bent, back buckled, taking a couple of hobbit steps behind him until he was launched.

More often than not the boy would sit alone on the tire swing and twirl and twirl, oblivious to whatever little playmate she'd handpicked for him. There was pain in that. Gerhard could see it in his wife's face, and he wasn't totally immune to it either.

Suzannah did her best to wear her disappointment lightly; she'd roll her eyes in Nikolai's direction, or maybe she'd use her hand to mime a gun to her forehead, an expression of mock, smug, self-satisfied despair. She would express her exasperation with her beloved child in the same manner as the other mothers, mothers of bright, attractive, precocious children, mothers who were married to bankers or lawyers or film producers — men who actually made money — mothers seemingly without a care in the world. Then she'd collapse back onto the bench and Suzannah and some other mama-in-yoga-pants — née actress or architect or tax attorney — would talk about whether or not it was actually child abuse to raise these kids in the city. The pleasure she took in these mindless discussions was glaringly, bafflingly obvious.

He turned the water on to very hot. He squirted a long stream of Lemon Joy onto the dish pile, the citrusy lollipop aroma first piercing, next flavoring the air. He plunged his gloved hands into the hot, soapy water, grease skimming across the top. Even through the latex, he could feel the water's temperature rise.

Their park was where Hudson met Bleecker. A little cement triangle bordered by an almost green space where a few sparse trees were planted among the cobblestones that led to the playground she preferred. Their apartment was so far south, so far west, that Suzannah probably could have opted to cross Canal and head toward the teeny-tiny playground there, a sand pit and some backyard equipment adjoining a square suburban lawn, remarkable only for its lack of grit. It was supposed to be a city playground! The encroaching sterility, the uniformity of Battery Park City was destroying Tribeca, Gerhard felt, as an urban entity, and this park was proof of his hypothesis . . . although the lawn there had been enticing when Nikolai was learning to crawl. Suzannah would let him loose on the grass and he'd paddle across the turf on the soles of his feet and his palms, no knees, in an ambulatory downward dog, while she pretended to read the paper.

Who was kidding whom? Suzannah never read the paper; she was too afraid to take her eyes off of Nikolai, and rightly so, Gerhard supposed, because the kid liked to put everything he could find into his mouth. When he was small, they had fished out bottle caps, cigarette butts, pieces of glass, and at one sickening instance, which Gerhard recalled now with a shudder, a small brown dog turd lolled about on the bed of Nikolai's little pink tongue.

He opened up the door of the dishwasher and began mapping out its internal composition.

Gerhard loaded plates first, next glasses, lastly it would be cutlery. Then what? His mind raced ahead. What would he do next if Shingshang still hadn't gotten back to him? It would be insanity to ring the man himself. The act would look weak and desperate.

There was a drawer in the module that he'd been meaning to

organize. Suzannah threw her odds and ends in there — Scotch tape, stamps, pennies. He could roll the pennies into penny rolls; he could ready them for the bank.

Gerhard finished with the knives, the forks, the spoons. He poured the soap into the little soap cup, he closed the door and started the short cycle — just as effective as the long or even the pots and pans cycle but not as wasteful in terms of hot water. He turned his attention to the drawer, which was in worse shape than he previously thought. Nails, a screwdriver, pens, old mail, a dishtowel — was she out of her mind? And in the corner of the drawer, one of the novels that she'd hidden from him. Gerhard picked it up. A dog-eared copy of Paula Fox's *Desperate Characters*. He'd seen Suzannah perusing the open stalls at the bookstore across from the playground from his spying spot at the café. Why she thought he'd disapprove of this choice was totally beyond him — perhaps she was afraid he'd expect her to discuss it.

Suzannah had never gone to college. Gerhard knew it was insecurity that kept her from the book groups that the other ladies of leisure in the playground partook of, discussion sessions she clearly would have enjoyed. She'd barely finished high school, buying a degree from the Professional Children's School with the money her mother earned as a guidance counselor in the public schools. Suzannah's father died shortly after the Falktopfs married. He was a pharmacist and made a decent living. But not the kind of living that supported private school and dance classes and new toe shoes two or three times a week. Suzannah's mother had done this for her, her ballerina, one daughter among three brothers. But Suzannah had barely earned her Regents diploma. Junior year, she'd gotten her first job, with the Joffrey, in the corps. What sway could "Bartleby the Scrivener" and trigonometry hold once her life's dream came true at seventeen?

Gerhard understood. You killed yourself in the studio day

after day, year after year, for a brief period of soaring flight. It would be foolish to waste a moment of this intense, golden, and achingly short stretch of time. If he had known Suzannah at seventeen he would have beseeched her to cut the classes, take the job, seize the day! Books could come later, after the torn cartilage, the glass Achilles, whatever, had retired her to the advisory board and the teacher's chair. What he didn't understand was the shame his wife felt in her lack of formal education. At first he'd played a little Henry Higgins. But Suzannah had felt monitored in her literary explorations — that was the problem. She'd felt judged, she'd said once, apropos of nothing, in a fight about sex, a fight about how and when and with whom to have it. Suzannah had turned the tables abruptly to an unpredictably touchier subject. So now she did her book buying on the sneak, her unemployed husband spying on her from across the street. It was almost pitiable, the two of them, that they'd come to this.

Gerhard began to roll the pennies. Why not? It was better than spying on his wife.

Gerhard was an autodidact and quite proud of it. He'd read all the great books on his own. He'd learned English and Russian and French as a boy in school, but his Italian was self-taught, as well as his Portuguese, and he possessed a smattering of Japanese he'd picked up hanging out with Yuki — although Gerhard had found the Japanese language lacking. He was astonished by the fact that it had no swear words, nor derogatory terms for women, which, in his own native tongue, he wasn't above teasingly whispering into the neck of a girlfriend writhing in pleasure.

"*Du Schlampe,*" he'd curl into her ear. "*Du Hure,*" he'd murmur.

All his years in America, and its affection for profanity, had sapped the German terms of their indigenous sting.

Art he'd learned about in the world's galleries and museums. Piano he played instinctively—he heard the music in his head and then it poured out of his fingers. Gerhard passed on what he could to his wife, as a form of tutelage—and then, when that had worn out its welcome, by osmosis. The combination had produced in Suzannah a sharp, satirical tone, defensive as well as incisive, pure sophisticated treble without the deep bass notes of a well-stocked mind. Strip her of that and Suzannah was all academic uncertainty and native instinct. It was this intellectual insecurity that kept Gerhard's wife from the book groups she would have enjoyed, when in fact she was smart as a whip. Lack of confidence kept her home. That, and she hated to leave Nikolai at bedtime.

Oh, the drawn-out, ritualized procedure that was bedtime in the Falktopf household: first music, book, bath, warm milk, teeth cleansing, back rubbing, then book, music, Suzannah's whispery attempts at singing, then Gerhard's stern bark, another book, music—a cycle as complex, long, and varied as Wagner's Ring. What had become of them?

Gerhard paused in his penny rolling efforts; he stared at the phone. Should he pick it up? Should he ring Shingshang? Or should he wait?

He should wait.

You'd think, thought Gerhard, staring at the contents of the drawer, which were now neatly piled on the countertop in some semblance of order—glue, tape, sticky stuff in one pile, implements of correction, such as screwdrivers, scissors, pliers, in another, the book shoved back in its silent corner; perhaps she'd think he'd overlooked it, its soft spine mangled and bent—if Suzannah were so determined to be Miss Mommy she would turn her attentions to some of these domestic details instead of leaving them to fester here, instead of leaving them here for him.

For a moment, Gerhard glimmered with an enjoyable righteous anger. Perhaps there was indeed a way to blame all of this on her. Wasn't that what a wife was for? Isn't that why people married? Someone to blame things on. The drawer. The dissolution of his company. Of course the dissolution of his company; what was his company without his star dancer? All of this to play house. And it was not like any of it became her.

As a mother, Suzannah was envious and competitive and in need of endless reassurance — none of which had been true of her when she was dancing. When Suzannah was dancing, she was queen of the stage and didn't she know it — she radiated it! Since she'd given all that up, she was obsessed with the nattering of the park bench, with the minutiae that preoccupied the other stay-at-home mothers. "Stay-at-homes." All this new jargon in their lives! The clumsy and stolid terminology. "Drop-off." "Pick-up." "Occupational therapy." Occupational? The little monsters weren't even of school age yet! These word choices made everything and everybody sound like they belonged on a locked ward. The stay-at-homes often were ex–tax attorneys, for evident reasons, Suzannah told him, as if he cared. As if he cared about any of it! When was the last time they had sex, Gerhard wanted to know. That's what he cared about. He was trying very hard now, in his anger, to remember.

It was after Elspeth died — she died in April — but before they'd left the town for the country, that they had last had sex; it had been before, while out in the country, fishing for God's sake, that the president of the board had called him on his cell. Gerhard had been alone out on the ocean on Elspeth's boat, Gerhard and all that water. Alone on all that water when he got the news. There had been, sadly, temptation in that.

Which was why, Gerhard supposed, in his most chary moments, the president of the board, *his* board, had told him this way, to tempt him. The company was remaining intact — most of those traitorous dancers staying on, although who could blame them? It was continue and dance, or take a stand and temp—*his* company would live on with his name, perhaps performing some of his classics, just without him at the helm. They were going to replace him with someone "fiscally responsible," someone with a "clearer vision." Someone "committed to the spirit of the early Gerhard Falktopf." A purist. Someone more Gerhard than Gerhard was. They told him all this, this way, Gerhard supposed, so he would off himself.

Truth be told, Gerhard hadn't much felt like sex with Suzannah since then. No, it had been some charmed night last spring, before, that Gerhard last made love to his own wife. They were in bed together; he was working. He was choreographing. Pen and paper. One of his special notebooks. He was finally regaining his wind after Elspeth's death, and the air was sexy, and his imaginings were fecund and dynamic, and the ideas kept coming. He was cooking; *Day at the Beach* was taking shape inside his head.

Outside his head, his body was responding; he always got aroused when he was feeling most creative. The nocturnal May air was uncharacteristically warm and sultry, sexy, sexy if the damn kid would stay in his own room, and they were both sitting beneath their cool linens, tenting the top sheet with their knees. Gerhard could see the outline of her body, still bony and strong. The color of the sheets alone, *willow*, a pearly gray—he'd chosen it—was sensual and suggestive against her skin. Everything was still possible that night—choreographing the greatest goddamned modern ballet of the millennium, coming twice within an hour, getting his wife, not his girlfriend, to let him stick his penis up her bum—everything was still possible then for Gerhard.

He had come to bed in boxers, a wife-beater, and half-glasses —a look he knew she liked—and was perusing musical scores. *Smile.* Gerhard had gotten hold of a studio musician who was willing to transliterate the music into notation. Some of the finished cuts were magnificent, beautiful, haunting, religious, brimming with youth and hormones. Gerhard had gone nuts trying to adapt it, but now *Day at the Beach* was taking new form in his head. Next to him, Suzannah was in an old company T-shirt, embossed with an image she herself had posed for years before. The image alone was enough to get Gerhard hard. A young, taut, rail-thin but gorgeously strong Suzannah, partnered by Rafael Aguado, who'd been guest starring that season—before he'd decided to become artistic director of the Ballet Cubanico, before his drug addiction, before he died of AIDS—his powerful, elongated black limbs braided dramatically with her powdered white ones. He'd worn a dance belt and body oil for the shoot, Suzannah the most gossamer of body stockings and then all that talc . . . the theory being what? She matte, he shiny, yin, yang, and all that rot. It had been difficult to hold onto the helix, Suzannah in a *ponche arabesque split en pointe*, each of Rafael's feet meeting hers in a splayed kiss, one anchored to the studio floor, one grazing his left ear. Gerhard remembered the giggles as all that oil kept making them slide. He remembered how the sliding had gotten him to wondering if it were worth the risk of trying to convince them both to enter into a threesome, his wife and his principal danseur—good thing he'd lost that internal battle! What with Rafael's illness and Suzannah's increasing possessiveness, Gerhard congratulated himself now, in this knowing moment, on his prescience, on keeping his mouth shut.

Suzannah was wearing that T-shirt, all stretched out by wear and tear and multiple washings, and full of holes. Gerhard remembered now that he could see one nipple through a small rip and through the armhole a tuft of black hair, which he adored; it was so Italian, he loved it when Suzannah went feral. She had a fashion magazine in her lap, the television news, like the whitest of white noise, on in the background.

He stroked her leg, his signal, but she was going on and on about something. What was it? Dux beds? Global warming?

Some other stay-at-home's former lucrative career? She was jealous and insecure. A celebrated ballerina intimidated by accountants!

"Ssshh, Suzie," Gerhard said, and pulled back his hand. He said it gently but with irritation. She irritated him. He was working. He was a man at work. He was concentrating. If he wasn't going to fuck, he wanted to work. Suzannah was too busy talking to warm up to him, to respond to the stroke of his hand. Gerhard was gentle in his irritation, because he didn't want the irritation itself to mess with his head. Suzannah was his wife, and his child's mother, and he himself had had no mother. Suzannah was, and had been, his muse.

At this point in time, on that warm spring evening before, Suzannah was somehow spanning the gap, balanced in the middle of "was" and "had been" in the muse category, existing only in the vigorous nonbeing of process and evolution, as she used to sit in the air in the center of the grandest of grand *jetés*; this was her calling card, her signature crowd pleaser. "Defying gravity and time, suspended between the beginning and end, frozen and yet miraculously dynamic," said Anna Kisselgoff of the *New York Times*. It was hard to know exactly how she'd land; she was that balanced. He had to honor this; Gerhard always honored her brilliance for its own sake, out of his own heightened aesthetic and appreciation, and selfishly, for its catalytic effect on his productivity, his own work. He made dances. She was his inspiration. Suzannah was the mother of his child, too, which disarmed him, ruining a lot of things.

Gerhard was not the type to insult his child's mother — after all, motherless waif that he was, it was a miracle, he knew, that his child had a mother! — to grow irritated with her, in the openly snappish manner with which he had license to grow irritated with his other dancers. But at that moment, in bed, tired, intent, lost in the sequence of steps that were magically and mathematically reformulating inside his head, he had had enough. Suzannah was prattling on about petty domestic non-sense, which was not sexy, the air was sexy, her torn T-shirt was sexy, but the prattling . . . clearly she knew she was prattling, she had that wild look in her eye. She often felt like a moth —she'd told him this, in moments of insane vulnerability— when she was crying and open and her nose was running, when it was awful to bear witness to her defenselessness. Gerhard would never expose himself like that! Especially to a spouse! Did she not know that the secret to a happy marriage was power?

She said she felt like a moth fluttering around a light. She said she sometimes felt that way around Gerhard when he was working, anxious and incapable of *not* being drawn to him, of staying away, burning her wings as she flew close. Unless he was literally working on her. When she was his instrument, oddly enough, then she felt in control. They both knew this to be true. Then she *was* in control. But that night last spring, in their marital bed, she was no instrument. She was a lonely wife and mother, obsessing about the parameters of her own subscribed little universe, prattling on in a paranoid, neurotic manner about the playground, and Gerhard found the playground excruciating.

"Like a cocktail party without the cocktails," he said, and so many of the women in sweatpants. Why? Why would any woman go out of the house in sweatpants unless she was under threat of foreign invasion and was frantically escaping to save herself? Gerhard, on principle alone, had banned sweatpants from the studio, the plastic kind included, for all you shed was water, not fat; in those things, the girls who were endlessly starving themselves fainted in the summer, those pants did nothing to build muscle. Dance was about what? What stupid inadequate axioms could he dig up and expound upon, his accent chafing the air, his European steeliness giving him authority at any Manhattan dinner party, Suzannah liked to note, wondering aloud if the other guests went home impressed or just intimidated.

"Dance is disclosure," Gerhard went on, a revelation of the soul, no matter how muscular and precise, a forceful opening of the audience to the distinctive cosmologies of what it means to be a person, the soft, vulnerable, gray-white, puddled little clam belly of the psyche, bared through the actuality of the human form. Exposure. Sweatpants were so submerging, so suburban, so Upper West Side.

"We live in the West Village," Gerhard had said that night, putting aside his notebooks and sitting up further in bed, "solely to escape sweatpants, and then in our playground, there they are."

He pounded his bolster for emphasis, and to fluff it up, before setting it back against the headboard and returning haughtily to his papers.

"An infestation of sweatpants," Suzannah stated dryly.

Gerhard couldn't help but smile, smile around his eyes, behind the half-glasses, the crinkly spider web of laugh lines giving him away, he knew they were giving him away—Suzannah made him laugh, he adored this about her—as he went on, leaning back against his pillows, unloosened and impassioned now. Most important, he said, he couldn't understand why anyone would stay at home, given options; it was so dull and dreary to stay at home, face facts, Suze! Kids are a delight and all, but taking care of them is frankly a bore. And then, "Suzannah, Suzannah!" like an incantation.

What he'd wanted to say was: "Me. Me. Turn your lens solely on me again," because wasn't it all about that? How much he missed her?

"I'm too old now anyway," Suzannah said, and she was and she wasn't, she was lying and she was telling the truth; Suzannah was and she wasn't too old to perform. She was thirty-six. Here, too, she existed in the inhalation, the bridge before the next note, in the *and*. What she was was on the cusp of being too old, she was at the last-chance mark, the moment in time Gerhard believed all dancers did their best work, when they were just past the height of their powers, physically, technically, and yet had the wisdom of their experience, a deeper and more profound understanding of being in the world and were therefore reckless in their resolve not to waste any of it—when they were under the spell of the ticking clock. *When they were desperate.* He wanted Suzannah on the stage. He wanted her back the way she was.

"I'll come to the studio," she'd said, throwing him a bone. She allowed him this, once in a while, to keep him hooked, to keep him happy; she allowed him to work on her. Gerhard knew this to be true.

"The stage, Suze," said Gerhard. "*Day at the Beach*, Suzannah. You know I'm choreographing this for you."

She'd been dazzling just before the kid was born, when she'd dropped out to bear him. If she were still training, instead of taking class several times a week like a dilettante, not just running to the studio in moments when she "could not take it"—being away, from the dance, from Gerhard—now that she knew something about grief and suffering and joy for God's sake, or whatever one called this bewildering devotion she had for the kid, she could unravel, he said, she could explode.

Why? Why on Earth would Gerhard want his wife to unravel? To explode?

He was ashamed of this, but he did. He wanted to behold the magnificence of the spectacle.

She hadn't gone back to the stage, had she? Of course, *Day at the Beach* was still unfinished . . . She hadn't even gone back to the studio.

"You have a full-time au pair," said Gerhard, "who's in the clubs all night and sleeps till noon. If it's going to be all-mommy-all-the-time, what's the point of that? What's the point of any of it?" Then he picked up his notepad and went out into the module to work. Gerhard loved the kid, sure, but he loved their life before more.

No, they had not had sex that night. When had they last had it?

The phone rang. Gerhard closed the storage drawer with relief before picking it up. It was Shingshang.

SUZANNAH was in the shower while the world changed. The world probably changed on many mornings while Suzannah was in the shower: floods, plagues, coups, murders, and so on, all wreaking havoc while she conditioned her hair. Downstairs Gerhard was on the phone with his lawyer and Celine, the au pair, was still asleep in bed. She was twenty-one and luscious and kept the hours of a teenager. Often, Suzannah was in the park with Nikolai and back at the loft for a snack — a little rice cake and soy butter since their playground was nut-free and the preschool would soon be, too — and still she had to knock at Celine's door to rouse her. In the shower a musical phrase was playing inside Suzannah's head, what was it? Coltrane. Gerhard had put it on the stereo when he first made the coffee. No more *Pet Sounds* in the house, no more bootlegs of *Smile*, no more sand and surf and cute young chicks and surfer dude tunes bouncing sunnily around the apartment like musical beach balls, and then the eerier mystical stuff, the stuff that made her feel like her spirit was lifting sideways to her body, like her soul was escaping — where would it go? She'd had a year and a half of the madness of Brian Wilson and Gerhard choreographing, first in his head and then in his notebooks and finally dragging her into the studio, working out the most baffling elements on her when he supplicated himself to her, needing her, sucking her dry, and then leaving her in the dark when she was most desperate to be in on it, the whole shaky and dazzling endeavor, until even Suzannah could no longer escape nor bear the anxieties behind the cheer. The whole fucking thing came crashing down five weeks ago, and now mercifully they were back to Coltrane and Beethoven, to Mahler—thank God for the wordlessness and the weight.

She would never admit it to anyone, but in some weird, horrible, indefinable way, aside from being absolutely terrifying, losing the company had also provided a strange and unmooring sense of relief. Of course, the irony was that starting in grade school it had been dance that had saved her from the horrible, airless bell jar of her family—all those boys, Barry the oldest, that monster; her father and his surrounding little dust cloud of failure; her mother's resolute blindness to all of it—always it was dance that had rescued Suzannah; she'd thrived on the discipline and the structure all those classes provided for her. Why, they'd taken her away from home—thank God!—out of the Bronx, and planted her safely in the studio, her mind and body focused on one thing: making that body work. And when her body did what she wanted it to, the mind, her mind, that torture chamber of Suzannah's own mind, well, it wasn't set free exactly, it was *disappeared* almost, it was pushed outside of her by moments of pure being. All that pain, all that self-abnegation, was for a long time closely entwined with joy. She knew in her heart that she deserved to suffer. Even the eternal exercise that not-eating became—try to focus on something aside from food when you're starving, Suzannah thought—well, even hunger had its rewards. She prided herself on her ability to whittle herself down, to take up less and less space, reduce her presence in the world, make herself a tinier and tinier target at home. And then when she was on the stage—when all that training added up to something!—when she was dancing, she felt miraculously not even human sometimes, not earthbound, not ruled by need, not like the farting, fat-producing, bleeding thing she could so easily become (her periods would stop for months at a time, which she loved, she loved being free of their constant reminder of her sex). When she was dancing she felt beautiful really, she felt a little like liquid light.

But all *that* took so much effort. It was a treadmill of work and self-control, harder and harder to maintain, especially as age taught the body to rebel. And so when she finally willed Nikolai into being, when he had come—finally he'd come to her, she was so, so grateful—he could be nothing less than an angel sent to save her.

When Suzannah first heard that Gerhard had lost the company she'd had a momentary fantasy, a thrilling little heartbeating daydream, an adventure of her imagination, that now she and Gerhard could embrace another life together, something less exacting, less full of scrutiny, less precarious. We could go live in Sweden, she'd thought, where nobody judges you. (Why she thought nobody would judge her in Sweden she wasn't sure, but someone had told her something like that once, maybe on the park bench, one of her mommy friends had told her this . . .) When they'd first started dating, she and Gerhard, that first spring they'd taken a walk in the Conservatory Garden in Central Park when the cherry blossoms were at their peak, white petals weeping like snow into the breeze, and even though it had been his idea to take this walk—this seductive Gerhard-walk through the petals—his allergies had acted up and he had been overcome by sneezing. Gerhard sneezed so many times in a row they'd lost count, and he'd actually had to find a bench and sit down. Sitting on the bench, sneezing and sneezing, he'd grinned at her between sneezes, like a little boy would, and Suzannah had burst out laughing, he was so sweet, so sweet in the moment, so helplessly sneezing and smiling away at her, in no hurry to leave. Sometimes she let herself imagine that without the company Gerhard would be different, he would be like he was that day in the park so long ago now; he would relax.

In the shower, beneath the sound of the music in her head and her young son's humming and the water running, Suzannah swore she could hear Gerhard shouting Shingshang's name.

"Shingshang!"

Her husband had been on the phone all morning, sitting in his boxers and T-shirt on a tall metal stool at the kitchen counter, running a tan hand through his thick mop of silver hair, his blue eyes so cool that even now, after all these many years of cohabitation, when Suzannah was away from him, as she was in this moment, and trying to conjure up his face, she remembered them in her head as pupil-less, just shafts of sea-blue light, like round little swimming pools in a doll's world, so lacking in human qualities that they never ceased to draw her toward him.

"Shingshang!"

Suzannah pictured Gerhard shouting into the receiver. His strong jaw was stubbled with morning silver and he must be stroking it, he was always stroking it, and the rogue nerve in his left leg—a leg so striated with muscle even in middle age it still looked like sculpture—must have been pulsing wildly. Was it just a few weeks before that Suzannah had noticed the gray hairs had spread from his chest to his legs? And wondered idly if his pubic hair was changing; she'd have to check. She'd have to pay attention. Shouldn't a wife know whether or not her husband was going gray where it counts?

Suzannah squeezed out a little worm of kiddie shampoo into her palm and carefully began to rub it into her son's wet curls. The air smelled like melon—the color, not the fruit. It smelled like what one now associated with melon from all these shampoos and fragrances, but nothing like a real melon would, when you placed your fingers and your nose on its little melon belly-button and pressed. As she soaped and rinsed Nikolai, she began to plan the next course of action: towel, powder, a quick padding down the hall to Nikolai's room where the clothes she'd chosen so carefully the night before—because it was a big day for her boy, a memorable day, his first day of school—were laid out on his bed. She'd selected jams and the "Life's a Beach" tie-dyed shirt they'd picked up in East Hampton this past summer, when they were staying at Elspeth's cottage after her death. Elspeth had always given the Falktopfs the last week of July and the first of August, every year, as a gift, and so this year, for the final time, her squabbling children had allowed them to keep to plan, too squabbily themselves to figure out how to share the oceanfront manse anyway.

Suzannah felt that through these beachy choices of clothing for her son's very first day of school she was making a statement that she was opting for the carefree, joyous childhood she was so steadfastly determined Nikolai would have—although how she'd go about arranging such a thing, "carefree joyousness," she did not know.

Even with the water pounding from the showerhead, even with Nikolai's constant humming (he was playing with some toy boats at Suzannah's feet, the dark blue faux-marble tile of the partially renovated shower stall with its white veining, like fat-streaked blue beef, providing him with an oceanic surface), Suzannah thought she could hear Gerhard yelling into the phone. Although of course she could not, she realized this minutes later, she could not possibly have heard Gerhard yelling into the phone from the module—because, after all, she hadn't even heard the plane, had she?—it was only when Gerhard ran halfway down the hall that she truly determined that he was shouting for her.

"It's Shingshang. He's at a breakfast at Windows on the World."

Windows? thought Suzannah. Weddings, bar mitzvahs. Why on Earth would anyone eat breakfast there?

"He said a bomb just went off in the building. They are evacuating him now. Look out the window!" Which she did. Suzannah obeyed Gerhard unthinkingly. Unthinkingly she leaned over and picked up Nikolai, his small body slippery and wet, and held his naked skin next to her own, his short, stocky, oddly muscular little legs wrapping around her waist, his little penis and scrotum smushed up against her wet lower belly, so that he sat on the shelf of her hip bones. Forever after Suzannah would ask herself, Why did I take Nikolai with me to look? She'd be plagued by this question, once she crossed the bridge from that life to this life, as if the trip to the window were so plainly a foolhardy journey, like taking him to a biker bar, or climbing some dumb mountain in Nepal, or bringing him to an Ecstasy party where she and Gerhard had had sex with multiple partners—all foolhardy endeavors that she had committed, but not with Nikolai in tow, never with Nikolai there. But this day she'd bent down and picked him up and stepped with him in her arms out of the shower stall. The apartment had big, industrial-sized windows, so the changed world, the world still changing, stood as nakedly before Suzannah and her boy as they stood before it.

"The birdies are on fire," Nikolai said.

Suzannah watched the people fall from the wounded, burning tower, a huge, gaping hole where the bomb must have gone off. There were several blazing human fireballs, then a man and a woman holding hands, the woman's skirt inflating like a flaming bell, an inverted tulip.

Would Gerhard hold my hand, she wondered, if we were to leap like that?

And next, one man headfirst, in his shirtsleeves. Was that his tie floating behind him?

He didn't take his tie off, thought Suzannah, before she put her hands over her son's eyes and turned him away. Why didn't he remove his tie before he dived?

FIRST, Gerhard put on his pants.

One glance out the window at the injured tower and then at Suzannah's face, and, well, the vulnerability of boxer shorts, those naked knees and ankles, was not going to cut it. His wife's hair was plastered to her skull; she looked like a kitten that had fallen into a tub. There was a towel barely draped around her and the boy, their naked bodies entwined like the twisted dough some neighbor kid's mother baked into crullers when Gerhard was a child—pasty and still damp from the shower, Gerhard's family looked ready for the oven. Nikolai's little monkey arms were wrapped tightly around his mother's neck; her eyes were telegraphing terror. It was enough to send Gerhard straight into the bedroom, where he quickly pulled on a pair of khakis.

In the back of his mind, like a pilot light, the notion flickered that, possibly, he could be of help escorting people out of the tower. He pictured himself clasping Shingshang's shoulders—"The Stairmaster paid off, hey, buddy?"—because the building must be at least one hundred stories high, and the restaurant Windows on the World, where he had never been (too afraid of heights), the jewel in that touristy crown, was on the top floor. The itch to lend a hand startled Gerhard. Could it be, as Suzannah used to insist (when had she stopped?) late at night, in bed, after sex, when he was naked, when he'd allow himself to openly wonder, that he was actually good at heart?

Suzannah followed Gerhard down the hall, to their bedroom. The blood was rushing to his ears in the oceanic oscillations he'd long associated with internal panic, as well as, oddly enough, erotic arousal and euphoria. Beneath this corpuscular micro-roar, Gerhard knew his wife was singing some sweet, dopey kid's song softly into the child's ear; he could see her lips move — "The Wheels on the Bus" — Nikolai's face burrowed into her chest, Suzannah watching big-eyed as Gerhard dressed.

After Gerhard pulled on his khakis, he tried dialing Shingshang again. The phone had never left his hand, his knuckles, gripping the receiver, were the blood-streaked yellow-white of chicken bones — how had he possibly negotiated the pants' legs?

Shingshang didn't answer.

Gerhard went to the closet and pulled out a white T-shirt from the top shelf and a belt, all without a word to Suzannah. He was thinking, or trying to. He ignored her silent pleading — for what? Reassurance? Guidance? Shingshang should make it out of there; it looked like the bomb damaged only one side of the building and that building must be filled with staircases and elevators, emergency exits, multiple modes of egress. A helicopter could airlift people from the roof until the fire was under control, Gerhard thought. Why, there must be a team of pros whose job was simply to evacuate that place . . . Wasn't there always a team of pros for . . . whatever? Especially after what had happened there a few years back — Gerhard and Suzannah had been away on Winter Tour and so the images were somewhat fuzzy in his recollection — what was it? Some bomb in a parking garage; had anybody died?

The towers were like twin mountains in his personal landscape, though the northern one practically obscured his view of the southern. Gerhard gazed at them every morning and every evening outside his window without much thought; he rarely went over there. Frankly, he found their monolithic inscrutability somewhat creepy. They were two of the ugliest buildings in the world—Gerhard disliked ugliness unless it was illuminating, unless it rankled and revealed—and all those people scurrying within, like chiggers beneath the skin, like chiggers you couldn't see . . . well, the concept, those parallel stacked and soaring municipalities, vertical conurbations, was to Gerhard extremely unappealing. They were just too tall.

The farmers' market in the World Trade Center Plaza was nothing compared with Union Square. Gerhard had some vague memory of buying Elspeth a leather lipstick case as red as a dog's dick at the Coach store in the subterranean shopping center, after a harried afternoon spent at Century 21 with Yuki, otherwise he'd had nothing to do with the place. He remembered when Philippe Petit did his famous unscripted tightrope walk between the two towers. Gerhard hadn't been living downtown all that long then. It must have been the early to mid-seventies—he'd still been cooking on a hot plate. He'd gone out for a coffee and toasted bagel and seen all these passersby looking up—the towers weren't even finished yet. Gerhard had gotten vertigo just bending his neck back to gaze that high. Petit walked back and forth half a dozen times, at one point he'd even lain down on the rope for a little rest, but it was Gerhard who had his heart in his throat.

Gerhard still remembered Petit's quote in the *Times* the next morning: "When I see three oranges I juggle, when I see two towers I walk." His own fear of heights aside, Petit's compulsion, his aching, driving need, was something Gerhard could understand. Wasn't he himself mostly propelled by impulse and desire? Leaving Germany alone at seventeen, getting on a plane to New York where he'd known no one, to master an art form he knew nothing about?

Gerhard admired Petit's feat, more so the preparation and discipline invested in carrying it off. Petit, with the assistance of various accomplices, had fired a fishing wire between the two towers with a bow—a fishing wire, a bow, and then a cable. Gerhard had never forgotten the daring. The hubris. He'd loved that. Petit and his crew, they'd entered the building during daylight in disguise and spent that night, allied and alone with their secret, like lovers, before dazzling the sleepy-eyed world with a morning surprise.

Is that what this was? A morning surprise? An eye-opener? Why attack so early—Gerhard looked at his watch, a Rolex, a birthday gift from Elspeth, hockable—it wasn't even nine o'clock? The secretaries were still on the subways. Shingshang had said a bomb. Is that what happened the last time the buildings were attacked? A bomb in the basement? Surely security had improved in the intervening years. Was this bomb the product of a disgruntled employee—a trader gone postal, a fired security guard? Or some nut with some psycho agenda like the last one? A blind sheik . . . It was coming back to Gerhard now. The attack had been masterminded by a psychotic blind sheik who seemingly mustered enough appeal to inflame a bunch of zealous retards to rattle the towers. Gerhard couldn't even remember the purpose of that mission. But they were still standing. The towers were still standing. Gerhard could see them standing outside his bedroom window.

The North Tower was billowing flames and smoke. It looked like there were people hanging out of the building's rent edges, clinging to open windows above the gaping hole. It was as if they were watching a parade. Go down the stairs, Gerhard wanted to bellow. People were sheep. They needed someone to tell them what to do every minute of every day of their lives. Gerhard knew how to make decisions. He was a choreographer. If he were in that building he'd make those lost souls move.

Gerhard calculated quickly. The bomb seemed to have detonated about eighty stories up. Was Shingshang past the boiling point by now?

Suzannah murmured something and then took the boy out of the room and down the hall.

He'd been so lost in his own private Idaho, Gerhard had forgotten all about them, his family, his custody. Still, their absence changed the tenor of the room. He was lonely without them. Somehow they'd absorbed a modicum of the electrical charge that was now surrounding Gerhard like icy air, turning his blood cold, causing the hair on his arms, his chest, his legs, his genitals, his perineum, to stand up, making him buzz. For a moment, he wanted to call out to them, to Suzannah and Nikolai, come back! Come back! But the instinct itself was absurd. Mother and child were safe in the next room; he was safe alone in here. Gerhard's heart was racing and his adrenaline surged; it was as if he actually felt his blood traveling through his veins. He was as keyed up as if he'd just snorted coke. Gerhard was afraid and he was excited, and almost instantly that feeling of being excited became energizing.

He turned to the television. He was looking for more details, interpretation, spin. What was outside his window was so oddly uninformative. Shingshang. He was looking for Shingshang. Shingshang talking into a mike, outlining the rigors of his escape, a middle-aged Lazarus, sharing his good fortune with some ambulance-chasing newscaster. Shingshang aglow. Shingshang wiping the sweat from his brow, Shingshang happy, simply happy to be going home to his wife and kids, a changed man. For a minute the fantasy was so alive, Gerhard almost envied him. He almost envied Shingshang the life-altering experience that provided him with the capacity to grow.

Gerhard picked up the clicker from his bedside table and turned on the television that perched on his dresser. He turned on *The Today Show* and saw the same burning visage of the North Tower that he could just as easily see outside his own window. The horror of the bomb and that gaping hole was less difficult to process on a small screen than it was in life, where it was so much larger and more visceral. So real.

Gerhard went from the television that sat on his dresser and then back to the window, dialing and redialing Shingshang as he went.

Outside the window, it was a beautiful day. But now the air was filled with smoke and flames. Not as beautiful a day as it was on television. On television it was celestial. Blue sky, brilliant light. On television the sun shone off of the towers like it does on the seas he noticed sometimes when he dared to look out the window of an airplane. Indeed it was only over the ocean that Gerhard, as a passenger in an airplane, could venture to open his eyes. The North Tower shone with an undulating metallic radiance, a silvery blue skin, nothing to divulge what was going on beneath the surface, except for the smoke belching from its exploded throat, its skin like shiny snake scales encasing surging muscle and inner organs. Gerhard had always admired the buildings' reflective powers. At the edges of the day they were more tolerable. At the edges of the day the towers took on color, they emanated color, they embraced color, like a Rothko they stacked and bled it. At sunset they glowed orange and black. At daybreak sometimes they were pink. Gerhard looked at them every day of his life. Every day of his life; who knew or cared about what went on inside?

Suzannah came back into the room, now in her robe, with the naked kid in hand and his little pile of clothes tucked beneath one arm. The tie-dyed shirt that Gerhard was so fond of. A hippie beach boy. A future surfer. Sun and sand and water. Volleyball? Guitars and girls and clambakes. Bikinis and jams. Fun, fun, fun. He wanted all this for Nikolai. His American offspring.

Nikolai.

On the television Matt Lauer said, "A small commuter plane has hit the North Tower of the World Trade Center."

"A plane?" said Gerhard. "Shingshang said it was a bomb."

Suzannah sighed a sigh of relief. A little color came back into her cheeks and her mouth was no longer frozen in the shape of an O.

"Thank God," said Suzannah. She ran a hand through her wet mop of curls. She was pretty, too pretty, almost inappropriately pretty for the moment, with the pink rushing back to her cheeks. Suzannah looked ready for a picnic, like a willowy girl you might grab and kiss, not a mature, intellectual force, handling things. It was as if his wife were living in some sideways reality; there was a bubble around her formed by her own exhalations. Her relief. It isolated Gerhard in the truth of the circumstances, as if he were the only one beginning to grapple with the enormity that was before them.

"If it was a plane that hit the building then it was an accident," said Suzannah. Her eyes were big and open. They were beautiful. Innocent and vaguely stupid. Her robe gaped, and he could see her small breasts. He'd always liked Suzannah's breasts. They were flat with rosy nipples even after the baby's birth, very nearly like a child's. That was one of his secret fears about having a baby — that Suzannah's nipples would darken. Most of Gerhard's lovers who had given birth had nipples that were brown or the color of wine. Hers were still peachy; the bosoms themselves almost like a young boy's. It was the almost, the little rise, perfect for a champagne cup, that made them sexy.

"Sowry," said Nikolai. He was playing with a loose knob on Suzannah's Moroccan dresser, red with intricate swirling designs, a patterned, painted filigree — Gerhard dropped three grand on the thing in Soho and then saw similar chests for mere pennies while tooling about Morocco. Around and around the knob went between Nikolai's tiny fingers, wearing away at the soft wood, weeping dust.

"It's not your fault, honey," said Suzannah. She looked stricken.

"It was an accident," said Nikolai. He said it over and over again as he turned the knob. Suzannah melted to her knees and stared at him. "Nikolai," she said. He didn't turn. He didn't respond to his name, to his mother. "It was an accident," repeated Nikolai. All that repetition was driving Gerhard insane.

"You think this is an accident, Suzie?" said Gerhard. He was surprised by the anger in his tone. He'd raised his voice to her, but it was the kid he wanted to slap. "How do you accidentally fly into the World Trade Center?"

Gerhard dialed Shingshang again. No answer.

Gerhard was a bastard. He knew it. The morning was proving traumatic for everyone and yet he was cruel to his frightened, too-beautiful wife and his idiot child. He probably wouldn't save Shingshang either, after all. Or maybe he'd save him, if the fucker would just answer the phone and let Gerhard know where to find him. Gerhard didn't have the first idea how to be a husband or a father. Let alone a hero. Outside, the tower burned.

INSIDE, Suzannah stood in the corner of their bedroom, in her robe, dressing the boy with his back to both the window and the TV — a futile and pathetic gesture at providing him the very protection she had denied him earlier, screening him from the same horrific scene she had just held him up to see, an image that had scorched itself into her retinas. When she closed her eyes now, on the insides of her lids she saw that man diving, headfirst, tie flying, in a glowing red outline like some awful neon sculpture, a scorched negative, blinking and cheap. So Suzannah kept them open, her eyes, open and wide and focused on the TV, across the room and over and behind Nikolai's small, blond head, the hideous information momentarily safeguarded away from him.

The tower was emitting more and more smoke on the TV screen. A confetti of papers swirled around the buildings like snow in a snow globe. That was television. Out her window, when she swiveled her gaze, there were flames and smoke and the air was full of garbage. People—it seemed there were people pressed up against their office windows . . . Were they actually hanging out of the tower, that far up? Were they trying to get a better view down below of the street? She hadn't realized the windows opened . . . Had they opened before? Had someone kicked the glass out? Had it blown out? Is that where all the paper was coming from—out the open windows? Were those people throwing that paper into the street? Why on Earth would they do that? Were they afraid the paper would catch on fire? How much paper was in that building? There must be a hell of a lot of paper in those buildings, Suzannah thought.

Suzannah turned to the television. On the screen there was more perspective. The two buildings were foreshortened by distance, while outside her window she was forced to rake her gaze up and down to encompass their totality. She could take them in only in sections and that meant contemplating each segment, which possessed its own specific awfulness, the rising smoke, the falling bodies, the people hanging out the windows, whereas on TV, oddly enough, the North Tower took up less space—it was smaller but somehow more soaring. More like a strange object of art. Ordinary save for the flames and black hole of smoke that coughed out its wounded side . . . And then on TV there were no people around to worry about. The image itself was that much farther away, tucked into the display; it was already framed and turned into an artifact, like looking instantly back at the past.

"It's appropriate to surmise people might be in the building," Katie Couric said, her voice a calm, soothing, oddly polite overlay to the appalling image. Disembodied. Because the camera stayed fixed on that lustrous, blazing tower. For all Suzannah knew, Katie's expression was as blank and smooth as her voice; her Mickey Rooney face — so chipper and round and preternaturally youthful — never graced the screen. Instead it was filled with sky, the tower gleaming in the sun and belching smoke. On television it was easy to imagine the building empty but for paper, the swirl of origami snowflakes that danced in the crisp, shining air. It was only if you looked outside Suzannah's window that the air was filling with smoke and people plummeted from the gaping hole. People on fire.

My God, thought Suzannah, those people are on fire! They are jumping from the towers! The towers are too high! They could get hurt! Don't they know they are going to die?

Did she speak these words or was the force of her thoughts so loud that Gerhard heard her?

"It must be preferable to what's going on inside," said Gerhard. He said this out loud; she could hear him!

It was all too much to bear. She turned away from the screen, from the window, too awful to witness but impossible to block out. She turned back. On the screen the world was silent, except for Katie's cool, even voice, still merely surmising that people might be hurt, when Suzannah knew for certain they were. She looked out the window again. She kept shaking her head in disbelief. She kept opening her eyes wider. She felt her eyes widening in their sockets. She felt her head trembling like she had Parkinson's or something.

"Gerhard."

He turned to her, looking for a split second like he'd forgotten she was there, maybe, like he wasn't exactly sure who she was, but then he remembered himself, his role in her world as protector and choreographer, husband and father, and he put his arms around her. They were strong, Gerhard's arms, still hard and muscled, and his touch wasn't calibrated but firm. He held Suzannah tightly, perhaps too tightly; it was difficult to breathe in Gerhard's embrace, but the steady *thump thump*

thump of his heart was reassuring, and the smell of his armpits, his sweat, was familiar, soothing. Now she pressed her face into his chest, the gray curly hairs peeking over his shirt's crew neck, tickling her forehead, the body of the shirt still fresh and smelling clean but wilting a little near her mouth, from her breath, stained by her tears. She was shaking and sobbing into her husband's chest, and he had his arms around her because *people* were on fire, not birds, and outside their window these people were diving to their deaths. On TV it was so fucking quiet. Here in Suzannah's home, sirens screamed. They'd been screaming for at least ten minutes now. She hadn't noted when they'd started.

Good, she thought, help is on its way. Rescue.

Gerhard grabbed Suzannah's shoulders with his hands. He pressed her gently away from his body. A little string of drool, like a spider's web, wobbled from her mouth to his T-shirt before breaking. Suzannah brought the back of her hand to her mouth to wipe it, but Gerhard didn't seem to notice. He had his hands on her shoulders and he was looking intently in her eyes.

"Okay?" said Gerhard.

Okay, Suzannah nodded.

Gerhard let go of her and dialed Shingshang again.

"He must be going down the stairs," said Gerhard. "He said they were being evacuated. He must be ten, twenty, thirty stories down by now."

Gerhard looked at the screen; he did the math. Shingshang needed thirty stories to be safely past the thing.

Suzannah glanced furtively around the room. Her dresser, Gerhard's coat tree, a wooden hanger. The bed frame. Her knuckles lightly rapped the wooden bed frame. Gerhard's eyes were on the TV anyway.

"Thirty, thirty-five stories, the guy works out on a Stairmaster, he's got his own Nordic track."

"Birdies," said Nikolai. "The birdies are on fire."

Oh God, thought Suzannah, Nikolai.

He was looking out the window.

Suzannah gently steered him away. Grabbed at the tiny pile of clothing she'd stacked on the bed. She'd already succeeded in pulling on his pants. He was standing at her hip now, bare-chested in his shorts, his little belly swelling over the elastic waistband, his ribs and veins visible, his nipples like two tiny copper pennies.

"There you go, buddy," Suzannah said, pulling the T-shirt down over Nikolai's curly head. She could hear her own voice as if it were coming at her from the end of a tunnel and it wavered in its certainty. The neck of the shirt was a tad too small, and she pulled a little too hard, so that his head bobbled a bit when it pushed through. It snapped back and then bobbled, like one of those toy dogs you saw in the rear window of a taxi. She was so rough! She could have injured his neck. His spine. What was more essential than a person's spine? In yoga they yammered away about the heart center; in Graham technique it was the contraction of belly to back; and Gerhard in the studio, Gerhard in the orchestra pit, Gerhard in the wings, in the wings of her mind—she couldn't get him out of *those* wings—Gerhard said over and over again: "Darling, use your brain!" But Suzannah knew it was the long, knobby staircase of nerves and function leading step by step to the head that was the source of everything that mattered for survival. Suzannah ran her hand up the downy slope of Nikolai's neck, palming the back of his skull, spreading her fingers through his curls, and kissed his forehead.

"It was an accident," said Nikolai. She felt a surge of love for him mixed with relief that dissolved everything else but that, her love and relief. He was forgiving, Nikolai. It had been an accident. He knew she'd not meant to harm him. He could give!

"Remember the Center was the location of a terrorist bombing some years ago." Matt Lauer narrated the picture now, as inert and fixed a frame as the yule log at Christmas time. Gerhard adored the yule log, burning merrily for hours on Channel whatever, the same tinny tunes playing in the background repeatedly. To save her life Suzannah couldn't understand if Gerhard was keen on it because it was ironic, the yule log, or if he liked it because he just liked it, period—and which of these two choices made him more cool.

Because he would be the cooler of the two, Gerhard, he would always be the cooler of two choices.

The static image of the tower, however, was riveting. Like O.J. and the white Bronco. Suzannah had watched that one for over an hour in a hotel room in Boston, not breaking even to go to the bathroom, bored and mesmerized. How long would it take to put this fire out?

She reached for her comb on her bedside table and used it to untangle Nikolai's wet curls.

A helicopter circled and flew close to the burning tower. Could they douse it with water from up above? Could a blimp fly into the picture? Is that what blimps were actually for? Their swollen bellies full of water? Or was the helicopter there for the sole purpose of liberating the people inside? Suzannah wondered how many people the helicopter could recover from the roof at a time. Perhaps retrieval was the best way for people who didn't have the strength to walk down . . . the elderly . . . Were there elderly people up there? Were there pregnant women? Children? Oh God, no one would take a child that unnaturally high up, would they? When she and Gerhard had taken Nikolai to the Empire State Building sometime in July with a group of visiting French dancers, Gerhard, that fraidy cat, waited out the excursion in the lobby. He'd left it to her to point out these very same Twin Towers, plus the Statue of Liberty. "The Statue of Liberty was a gift from France," said

Suzannah, feeling like a tour guide, although Nikolai had not been listening to her, he was too intent on turning the knobs on the viewfinder. There couldn't be children up there, thought Suzannah. It would be way too scary for children up there now.

A silver airplane flew into the screen, low and large, and then circled behind the burning tower like a fat shark. There was a big swell of black smoke that bulged from behind the building and then a flaming red explosion fired up behind the North Tower's sleek surface, as if the building were obstructing the observation of fireworks.

"Oh my God, another one just hit," said Matt Lauer.

Another what? thought Suzannah.

"This is so shocking," said Katie Couric in a flat, flat voice, not sounding shocked at all. It was as if her voice were two-dimensional, written not spoken language, as if it had been planed.

The view of the buildings switched on *The Today Show*. Now Suzannah could see the South Tower, newly maimed, flames blazing and thick black smoke catching the wind and rolling up into the sky like toxic clouds.

"Gerhard!" Suzannah's scream stumbled in her throat. It came out raspy and low, like a net of panic was restraining it. "Gerhard, what in the world is going on?"

"What in the world is going on?" said Katie Couric. There was wonder in her voice.

Gerhard looked at Suzannah wild-eyed. He rushed to the window, but the North Tower pretty much blocked their view of the South Tower. Still more and more smoke saturated the air; there was more and more paper. Sirens screamed. Everything was screaming. Nikolai was screaming.

"I wonder if something is going on in air traffic control," said Elliot, a *Today Show* producer calling in an eyewitness report to the news show from his loft downtown. Elliot's loft, that was probably in the same vicinity as the Falktopfs'—who the fuck was Elliot? Suzannah knelt next to Nikolai. She hugged him hard, pressing down on his shoulders and hip joints. His screams were so awful, worse than the sounds that were going on outside.

"We're getting out of here," said Gerhard. He put on his shoes.

"What?" said Suzannah.

Gerhard took his wallet and his car keys off his dresser and put them in his pocket.

"Pack up the baby," said Gerhard. "Where's Celine?" He looked systematically around the room as if the au pair were hiding somewhere in plain sight. "I cannot believe she's slept through all of this. I'll get the car."

"What?" said Suzannah.

He turned to her, blue eyes blazing.

"We are getting out of this hellhole," said Gerhard.

What hellhole? thought Suzannah. The apartment? The city? She instinctively looked around her in an effort to understand him, to get her bearings. Her eyes fell on Nikolai.

"But Nikolai has to meet his teachers today; it's the first day of school." The sentence came out of her mouth like a little girl's entreaty. She felt small and thin when she said it. All summer long, Suzannah had been meditating on this date. All summer long, she'd been full of anticipation, of hope, eager to have Nikolai proved normal. September 11th. Nikolai starts school.

Gerhard was incredulous. His voice full of amazement.

"Suze, don't you get it? We're under attack!"

"We're under attack?" said Suzannah.

"We're under attack," said Gerhard.

"Why?" said Suzannah. "Who would attack us?"

Gerhard shook his head at her in disbelief.

"Why don't Jews ever know when to leave?" he asked.

Suzannah stared at him. She stared at her husband as he headed down the hall. After a moment or two, Suzannah was following him, but he was too fast for her, and when she couldn't see him any longer, she heard the front door of their apartment slam shut.

I've ruined my life, thought Suzannah. I've ruined it and the world is coming to an end. She picked up her son and went down the hall to wake up Celine.

Celine would help her pack.

OUTSIDE, it was a beautiful day. So surprisingly beautiful that even saturated as he was by urgency, Gerhard actually noted how distinctive and fine a day it was as he used both palms to push open the building's heavy metal door and stepped out over the ubiquitous pile of Chinese takeout menus into the sunshine. Something about the quality of the breeze, the light . . . This morning was exceptionally, uselessly gorgeous.

Out on the street the air felt so glassy, stiff, and clear, Gerhard had the peculiar sensation that he could fold it. The colors of the cars, the mailboxes, the restaurants and storefronts, the trash in the trash can, even the gritty grays of the cement and the pearlized silver of a truck's side view mirror, all seemed heightened somehow, hyper-real. Like the world was all a canvas by Richard Estes, or Gerhard Richter, newly painted and still wet, and hence mutable, like he could take his finger and smear it. The sidewalks were full of people, people gathering around open car doors listening to news reports on the radio, people bunched together facing a little portable TV balanced on a café table in front of the corner bistro, people rushing toward the towers, drawn by their magnetic pull. There were people rushing away, too, people with sense. People like him. Some just stood where they stood and looked up. Not Gerhard.

Gerhard looked down at the pavement and he looked across; he looked where he needed to look. As he traversed Hudson Street, fire trucks, ambulances, emergency vehicles careered down the boulevard; red, white, blue, their sireny bright patriotic colors taking on a new clarity; their various alarms and horns, clamorous and insistent, begging for attention, when no one for miles seemed to have any attention left to spare. There was so much noise the racket itself became something sort of solid, a recognizable, specific hullabaloo—my whole life I will be able to conjure up this impossible chorus, thought Gerhard, I will remember exactly its detailed howl—and within that context there was little that could pierce the continuous braying. This was the background sound effect to the attack on New York, signifying the end of what? That much he wasn't sure of. The end of two buildings? The end of a way of life? The end of the world? Certainly not the end of him. It took some sure-footed savvy on Gerhard's part to dodge the moving vehicles.

Like bumper cars, some of the cars and trucks and things that go—"cars and trucks and things that go," what was that from, one of Nikolai's distressingly dimwitted books?—seemed to be bouncing into and off of one another. Gerhard took note: some cars and trucks and things that go appeared to be crashing. They *were* crashing. Gerhard's heart felt like it was pumping its way out of his chest and up into his throat. Still he remained calm. His skin held him in. Stay clear, thought Gerhard, stay focused. Emotionally, he zipped himself up.

Gerhard headed straight for the bank on the corner. Money first. They would need money in their pockets. Then the car, the silver Mercedes SUV, still leased out to what was no longer his company. "You'll cart dancers around in it." Suzannah had insisted upon it once the kid was born. She was thinking about Nikolai's well-being. "It's a legitimate business expense, *and* the safest car on the market. What do you think the cabbies drive in Tel Aviv?" The Krautmobile she called it. "Das Boat" she'd say in public, needling him.

Gerhard was his wife's ultimate rebellion. Suzannah had gone and married a German. A *yiddishe maideleh* with her very own storm trooper. A ballet dancer–storm trooper. It was ridiculous. Her father had refused to come to their wedding. Gerhard had refused to lick his boots. Wasn't it obvious, Gerhard had maintained, he himself had eschewed the land of his birth! He had cut himself off from his own father! His drive and desires were infinite. Although he was not a superstitious man, the fact that he found himself in New York, doing what he was doing, living with Suzannah, well, there were mystical properties at work. He was meant to be where he was. It was un-American, Gerhard claimed, to vest the sins of the father upon the son.

As he rushed toward the bank, Gerhard reflected on his parting comments to Suzannah minutes before—*why don't Jews ever know when to leave?*

Is this the way he wanted to behave during a catastrophe? If another plane, a bomb, some flying debris were to hit right now, would these be the words she remembered him by?

But what was she waiting for? An airplane with her name on it to sweep into their living room?

Just because he was German did not mean he was heartless. Just because he recognized evil did not make him so. She loved Thomas Mann. Mahler. Freud was a German. A German and Jew—the most exalted combination; Gerhard kept this thought to himself when Nikolai was born. The brains and rigor, the warm emotions, the cool approach. He'd secretly applauded himself for mixing his genes. Mendelssohn, Marx, Einstein, all marvelous mongrels. Suzannah loved many things German—him for one. She loved him. Gerhard. He counted on this.

After the bank, Gerhard would meet them at their car. The

car was German and it was the safest SUV on the highway, Suzannah said so herself. She'd done research on the car, the car seat, the sippy cup. Guarding against fender-benders and buckteeth, always on the lookout for hazards large and small. Why didn't Suzannah in all her zeal guard against airplanes that behaved like heat-seeking missiles? The world was literally falling to pieces around him. He looked downtown. Fire and smoke, a snowstorm of paper. The populace amok. Somehow, for a brief insane moment — Gerhard knew it was insane — he convinced himself it had been *her* job to protect him from all this.

He headed toward the bank. The bank and the car. Where had he parked it?

Usually Gerhard garaged the car, but late last night he'd parked it on the street. He'd just gone shopping. Fairway Uptown. Once or twice a month, Gerhard got behind the wheel of their souped-up truck, took the West Side Highway up to Harlem and did his shopping like a suburbanite, in bulk. He enjoyed this. He enjoyed opening his closets and seeing row upon row upon row of paper towels, toilet paper, Diet Coke. Then there were the foodstuffs. Wonton wrappers. A rotisserie chicken. He'd pull the meat off the back with his fingers in an act as intimate and private as jerking-off, late at night, sandwiched in between the composition of his livid correspondence — those poison letters to the board, to the critics, to the dancers who'd betrayed him — his pacing, his fuming. He'd pull the meat off the chicken back with his fingers in an animal act, but he'd still lay the white strips out nicely on a plate — presentation being ninety percent of anything. He'd still use cutlery to carefully place the meat in his mouth. Pink peppercorns. He'd bought pink peppercorns because they looked like a party — confetti, balloons, something celebratory, housed in a graceful glass jar that pleased him. Gerhard had done the shopping late last night when he was restless, he'd called the garage around 9:00 and was fully loaded up before the store closed at 11:00. He'd spent the bulk of his time at the cheese counter. September. This was the best season for farmstead Vermont cheeses. You could taste the meadow, the *terroir* in the milk.

The parking lot across the street from Fairway sat right on the Hudson River. Gerhard had eaten a sesame bagel plain, leaning against the hood of his car and marveling at the hideousness of New Jersey. The looping diamond necklace of the George Washington Bridge. The thick, rich, humid night air enveloped his skin, a protective layer between him and the world. It was a peaceful interlude. Gerhard, for once, not fully engaged in the orchestrated jam-packed strata of his thoughts. Those multitudinous chords and arpeggios, the warring impulses and urges, creative bursts and spikes—he once surmised that if he could chart his own thought processes it would read like the EEG of an epileptic—the anger and fear that had ruled him of late. There had been a party to celebrate Marc Jacobs's new line that night—Yuki had invited him—and he'd blown it off. Chewing his bagel, he'd had no regrets.

After, he'd barreled down the West Side Highway and parked across the street from the loft, the cobblestones jostling the bags as he navigated—after all these years, Gerhard still hadn't mastered parallel parking. So the car was right where he needed it. A mile from the curb perhaps, but across the street from their building. Money. Money was Gerhard's problem. Nothing new there.

The door to the bank swung open as a white man with a red face and an expression of total astonishment blasted out of the glass-enclosed storefront. Surprisingly, the tier of ATMs was fairly empty. Gerhard sidled up to a machine right away, not wavering for even a moment before electing to withdraw one thousand dollars from ready-credit. It was the end of the world as he knew it. No amount of debt could possibly matter now.

Turning rapidly away from the ATM, still folding the crisp

bills into his money clip, Gerhard saw a young woman with short, sleek brown hair hunkered down on the floor in the corner of the bank. She was on her knees, near the banking receipts and deposit envelopes, at the foot of the little Plexiglas stand that housed the bank slips, where the pen chains always hung empty of pens—a personal pet peeve. Gerhard carried his own pen, a Mont Blanc that Elspeth had given him for no discernible holiday or occasion but solely because she wanted him to have it. Gerhard Falktopf carried his own pen; why couldn't the rest of the world? The young woman knelt next to this abominable-looking apparatus, her back to him, and her back to humanity. She was hunched forward, her spine was rounded, but he could still see the curve of her waist. Her jeans were cut low, and her striped top ascended the beads of her spine, the vertebrae rounded and countable as rosaries, so that Gerhard could see the soft down at the base of her back. Above that her cropped chocolate bob was as glossy as mink. If she were an American girl, this young, this stylish, she would have been sporting a tattoo on that small, flat plate of her sacrum. One of those thick black designs that looked remotely like Sanskrit, or a sunburst full of color. Obviously, she was not an American; she was a foreigner, a European, like him. Her clothes were so casual and so polished. This young woman was down on her knees on the floor of the bank, the most undefended part of her exposed. Gerhard noticed her shoulders shaking.

At home, Suzannah, his wife, was waiting for him. She was waiting for him with his son. His family needed Gerhard. They needed him to make them move. To get them out. This great city was under attack . . . New York was under attack, Gerhard could hardly believe it. He was a man who was needed at home, so Gerhard started to stride by her, this girl on the bank floor, when something stopped him, something made him hesitate, and when you hesitate you're lost, he knew this. Gerhard waited when, strategically, it was the only smart response to wait, but he never hesitated. Hesitating invariably was an act of improvidence.

Still, now, when he most needed to do something, take action, perform, for the first time in a very long time, as long as he could remember, Gerhard wavered, something made him stop—who knew what? He would wonder later. That stupid flickering philanthropic flame lit by Shingshang and his escape, that newfound urge to help, to assist? The fact that this girl was kneeling on a floor, a floor that was probably filthy, a girl on the filthy floor, the city in chaos, under attack. Perhaps she was hurt . . . From behind, she looked young, very young, tenderly young, barely out of her teens it seemed to Gerhard as he drew closer, those dark golden hairs on her sacrum . . . early twenties. She was kneeling on the floor of a bank, crying softly in the corner, while New York City crashed and burned around her.

Gerhard took two steps forward and leaned over, about to touch her shoulder, but here hesitant, too—why the hesitancy? —and said gently: "Fraulein?"

His native tongue.

When she turned he saw a baby securely wrapped up in the denim Baby Bjorn on her chest. No Fraulein, but Frau. A mother. Is there a more exalted role in this human theater? Instinctively Gerhard had stopped to assist a mother. He *was* good! Suzannah had worn Nikolai in just such a contraption day and night, until Gerhard had come to think of the thing as part of her body—like a kangaroo. They'd once had sex while she was wearing the gadget, baby inside, Gerhard coming at her from behind, Suzannah oddly anxious that this would somehow scar the kid psychologically. We had sex when Nikolai was still inside the belly, what's the difference now, argued Gerhard, as long as the baby didn't see him, as long as the baby was facing out? Wearing him like that, constantly, in the little

frontward-facing sling, was the only way to keep infant Nikolai from screaming, Suzannah's hips swaying like a stripper's,
rocking him around in her pouch. Gerhard had worried that
Suzannah's constant reliance on the carrier would give her cur-
vature of the spine, that it would destroy her regal posture,
but that was one worry that had not come to pass; one wasted
worry.

Gerhard had said, "Fraulein."

He corrected himself in French, and then his beloved English, "Madame, are you all right?"

<p>

SUZANNAH knocked on Celine's door. No answer. She rapped
harder on the wood with her knuckles; Nikolai perched on the
ledge of her hip.

"Celine, Celine," said Suzannah. She tried the doorknob,
but it was locked.

She rapped harder; then turned her fingers into a fist. Suzannah pounded on the door.

"Celine!"

"No babysitting," said Nikolai. He said it into her ear — a
whisper, a seduction, a supplication — like a lover. His little
cheeks, as white and puffy and dense as pork buns, still wet
from all his crying.

"Celine, for God's sake," said Suzannah.

The door opened, revealing a sleep-tousled Celine in creamy
sateen pajamas, the duvet draped around her, her long black
braids cascading in a waterfall past her shoulders. Her eyes
were still closed, like a newborn kitten's.

"Did I oversleep again?" asked Celine.

She smiled drowsily at Suzannah. She leaned over and
scratched at the bottom of her foot, a pink satin slipper. Her
nails were painted pink, too, so much pink against her black

skin. When she smiled, the pink insides of her lips glowed as if the glossy vibrant lipsticks she favored were applied on the inside, not the outside, of her patent-leather mouth.

Looking at Celine, this long-stemmed beauty, yawning and scratching, younger and more vulnerable upon waking, was like looking at the world before, before whatever just happened. Drowsy, striking, lazy Celine—for a second, seeing her made it feel retrievable, that other life. Suzannah remembered for a moment, walking down the hall just half an hour ago, maybe less, the way her panties had crept up the crack of her butt, how she had so casually snapped the elastic back into place, the routine of it—why was this silly detail the one she focused on? She thought of *him*, the man in free fall framed outside her window, she thought of *him*, just hours before standing in front of his bathroom mirror, maybe in his briefs, maybe with a towel around his waist, tying his tie. Maybe his wife, or his girlfriend, maybe his boyfriend, had stood behind him, as she sometimes did with Gerhard—Gerhard hated wearing ties—and tied his tie for him. That tie. That emblem of his professional status, his class, perhaps his education, his responsibilities, his taste, the tie that he hadn't taken off, the tie that flew behind him like a loosed tether when he dived.

If it were possible to develop the picture of him that was now etched inside her mind—this picture of him headfirst, tie flying, diving—if it were possible to develop the image that was seared inside her brain, to take it out and print it, would some woman somewhere, some wife or lover or sister or mother, see it and bring her hands to her mouth and whisper: "That's my Johnny"? Suzannah stared at Celine, Celine who still lived in a world before that man took flight, Suzannah afraid to speak and break the spell. That was before Celine opened her eyes and saw the expression on Suzannah's face. Then Celine's smile dissolved.

"Oh my God, Celine," said Suzannah. "Two planes flew

into the World Trade Center." For a reason she could not begin to fathom she felt like an idiot saying this, like she had made it all up in her own mind. Like she was a crazy person. She began to cry.

"Two?" said Celine. She was looking at Suzannah like she was counting inside her own head. One, two. One plus one. Elementary math, yet unfathomable. "What are you talking about?"

"People are going to be dying, Celine. Parents." Suzannah's voice was hushed. She had her hands over Nikolai's ears. "Parents are jumping . . . They're already dying, Celine." She whispered it like a secret.

"Why did two planes fly into the trade center?" said Celine. "Is it raining outside?"

There wasn't time for this. Suzannah pushed Celine back into her room, she set Nikolai down and grabbed Celine's jeans off the floor where she'd left them; they still held the shape of her body, stove pipe legs and naturally ruched at the hips. She handed them to Celine.

"Gerhard thinks we're under attack. We have to move quickly, we have to get out of here." Suzannah felt like she was a character in a bad TV show, a character saying lines she herself would scoff at. Dude, thought Suzannah, inexplicably, *Dude*, we have to get out of here. It was as if she were outside her own body as she spoke.

"Where are we going?" said Celine.

Suzannah stopped. It was a reasonable question to which she had no answer. She shook the question off; Gerhard would figure that out.

"Get dressed," said Suzannah.

It was at that moment that she realized she was still in her bathrobe.

It wouldn't take too long for them to put their clothes on and, working in tandem, to throw some juice boxes and Goldfish crackers into Nikolai's backpack. It wouldn't take them too long at all.

They would be ready for Gerhard when he came back.

❦

GERHARD was squatting on the floor of the bank, next to the young woman; he was waiting for an answer. He'd never done anything like that before in his life, never asked an intimate question of a stranger. It's not like he'd ever cared to, really. But here he was, low to the ground, in the middle of a man-made disaster, waiting when he should be moving, waiting for her response, waiting for her to say yes, she was fine, so he could move on, get out of there. He should get out of there, out of the bank, Gerhard knew this, but he stayed.

"It is my husband," she said, finally, as if she had been searching for words. She was French. Clearly she was French. Her accent was French. She had a very good haircut. She was wearing fashionable sneakers. Jeans. A boat-necked striped T-shirt, white and blue. The baby had a little striped chef's hat, a toque, on its little infant's head. His eyes were blue as marbles, but the mother's eyes were brown and full of tears. Her face beneath the fear was lovely. Her lips looked swollen and there was a smattering of freckles across her strong nose — all the bones in her face were strong: nose, jaw, cheeks — that mercifully kept her more interesting than perfect.

"Your husband?" said Gerhard. He said it again in German, although she was not German, she was clearly French, and he was fluent in French, and she, after all, was speaking English. German, French, English, a tangled twist of tongues, and yet they understood each other.

"He is lost," she sobbed. "Or I am lost. Oh God, we cannot find ourselves."

Outside the sirens blared. More and more people entered the bank. They knew enough to take out their money. More and

74

more people with sense. People who recognized the urgency with which they needed to flee.

"Maybe you should go home," said Gerhard. "Maybe he will meet you at your apartment?"

The young lady shook her head, and when she did, her tears sprayed off of her face, like cat whiskers.

"We are here on a visit. We are staying in a hotel. Over there . . ." the young woman gestured toward the hell of downtown. "We were in the hotel and he went out, he went out to the World Trade Center to get some rolls, my brioche, to get coffee . . ." She sobbed, out of words.

"There, there," said Gerhard. He couldn't believe himself. Gerhard Falktopf, almost clucking. It was what Suzannah would have done in this instance. His wife with her paralyzing sense of compassion. Her empathy.

The young woman caught her breath. She looked up at Gerhard, her eyes open, much too open; something could fall into eyes open like that. A person could fall in.

"Then it hit. It hit, and I got us out of the building, something fell on our building, on our hotel, and I got us out. I ran and I ran and I ran, and then I stood and watched, and then the other one, it hit; it hit, too. I went inside here. We came inside here," and her hand instinctively cupped over the head of her baby, like she was blessing him.

The baby's eyes were blue. The bluest eyes in the world. Also, the baby was quiet. Gerhard liked a baby that was quiet.

Gerhard nodded. She'd done the right thing, this French mother.

"I have no money, I have nowhere to go, I do not know where my husband is . . ." and the tears began to flow.

Gerhard gave her his hand. She took it. Surprisingly, her hand was warm and dry. Like his.

"Come," said Gerhard. "You two, you come with me."

☙

SUZANNAH was out in front of their building waiting for her husband, her son in her arms, the au pair by her side, when Gerhard, holding some young woman's hand, came rushing around the corner. The woman was carrying an infant in a Baby Bjorn, its little arms and legs flapping as she ran, like a live bug pinned to a board on its back. Whose child was that?

Now Gerhard was beckoning for Suzannah and the others to cross the street and meet up with him and this unfamiliar person, pointing halfway down the block to where, for the first time, Suzannah realized their car was parked, Gerhard barking something inaudible. An order obviously. An order to join him and this woman at the car — Suzannah needn't be a mind reader to figure that out — their car that was parked about a foot and a half from the curb, how had she missed it? The Mercedes, it jutted out into the street, that silver boat Gerhard couldn't park to save his life. They were standing in front of the building: Suzannah, his wife, with his son glued to her hip, and Celine, Celine, his au pair, holding Nikolai's black backpack, all of them scared out of their minds, Suzannah noted, while Gerhard held the hand of a stranger. A stranger with a baby.

Gerhard shouted, "Over here, I'm parked over here," but they were already rushing across the street, Suzannah looking both ways before she'd cross with Nikolai, even though there was no traffic; there was never any traffic on their block, they were so far west. Still she always made the boy look, too, to get him into gear, to ingrain the practice into him, a muscle memory — it worked that way for her, at the barre and in the center. Enough repetition and Suzannah's body would perform the movement unthinkingly, freeing the passions within, allowing them to shine. With Nikolai, repetition, behavior mod, whatever they called it, seemed sometimes to be the only way to get through to him; it was as if Suzannah were engraving the movement into his brain, the way the patterns of sound were in some numinous manner imprinted into the vinyl surface of her old records. Reasoning with her child did not seem to work, nor did thoughtful, pared-down explanations. There were times when Nikolai literally didn't seem to hear her. "Earth to Nikolai, Earth to Nikolai," Suzannah would say playfully at the playground or whenever she had an audience. At home, in private, she'd say, "Goddamn it, why don't you listen to me?" He often seemed to patently ignore her. Sometimes, like now, she'd have to physically turn Nikolai's head, taking his little chin in her fingers, sometimes she'd have to manipulate him so that he would see her lips move; today was one of those days.

Suzannah turned Nikolai's head and said: "Look both ways before you cross," turning his head back again, a little late as she was already approaching the other curb. Gerhard was by now unlocking the SUV and helping the young mother get in the back seat with her baby.

"The car seat is for Nikolai," Suzannah called out, grabby and defiant. The city was under attack. They were in the midst of evacuating their family. There was no need for politesse. She approached the car.

From within the SUV she heard Gerhard speak, apologetically, to the woman in French.

What was there to apologize for? Nikolai was his child!

Gerhard reached over and pulled the shoulder strap over this young woman and her baby, and then fastened the seat belt for them. Suzannah was standing behind him when he backed out of the van. He almost knocked her over; she had to take two steps back.

"Get in," said Gerhard.

"Gerhard, who is that?" said Suzannah.

Gerhard took Nikolai from her arms. Instantly the child began to shriek.

"Not now, Nikolai," said Gerhard.

Nikolai began to kick and scream, reaching for his mother.

"Goddamn it," said Gerhard.

"Give him to me," said Suzannah.

"Shut up," said Gerhard.

Was he speaking to her or to Nikolai? How dare he speak to either of them that way! "Just give him to me," said Suzannah.

Nikolai dove into her arms. It was almost as if Gerhard had propelled him there—Gerhard looked so disgusted with the kid. So disgusted with her.

"Who is that woman?" Suzannah said to Gerhard. "Who is that baby?"

Suzannah had never been so angry with him before. The skin on her face, her cheeks, her lips, was on fire; everything beneath that skin, jaw and teeth even, felt molten. Suzannah had been angry with Gerhard many times before this moment, yet she could not remember ever coming close to the intense wrath she felt now.

Suzannah waited for an answer. As she waited, she jounced Nikolai in her arms like he too was a baby, when of course he wasn't a baby any longer. She did it without thinking. It seemed the natural response in a time like this, although of course it was totally wrong, what did she ever do that was right? The jouncing made Nikolai scream louder and more atrociously. What was Gerhard's problem? Who were these people? Why was he wasting time?

"Who are they, Gerhard?" Suzannah could wait no longer; she demanded an answer.

Gerhard gave a helpless little shrug. Gerhard?

That was scary.

"I don't know," said Gerhard.

"You don't know?" Suzannah felt her own voice rising, with what now? Powerlessness? Fear? All of the above? It would have to rise, to be heard over Nikolai.

What was that smell? Plastic, paper, metal? All burning. She was burning. The buildings were burning. The world.

Celine scooted past Suzannah, into the car, securing her own place with a seat belt.

"Put the kid in the car, Suzannah," Gerhard said. Again, a command. This time he sounded tired.

Suzannah stared at him; she was furious, but her options were limited. What else was she to do? Pitch a fit and waste more time? Furious at her own impotence, she leaned over and placed Nikolai in his car seat. She twisted at the waist and reached over to fasten his straps, but she couldn't get the little T-bar in the middle to catch.

"For God's sake, Celine," snapped Suzannah. "Help me out."

Celine reached over and threaded the metal piece into the little plastic receptor, the male piece into the female, that's how it read in the instruction manual. Once, in her former life, Suzannah had entertained an entire dinner party with a dramatic interpretation of the instructional manual of Nikolai's car seat, but now its cumbersome qualities were, ironically, an impediment to their safety. It was only when the T-bar was securely locked into place that Suzannah looked past the web of her own hair, which had fallen into her eyes, to see the young mother and baby in her car. The young woman was crying behind her hand. She was trying to shield the world from her tears.

Instantly, Suzannah felt ashamed of herself. This woman was suffering. Obviously, she was even further along the path of terror and pain than Suzannah was at this point. Would Suzannah soon arrive at the same place?

"Forgive me," said Suzannah. "It's just that I'm so scared."

The young woman nodded at Suzannah from behind her hand, from behind her hand she was trying to contain herself. There was some dignity in the gesture, although she looked ready to collapse.

Suzannah took a deep breath.

"I am Suzannah," said Suzannah.

The woman tried to speak, but could not. She shook her head regretfully.

Suzannah backed out of the car and turned to Gerhard, but

he'd already rushed around the front end and was entering the driver's seat. This left Suzannah to open her own car door and haul herself into the vehicle. If she didn't hurry, if she weren't fast enough, would Gerhard take off without her?

As if in silent response, Gerhard peeled out of the parking spot even before Suzannah had the safety belt securely stretched across her chest.

"She was on the floor of the bank," said Gerhard quietly to Suzannah, as she looked at him imploringly over the plastic drink containers. Nikolai was, of course, still screaming. "She was on the floor of the bank with the baby."

"Shut up, Nikolai," Gerhard yelled into the back seat.

"Is the duck back there, Celine?" Suzannah tried to speak above the din. "For God's sake, Celine, try the duck."

Gerhard took a left turn and the Mercedes swung uptown, against traffic. He indicated to the right with his head, to downtown and the twin infernos: "Her husband, he's somewhere in there."

More and more emergency vehicles whizzed past, fire trucks, ambulances . . . EMS. They were all heading south, to the tip of the city, to the towers. No one was going uptown, it seemed. No one save a lumbering bus, a befuddled taxi. Foot traffic. People walking. Some of them walking backwards, eyes up, riveted, unable to tear themselves away, like Stepford wives, automatons. No one armored was going where they were going, not rescuers, liberators, saviors. The Falktopfs tore uptown at record speed.

Gerhard raced through a red light, then another, driving fast, way too fast for the city, for the city and its laws and its traffic. Except there wasn't much traffic. And what laws? They were at war! They were under attack. Were they at war yet? There was traffic only when they crossed major arteries, which they did now, Madison, Park, Lexington, each avenue a dangerous dash through the onslaught of the zooming vehicles with sirens, rushing to help, rushing to save. A battalion of rescuers, brave, kind, just, while the Falktopfs were running away as fast as they could, getting the hell out of there.

"Oh my God," said Suzannah. The world made no sense. The world was flashing by her. It ticked past like so many cartoon cels, in a staccato charge, a herky-jerky, headlong, forward motion. Like one of those little flipbooks you got as a kid, turn the pages quickly and you make a movie. Today the world was like a movie. Like CNN, *Nightline*. The media, entertainment—they were the only reference, the only way to make sense of the thing. What was happening here, now, would be broadcast somewhere else, later. Later, somewhere else, a compassionate almost-young mother would be lying in her bed watching the mayhem, the madness, and murmur, "Those poor, poor people," and then she'd turn away from the screen, away from her husband, too sensitive to behold the sight, and say, "Darling, please turn it off."

Someone like her.

Suzannah turned in her seat to the sobbing young woman. "I'm so, so sorry."

The young woman nodded again through her tears. Her face was wrinkled and swollen from all that repressed crying, the tears fairly oozing out. Her nose was red. The baby's eyes were open. God, they were blue. They were so blue, it was weird. So blue it hurt.

The poor thing, thought Suzannah. The poor tiny little unknowing powerless baby.

Nikolai kept screaming. There was a numbing metronomic simplicity to his cries. Like chanting. Suzannah chanted now and again. She chanted because why not? She chanted in yoga class because everyone else did it and sporadically it suited her, relaxing her with all that soft East Villagey philosophy, making her less twitchy, less nuts; for a while she'd even thought about becoming a Buddhist—because, unlike neurotic New

York Jews married to difficult, demanding, genius manchildren of Nazis, Buddhists seemed calm. Nikolai's screams had a rhythm all their own and they corresponded with some tidal pull inside her. Or maybe she was just used to them, used to them in theory, because Suzannah felt as if she could stand them right now, Nikolai's manic cries. Still, the veins in Gerhard's temples were pulsating wildly. He looked like he might have a stroke. Which wouldn't be good, would it? It would not be good for Gerhard to have a stroke right now.

Suzannah took hold of herself. Or rather it just happened to her, a sudden surge of control, God-given and out of the blue, rising up through her body, while she gazed at her husband's pulsating veins, the untamed muscle wild in his jaw. This had happened before to them in crises—as if collapsing was something you could take turns with. It was what marriage was, Suzannah thought, when it was working: one person handling what the other cannot.

"The duck, Celine," said Suzannah, with a dry, sandy firmness that came from someone who was just past the point of losing it, someone who had crested and then crossed over to another peak, pulling it together, turning the corner to the other side. "I think it's in the black bag."

Mercifully, Celine fished the duck out of the bag, a plastic backpack with its own foldout changing tarp and bottle holder, and gave it to Nikolai. The gift had been from the girls and boys in the corps—they'd thrown her a surprise shower one day when she'd stopped by rehearsal to teach the warm-up barre. She'd been eight and a half months' pregnant at the time, Nikolai like a little bowling ball in her belly—she hadn't even looked knocked up from the back, her arms and legs still thin and muscular, like an ant with its swollen torso and spindly limbs. Suzannah had had trouble gaining weight—nausea through the eighth month; is that what Nikolai's "stuff" was all about? About her and her inability to nourish him? How could a baby develop properly on soy lattes and rice crackers? All those tuna sandwiches on dry rye toast. Was it the mercury? Was it the mercury in the canned fish that made him scream? After his birth, Suzannah could no longer stand to even read about tuna sandwiches on a diner menu — a wave of nausea would hit her.

Now Nikolai began to chew aggressively on the duck's beak. He couldn't really scream and chew simultaneously — it took him a few halfhearted attempts to realize this — and so he just jawed down on the thing, Suzannah watching in the mirror of her visor. She snapped shut first the mirror and then the visor back into place. She reclined in her seat and rested her head on the seat back.

"Where are we going?" said Suzannah.

"Elspeth's. I still have the keys," said Gerhard.

"Elspeth's," said Suzannah. Elspeth's "cottage." That handsome, sprawling manse on the sea. From another life. Why not? It was a beautiful day. Why not go for a ride? Why not go to the beach? East Hampton. The irony in that hit Suzannah sideways, so hard she started to laugh.

"What's so funny?" said Gerhard. He turned to look at her. His face was worried, his eyes intent. But he was courting a little half-smile on his mug, like he truly wanted to hear something funny. Like he wanted to laugh himself. Like he wanted her to entertain him. Like he wanted for them to be the way they usually were, Gerhard and Suzannah, their usual standard way.

"It's just that when my grandparents fled the pogroms, they ran to a neighboring shtetl. You and me, Gerhard, we're refugees to the Hamptons."

Gerhard smirked. The situation was so frightening and yet so patently absurd.

"So they loaded up the truck and they moved to Beverly," Suzannah sang a little under her breath.

She reached out her hand and patted Gerhard's forearm. The curly silver hairs. Gerhard caught her hand and brought her fingertips to his lips.

"What?" said Gerhard. His lips felt dry, like rice paper. He brushed them next against her knuckles, her wedding ring. "What's that song?"

They approached the Midtown Tunnel, both of Gerhard's hands back firmly on the steering wheel. Police cars stood at the entrance with a small crowd of people on foot waiting next to them. The cops seemed to be waving cars over and then randomly placing some of the pedestrians in the halted vehicles before sending them carpooling through the cavernous warren that wended under the East River to safety. Gerhard slowed down as he approached the little knot of people, but with one quick glance at their crowded SUV, a police officer waved them on. A black man in a blue uniform motioned for the Falktopfs to leave the burning city while he himself elected to stay behind and make it safer. For the first time in her life, Suzannah felt grateful for the police, for the first time she felt aware of them. It was 9:20 in the morning. Suzannah knew, because she looked at the dashboard at the moment the SUV left all that mad, natural light and entered the artificial fluorescent glow of the tunnel. It was 9:20 and then it was 9:21. The numbers glimmered digitally, which made them easier to see in the dimness, the yellow.

"It's from a TV show when I was a kid," said Suzannah. She meant the jingle.

The tunnel seemed obscenely narrow to her today. She wondered about the empty lane on their left. Was it supposed to be empty? Was it always empty? Why was no traffic coming in the other direction? Was it because nobody wanted to?

"Oh," said Gerhard, losing the thread. Apparently they did not have *The Beverly Hillbillies* in Germany when Gerhard was a child. He was so much older; he was so different from

Suzannah in so many ways it was hard to take inventory. The only reference points they sometimes appeared to have from the life they hadn't spent together was the language of the studio. Every once in a while this disconnect hit her like a cold wave. Gerhard and Suzannah had nothing in common, nothing except dance. Except absolutely everything.

"These hillbillies, they struck oil in their backyard, they made millions. 'Black gold, Texas tea,'" Suzannah said, remembering. The tunnel, it seemed to go on forever. Was it dug out of bedrock? Or was it surrounded by water? Why hadn't she ever wondered about any of this before? Why hadn't she noticed? She and Gerhard had once driven the tunnel under Mont Blanc, twenty miles, forty minutes, burrowed through mountain between Italy and France, no means of escape, no way to get out. She'd gone insane with the claustrophobia of the journey. That singular, specific panic was newly awakened in her memory. It roared to life inside her. Would she ever again taste outside?

"'They said California is the place you've gotta be, so they loaded up the truck and moved to Beverly.'" Suzannah sort of half-sang the theme song. It warbled within her throat with her latest surge of fear. The words were moronic. She knew she sounded like an idiot, that she went on too long, but she couldn't help herself. Reconstructing the queer little song kept her from screaming.

In the back seat the baby began to babble. Perhaps the silly television jingle was working for somebody. Nikolai was still chewing on the duck. The light at the end of the tunnel got brighter. As they sped away from the mouth of the sarcophagus, the Port Authority guys and the NYPD began blockading the entrance to the tunnel. The Midtown Tunnel was being blockaded behind them. The Falktopfs' car was the last car out it seemed . . . Wait, there was a Town Car she could spy in her side mirror. Was it still the driver's job to whisk some fat cat out of town as if his own safety didn't matter, or was salvation an added benefit to the job? A yellow cab crossed lanes behind them as the tunnel was being shut down, the city shut off, a major artery cut, isolating everyone (all those people!) trapped on the other side.

"What?" said Suzannah, unlocking her seat belt and turning around to stare. "They're sealing off the city!

"Look, Gerhard," said Suzannah.

Gerhard did not turn his head; he did not glance in the rearview mirror. Instead he leaned into the gas.

"Look, Gerhard," said Suzannah.

As the car moved forward, curving down the elevated expressway, Suzannah saw the skyline. It was spectacular. The Empire State Building. The Chrysler Building. The World Trade Center. Those two big, beautiful skyscrapers, silver and familiar, bright in the sunlight glancing off the lower stories and above progressively shrouded in a great big swath of shadowy black smoke. The towers were bleeding the stuff. The black smoke was wrapping around the throat of the two buildings, and the tails of the smoke, like long scarves, were unfurling across the city. Like the Angel of Death it seemed to her. What was that movie? *Ben-Hur?* Yul Brynner, Charlton Heston as Moses. Moses! Exodus. Even from Queens when Suzannah looked at the towers she could see the feathers of red flames piercing the black clouds — so the fires weren't out yet.

Soon, thought Suzannah. Soon those firefighters will put that fire out. They are probably doing exactly that this very minute. They are probably doing their jobs.

"My God, Gerhard, look!"

Gerhard's eyes floated up. She could see them in the rearview mirror. She could see them memorizing the destruction of the towers. His blue, blue eyes.

The baby in the back seat had blue eyes, too. Unearthly blue blue.

Suzannah turned in her seat to look at them.

At the moment, the baby had his eyes shut. He was sucking on his mother's finger. His mother looked literally scared to death.

Celine was shaking next to her. Her teeth were chattering and her whole body was vibrating.

"Don't worry, Celine," said Suzannah.

She reached out her arm to the girl, to pat her leg. It shook beneath her hand. Celine grabbed her hand; she squeezed it hard.

"We can't go back," said Celine. Her teeth were going so fast her words came out choppy, staccato. "They've locked us out."

"We don't want to go back," said Gerhard.

"Not yet," Suzannah murmured, reassuringly. "We'll go back soon," she said, "when the fires are out."

Suzannah spiraled even further in her seat. She looked at the mysterious French woman.

"When the fires are out, we will return and find your husband, okay?" she said.

The woman stared at her. She did not appear to comprehend what Suzannah was saying. Her eyes were open and wide and her head shook a little from side to side.

"Does she speak English?" Suzannah asked Gerhard.

"Of course she speaks English," said Gerhard. "All of Europe speaks English. The whole fucking world, we speak English."

Gerhard took a turn, over a rise in the parkway, past some industrial buildings, a big cemetery on the right rising out of the ground, a sign for assisted living on the left — did the two go hand in hand? Nursing homes and a boneyard?

"She's just too afraid now to speak," said Gerhard.

Was he now an authority on this stranger? How did Gerhard know what she was feeling? How did he know anything about the woman in Suzannah's back seat? Who was she to him?

Suzannah turned around again to look at her.

Celine, still holding Suzannah's hand, began to murmur something in French into the woman's ear. Suzannah's back seat was filled with frightened French girls. Beautiful, frightened French girls, more delicate and deserving of understanding and consolation than she was.

"Celine," said Suzannah. Celine's grip was cutting off her circulation. She gently tried to extricate her hand. "Celine, please translate for me — tell her we'll come back to find her husband as soon as the fires are out." Suzannah wriggled her fingers free.

Celine whispered to the woman in French. The woman nodded gratefully at Suzannah and then whispered in English, "Thank you."

So Gerhard was right. She did speak English.

Suzannah tried to smile. She wanted to be supportive. The woman tried to smile back. They were all trying now. Even the baby opened his lids and flashed Suzannah his blue, blue eyes.

Suzannah turned back to the road ahead. Another rest home on her right. Was Queens the capital of these things? she wondered. Maybe she should have moved her mother out here. Her mother! Was her mother safe? Would the health care attendants and nurses' assistants at the Hebrew Home for the Aged stay and watch over her mother and the other patients? Or would they flee, the way Suzannah was now fleeing? Would they save themselves and leave poor defenseless Judy Sucher in her foggy bubble? Whoever had done this, they wouldn't bomb a Home for the Aged, would they? Of course they would, they've just bombed two buildings full of innocent workers — and artists, weren't there some studios at the top of one of those buildings, didn't Stan that sculptor guy who used to hang out with her friend Eve, didn't Stan have a studio in one of those towers? Was he up there right now? Stan with the painter's pants, Stan in his forties still wearing painter's pants. Was he climbing down? Would the workers at the Hebrew Home for the Aged just leave her mother to these merciless people? She had Alzheimer's. Could her mother still feel fear? Was she afraid now, up in Riverdale, was she frightened? Suzannah didn't want her mother frightened. Suzannah looked past Gerhard's left shoulder; the Bronx seemed not to be on fire. There was nothing to attack in the Bronx, anyway, thought Suzannah.

"Do you have your cell phone?" she asked Gerhard.

The city and its skyline had disappeared; the horizon in the distance was graying from smoke. There was some traffic, but nothing to impede their progress as they drove forward into the sunshine, nothing out of the ordinary. Bagels, karate schools, the Afghan Kebab House, McDonald's. In Queens everything seemed almost normal.

Gerhard glanced at her.

"My mother," she said. Her voice trembled a little when she said this.

Gerhard nodded at her. He understood. She felt grateful for this.

With his right foot still on the gas, Gerhard straightened out his left leg and withdrew his cell phone from his front pocket. He passed it over to his wife. Suzannah kept her head turned, hoping to glimpse the skyline one more time as she dialed, but it didn't happen. The phone call didn't happen. The cell phone seemed to be working, that is, it was juiced, but the line at the Hebrew Home for the Aged was busy, busy or it was broken; something, it was something that meant no one was answering it. So the phone call didn't happen and the skyline didn't happen either. The previous glimpse was the final time that she saw it, the skyline, the skyline as Suzannah had come so quickly to expect and remember it, burning and enwrapped with black smoke. With two towers.

GERHARD drove. He turned on the radio and then he drove and drove and the interior of his car was oddly quiet, save for the soft, shuddering moans of the French woman in the back, like a dove cooing, as they listened intently to the news that was whooshing—why all that *whoosh* in radio broadcasting?—as the DJs or whoever were interviewing all those sobbing bystanders—"It's a sunny day so it looked like a silver flash, and then we thought it was debris, you know, but it was people falling"—citizens of the nation telling Gerhard again and again what he already knew. Eyewitnesses crying into the microphone. How come they had time to talk? Nobody on the radio could believe it; no one could believe what was happening to their city. Every single eyewitness interviewed could not believe his eyes. What was not to believe? thought Gerhard. People were terrible. Look at the country of his birth. He had understood this from the moment he was born.

It was as if his whole life he knew this day was coming. Two planes had flown into the Twin Towers. Did it matter who flew them? Someone somewhere wanted other people to suffer. Why not? Someone somewhere was always orchestrating someone else's demise.

"I don't understand," said Suzannah. "Why not a military outpost, or a governmental compound—why an office building?"

An office building, thought Gerhard, because that's where people are.

"It is 9:43 A.M.," whooshed the radio announcer, "and a bomb has just exploded at the Pentagon."

"They bombed the Pentagon?" said Suzannah. Astounded. Even after what she just saw. "The Pentagon?" She repeated herself. Once again this morning, Suzannah was busy being stunned.

She looked up at him, again with those big brown eyes. It was as if her mother had mated with a deer.

"Gerhard," she whispered, shaking her head. "Gerhard."

"We're okay, Suzie," he said. "We're okay and that's all that matters."

Outside a Range Rover cut him off. Gerhard leaned hard on the car horn. After a while he heard Celine whisper; she was whispering in French. Not to Nikolai as he had hoped—Gerhard had hoped when he hired her that Celine would speak to Nikolai only in French—but to the woman sitting next to her. Celine was quietly translating the news, which was now being relayed rapid-fire. The White House was being evacuated.

"The White House?" said Suzannah. "Where's Bush? Who is running the country?"

Americans, thought Gerhard. What luxury. They think they are untouchable.

"Eyewitness reports a plane and not a bomb has hit the Pentagon."

Another plane? Gerhard drove faster and faster, farther and farther away from national landmarks and other strategic targets. No one would bother to attack the beach. His family would be safe there.

Gerhard ran a hand through his hair. It was damp at the roots—he'd been sweating and now the sweat was beginning to cool. It was drying on his skin. He took a deep breath. His heartbeat was slowing in his chest. He was little by little reawakening to an awareness of these things. His needs. Number one on Gerhard's list of needs was that he needed to pee. Gerhard needed to pee and he wanted a cup of coffee.

He signaled and took the next exit, pulling off the highway.

"Gerhard, what are you doing?" said Suzannah.

Gerhard slowed down on the off ramp and drove toward what anywhere else in the country would officially be a strip mall but here in Queens was just a shopping street—low-level chain stores, ethnic restaurants, a bingo palace, and a catering hall.

He pulled into a parking spot in front of a McDonald's.

"Gerhard?"

"I need to pee," said Gerhard.

Suzannah stared at him beseechingly. It was the kind of look that said: "Aren't we running for our lives?"

She was right, of course, but the urgency to their flight suddenly seemed to be draining away, leaving him feeling slightly weak.

"Look around you," said Gerhard.

They were in the heart of Queens. Or maybe Long Island. Who knew, somewhere around Exit 30. The sun was shining. The Earth was turning. There was traffic but not much. Trucks were lumbering by.

"No one is going to fly a plane into that McDonald's," said Gerhard.

He needed to pee. He needed caffeine. His head was beginning to hurt. In the caffeine spot, between his eyebrows, there was a widening crack of pain, a fissure.

He shifted around to look at the crew in the back seat. A car full of women. Women waiting for him to take the lead. Women and children. Like a lifeboat. It was preposterous that he should find himself in this position. What did he know truly about taking care of anyone?

He took a deep breath.

"Would any of you like anything to drink?" said Gerhard. He said it like an American father, like any American father.

"I'll take a Coke?" said Celine. "And some of those cookies?"

She'd been in New York long enough that most of her statements sounded like questions, her inflections those of a native teenager. She wasn't shaking anymore, but her face still looked ashen.

Gerhard nodded. He gazed inquisitively at the French woman.

"Martine," she said.

"Martine," said Gerhard. She had only partially answered him.

"Some milk for the baby?" Martine said. "And an Egg Mc-Muffin? He'll eat the egg—the baby will."

"One Egg McMuffin coming up," said Gerhard, trying for a smile.

Martine tried to smile back.

"And a coffee, please, for me?" said Martine.

"Sure," said Gerhard, "my pleasure." This time he smiled for her.

Then he turned back to Suzannah. She was still strapped in the other bucket seat. She was staring at him. Dumbfounded.

Just when Gerhard was beginning to wonder if he should bother getting worried about this, too—about Suzannah's state —she deflated.

"Oh, for God's sake," said Suzannah. She sank back into the car seat. "A Diet Coke for me—some of those Ronald McDonald cookies for Nicky."

Gerhard nodded. He opened the car door and swung his legs out, stood and stretched. It was a beautiful day. Still beautiful. Still the same beautiful day. Incredible.

Gerhard shut the door, leaving his family safely in the car, and walked slowly toward the fast-food restaurant, his legs stiff and wobbly, like a marionette's. But he was not a marionette, he was walking freely, walking not running, under his own steam toward a McDonald's. The sun was shining and on the street people were moving without fear or favor, unaware, it seemed, of the chaos Gerhard had escaped less than a half-hour before. It was as if instead of just crossing the East River, he had taken his family and driven them backward in time.

For a moment, Gerhard questioned his own sanity. New York was under attack, scores of people were dying, and yet at the exact same time that this catastrophe was occurring, this holocaust—and Gerhard was not one to use the word lightly, but people were burning to death, people were being incinerated!—Gerhard Falktopf was entering a McDonald's. In Queens. An SUV full of hungry, scared women and children waiting for him at the curb. He pushed open the plate-glass door.

There were three clerks behind the counter, two heavyset young women and a fry cook, all in the requisite uniforms, red and gold like drum majorettes, and a white-aproned young man behind in the kitchen. The girls were rather sullen in their heavy gold jewelry: earrings that stretched their lobes, you'd need lobes of steel for such finery, and thick, loopy name necklaces with thick, loopy names, impossible to read. Still, for all that gold you'd think there would be more of a lift to their collective mood. The single emotional chord here was boredom. Blessed boredom. One young woman wore her hair like Nefertiti, black bobby pins shaping her hair into a cone.

Is it possible that they still don't *know?* Gerhard wondered.

He elected to say nothing but requested the Cokes and Diet Cokes, cookies and coffees that would feed his charges. After placing his order, he walked to the back of the restaurant, pushed forward the red swinging door to the men's room, and entered the clean public restroom of the McDonald's. Were there more attacks in Manhattan since they'd fled? Was their building still standing? Gerhard stood before the urinal emptying his bladder—he was peeing and peeing and peeing, never before had so much urine left his body—when he realized that he'd forgotten to take the Agnes Martin. The Agnes Martin. He'd left it to the fires and the missiles. Would he ever see it again?

Gerhard washed his hands in the sink. The act itself seemed ridiculous, but oddly lifesaving. New York was under attack and Gerhard was washing his hands in a public restroom. Finally he understood the difference between knowing you are going to be sent to battle and then being there, being in battle, actively being shot at, and still somehow surviving it all and moving on. The accidents of time and space and luck; their cruelties and beneficences. Gerhard forgot to take the Agnes Martin but he didn't forget to wash his hands. Could he carry on without that painting? Its magnificence had sustained him these past heartbreaking weeks; the privilege of being able to gaze at it was what had gotten him up each and every morning. That and the jet propulsion of his rage. But now, standing before the sink, soaping up, lathering carefully between his fingers like a surgeon would, for the first time in a long time, as long as he could remember, Gerhard didn't feel angry. None of it seemed to matter anymore. Art never saved anyone from anything.

The idea hit with an intensity that startled him. The sweat on his body had cooled and his skin, especially on the back of his neck, felt stiff. He rolled his head and then washed his neck. Art never saved anyone from anything. The thought was both emancipating and unmooring.

Gerhard dried his hands under the electric dryer, and the back of his neck as well — the hot air felt good there — and then he kicked the restroom door ajar with his foot, and again, like a surgeon, used an elbow to push it open. He walked down the hallway and returned to the counter. He collected the drinks and the cookies in the little cardboard tray that one of the servers thoughtfully provided for him and paid up. Then he made his way back out into the sunshine, stopping in the doorway to say thank you (he'd forgotten) and when the young lady in question smiled a big "you're welcome" smile in return for his recognition, grateful really, for this human kindness, Gerhard, who was frozen in his exit — one foot in the bright outside world, one in the dark safety of the restaurant — felt for a single inexplicable moment as if he might cry out. He took a breath then, composed himself, and stepped out on to the sidewalk, blinking that world back into focus (and the world he was focusing on was Queens, multi-ethnic, workaday, bad-architecture Queens — thank God for it). At this point, his wife, his Suzannah, swung open her car door to take the refreshments from him; it was Suzannah who was reaching out her long, lovely arms to ease his burden. Gerhard was still alive. He was still alive and blessedly he was enveloped in a moment of fantastic mundanity, dispensing drinks to his passengers in the back seat of his car, passing the Diet Coke to his stunned, pretty wife. He *was* an American husband, an American father. The thought itself made him feel lighter. Almost giddy.

He waited until Suzannah sat back down in her bucket seat and fastened her seat belt and then with a gentleman's good grace he shut her car door for her. He walked around the SUV's front bumper and opened his own side door. Gerhard slipped into the driver's seat of the SUV, fastened his own seat belt, turned the key in the ignition, put the car in reverse, and pulled out. He pulled out onto the street, drove to the corner, turned around, and drove back so that he could reenter the Long Island Expressway two blocks over. In the back of the car was the symphonic sound of sipping and slurping, eating and drinking, burping and farting (Nikolai), respirating, swallowing. Life in the land of the living.

It was at this precise moment that Gerhard realized that he'd neglected to check in with Yuki. She must be scared and she would need him. She was just a kid. She'd be waiting for his call.

Gerhard reached into his pocket for his cell phone. Then he pulled it back out again. What was he going to say to her? *I'm sorry I forgot you? I made my choice?* And all of this in front of Suzannah? There was no point. He put the cell phone back into his jeans pocket.

They were going to the beach. The sooner the better. The salt air. The rhythmic rushing sound of the waves. The soft sand. Everything had changed for him. Gerhard pressed his foot down on the gas pedal. He bet the water in East Hampton was still warm enough to swim in. He could not wait to get there.

He reached over to turn the radio back on, glancing at the clock as he turned the dial. "It is 10:05," said the radio announcer, corroborating the visual evidence in front of Gerhard. "September 11th, 2001. The South Tower of the World Trade Center has collapsed."

THE SURF was up.

There was no one on the beach but Suzannah and Nikolai—and a trespasser. Nikolai wasn't exactly paying attention to his mother; he was busy building roadways in the sand, and the trespasser—who was skimming the surface of the ocean on his surfboard and therefore wasn't exactly "trespassing" anything—the *surfer* was out riding the waves. So for all practical purposes, Suzannah was alone. Alone with company, which was how she had spent most of her life.

For a moment Suzannah could not quite see him, the surfer, nor the Atlantic Ocean, for that matter, and it was splayed out and open, sprawling wide before her, not just a tiny black surfing squiggle on the horizon (the light refracting off the water was truly blinding, a blinding, brilliant white), but if she squinted and used her hand as a visor, Suzannah noted that the swells were spectacularly high and the surfer was making good use of them. She'd left her sunglasses—a love gift from Gerhard—back on her desk in the city. The waves were breaking a long way from shore now, first swelling glassine and dramatic, then shooting glinting shards of seawater as they crashed, sending harmless foam and lacy froth racing up the beach onto the sand . . . before sucking it all back out to sea again. Suzannah kept Nikolai at some distance from the water's edge. After the day they'd had, she swore she would never let him out of her sight again.

They sat together, the little boy safe between her knees — which were bent and spread, her elbows on her kneecaps, her body creating a shelter for him as he played — up the beach where the sand began to amass into a minor-league cliff. A bluff, she corrected herself. It was a bluff that raised Elspeth's cottage above the shore and the sea and gave every room in that monster-sized vacation home such a world-class view of Main Beach that the house itself was — Gerhard had assessed greedily after Elspeth's death — close to priceless. Or, correcting herself again, the priceless view was of what half a mile down the road was termed Main Beach, where the East Hampton proletariat did their bathing. Here at Elspeth's, the beach was private — it was "Elspeth's Beach" to the Falktopfs and to the locals — and since Elspeth was dead, and her offspring were fomenting, fighting nut-jobs, and the world was coming to an end, and the Falktopfs at this moment had possession, possession being nine-tenths of the law and all that, this beach was theirs. It was hers and Nikolai's.

They had their bare feet planted in the cool, moist sand, sand the grayish, brownish blond of the fur of her old Siamese cat, Buster. The air tasted saline, briny, with a hint of iodine; it smelled like a freshly opened oyster, and Suzannah inhaled the scent deeply, that thick, salty, enriched air somehow branching out and nourishing her body, inducing a sense of calm. Between the perfect weather — the air was cool but the sun was hot — the rhythmic in-and-out of the waves in tantric yogic breaths, the tickle of her little boy's fingers on the skin of the sand, underneath the surface Suzannah could swear the Earth was purring. She and her Super-Bunny, they had their pants rolled up past their ankles. Nikolai was busy, digging with a shell she'd found for him for just this purpose.

Up on the bluff in the cottage, Gerhard was probably pulling sheets off the furniture — she could almost see the dust motes dance in the sunlight as he pulled those drop cloths off the rattan and linen in the Florida room like a magician with a tablecloth: "Voilà, another ugly, expensive piece of furniture!" or when he unwrapped the heavy mahogany and silks in the formal living areas, the wainscoted dining room, book-lined sitting room, the redundancy of the sofa'ed parlor. Or maybe Gerhard was upstairs, turning on the various television sets in the various bedroom suites, searching for more bad news — although once the radio spit out the inconceivable information that not one but both towers had collapsed while Suzannah and her family were toodling along on the LIE, she'd had enough reportage, she thought, to last a lifetime.

What an idiot she was, Suzannah reflected now, as she watched the light play on her son's soft curls, her first disbelieving response upon hearing that initial communiqué had been: "I wonder why they didn't wait longer to demolish it," meaning the South Tower of course. (This one she'd said out loud! Much to Gerhard's incredulousness.) Even now, hours later, she couldn't quite believe it. How did a building that big fall exactly? It hadn't toppled over sideways, had it? The descriptions on the radio made it sound like one floor had just pancaked down upon another, *thunk thunk thunk*, collapsing in upon itself with clouds of smoke billowing out. In her mind, Suzannah pictured a mushroom cloud, but that couldn't possibly be what it was like . . .

She'd said to Gerhard, "I guess they must have already gotten all those people out," as if the disintegration of the building had been orchestrated, as if it had been ordained by the powers that be, as if the destruction of those two massive skyscrapers had been by design by people who knew better than she what the correct response was to any set of circumstances, by people who knew what to do next. (Were there still any "powers that be"? They'd heard the mayor on the radio, the mayor who had announced to the media that he was divorcing his wife before he'd even bothered to inform her himself ... Now Rudy sounded strong and fatherly in the moment, asking for calm, for good behavior, reassuring Suzannah and her fellow citizens with his composed and compassionate leadership. Isn't that what Suzannah was always craving, a good leader? A father? Isn't that what her stupid shrink kept on telling her? Her own father was dead, and he hadn't had much of that mythical fatherly gravitas, had he, when he was still living. He hadn't been much of a protector.)

Suzannah's palm carved out a small semicircle of sand; she decorated it with her forefinger, an *S* for Suzannah, and then she wiped that slate clean, before repeating the process over and over again, inscribing herself into the earth and then erasing her individual signature, for absolutely no reason at all.

She married an older man. A mentor. You need not pay a shrink to explore that one, although Suzannah did just that. She had paid three different shrinks buckets and buckets of money she didn't have solely for the exquisite torture of examining her relationship with her father over and over again, holding up its cracked crystal to the light. And what hay those therapists made of her decision to marry Gerhard! (And what about her decision to engage only male psychiatrists? Suzannah smirked as the thought occurred to her, envisioning the tens of thousands of dollars more she didn't have being spent on a new battalion of psychotherapists just to scrutinize *this* slice of her psyche, blowing Nikolai's tuition, preschool through college, in the bargain.)

According to Shrink #2, Gerhard was the mythic father she'd never had, "and all that," remarked Suzannah ironically, when she'd run home and reported this statement to her almost amused husband. Shrink #3 called Gerhard "the powerhouse creator of her universe." Gerhard had nodded heartily at that one—validated and not a little bit flattered that a stranger saw him as he saw himself, Suzannah supposed.

Well, it was true, she was crazy about him; Gerhard gave her direction and order. His genius had defined her purpose here on Earth (to dance, to satisfy him) and had given her life meaning, and perimeters — she wasn't going to go off to Great Neck and marry a dentist now, was she, or to Paris to apprentice to a fashion designer; she was never going to finish college or go to law school like her father had always wanted her to do; up until the fiasco with the company she'd just assumed that with Gerhard by her side she was going to remain the muse and erstwhile prima ballerina to one of modernism's great living choreographers, she was going to birth and raise his children, and when age ended both these exalted runs, she'd be a mythic emeritus, and sometimes she might teach. Period. Who knew what was going to become of her now?

With Gerhard, there was never a dull moment. Suzannah liked to state with a mordant logic that she hung in just for the entertainment value, not always ready to own up to the fact that for most of her life she'd been helplessly in love with him; Shrink #1 said she hung in out of fear. Whatever. Gerhard had all but refused the role she'd initially cast him for, the role of father. He wouldn't play Daddy to her; his own needs were just too clamorous and insistent. In terms of Nikolai, it had been enough to get Gerhard to agree to simply "father" him; the rest of it, nurture and all that, was outside Gerhard's social contract, his native ken. It just wasn't his strong suit. All three shrinks agreed on one point: she had no choice but to accept this.

So she'd have to settle for Rudy Giuliani in the father-figure department, Suzannah thought, while the world was coming to an end.

Up above, a flock of seagulls screeched across the horizon. One dove down to get some lunch, emerging with a wriggling fish. Fly and dive and chow down. It was that easy for a seagull.

As for the president, where was he? Soaring above the clouds and the mayhem in Air Force One — Suzannah instinctively searched the bright blue sky for his vessel, using her hand as a visor once again, the sun so close to directly overhead it must have been about 1:00, at the very most narrowing in on 2:00 — not a single plane marred the firmament. No planes flying now, not over American airspace, that much they'd heard on NPR while they were driving, Suzannah fiddling with the channels, the stations, as if she could change the information pouring out of the SUV's sound system just by turning the dial. It was so quiet on the beach — was it always this quiet? Did the surf usually drown out the roar of the jets overhead? Who knew, who'd ever, ever, paid attention before?

If he wasn't up in the air, where was he, Bush? Was he squirreled away in some underground bunker? Hiding out, like a Nazi, like a coward? Who was the decision-making "they" of Suzannah's naive and ridiculous consciousness? Why at this advanced age — she was almost almost-forty — was she still assuming somebody expert and right-minded, somebody with better sense than she had, was in charge of anything?

Suzannah had enough of the news; she'd gotten to the point where she could not tolerate it. And so, after the remaining potato fields of Bridgehampton had disappeared — grandfathered into the landscape like a legal clause, primarily she supposed, to provide context to the many sprawling McMansions that dotted the countryside, lending them that native agricultural "East End" quality — after the potato fields had disappeared along with the road behind them; after Wainscott and its Upper West Side outposts of the gourmet supermarket Citarella and the Levain Bakery, and the gooey half-baked chocolate chip cookies Gerhard ate until his stomach hurt, had been passed by them; after there was no longer any correlation whatsoever between the beauteous Candyland sprawling before her and the horror that just hours before had hit her like a tidal wave and then, by some weird alchemical miracle of dumb luck and cunning on her husband's part, had deposited her on this other gleaming shore, she turned the radio off.

At first Gerhard protested, but when Suzannah said, "No, enough is enough," because there was something obscene, almost, in hearing the vile, frightening information as they motored by farmers' markets where one could spend two dollars on a single heirloom tomato; because the news itself was too awful to contemplate as they winged their way past flower stands where the black-eyed little pansies were still trying to hold their ground next to the bold-fisted, ham-handed, monochromatic mums that harkened autumn; and because he'd probably heard enough himself for the time being—even tough guys like Gerhard could go on overload—Gerhard nodded in the affirmative, and took his fingers off the dial of the radio. The Falktopfs turned the news off because for them, for a time, it was still possible to do so.

Suzannah watched as Gerhard steered the SUV off Route 27, taking a right, just beyond the Jewish Center, but before the pond with the swans. Swans. On land they wore thick black boots, waddled about like fat people with thighs that rubbed against each other, and were ugly. On the water . . . well, enough bad poems had been written in an effort to capture their lyrical charms. Without the news on, one could contemplate the paradoxical duality of swans. No news, insisted Suzannah, again and after the fact, gratuitously; her husband had already acceded to her demand. They were almost home anyway. Gerhard could pursue his futile quest for knowledge at the cottage.

He drove up Ocean Avenue—or whatever it was called, Dune Street? Beach Road?—as he'd done so many times in the past and pulled slowly into Elspeth's graveled drive in near silence—that gurgling, cooing baby in the back seat and his heartbroken French-murmuring mother the only passengers producing noise, loving, heartbreaking susurrations, like fingernails on a blackboard, making Suzannah's teeth itch and her skin crawl. She'd wanted to roll back and forth on the ground and scream, listening to them, the gravel cutting into the exposed skin of her neck and arms. That's when Suzannah made a run for it. When their bizarre and motley crew arrived. When she pictured her own blood in the driveway with strange pleasure.

She quickly trundled Nikolai out of the car seat and thankfully he'd taken off like a shot, off the pebbled pathway (so hot from the sun she could feel the heat radiating through the thin soles of her Italian sneakers) and around the mammoth shingled saltbox, through the side yard where the screened-in porch was located and across the flagstone veranda, straight for the beach; he was like a little homing pigeon, Nikolai. He knew where salvation lay. She followed him. She ran right after her kid, like any mother would, not bothering to help the rest of their guests unload or to say another word to her husband.

Suzannah followed Nikolai across the lawn and down the steps that traversed the dunes and corralled him — that is, she tugged him gently back by the rear collar of his T-shirt — only when she was afraid he might run too close to the water. All of this had taken place about twenty minutes ago. No one had come looking after her little boy and his mother since then. No one had bothered to learn what had become of either one.

Now out on the beach, under the bright and faultless sun, Suzannah didn't have a clue as to what Gerhard was up to back at the house; perhaps he was digging around the pantry for old items of food or excavating one of the freezers — there were frozen hors d'oeuvres in there, puff-pastry mushroomy things, pigs in the blanket, she remembered leaving them behind for the Elspeth progeny, in case they ever came out again, in case they ever arrived hungry and at night, and pissed off, and cocktail olives wouldn't hold them. (She hadn't wanted Elspeth's kids pissed off; she wanted them on Gerhard's side — they were future donors, for God's sake, philanthropy was in their gene pool, might as well make use of *this* inheritance.)

It was possible Gerhard had already hit the bar; that was always fully loaded, stocked with brand-name booze of the highest order, heavy on the Johnnie Walker Black, Lafroig, and Dubonnet, Elspeth loved her Dubonnet; she had kept on reserve a lifetime's supply. Or maybe Gerhard was now comforting the French lady and her blue-eyed brat. How was he comforting her? Suzannah didn't care. The sky was blue, bluer than that kid's eyes were, and the sun was cool even though the air was not, and the swells were as large and voluptuous and curvy as one of Matisse's odalisques; the colors of the world that eye-popping and primary. It was the most beautiful day in the history of civilization. The most beautiful day she had ever lived through. Clearly, on this specific day, where Suzannah was was exactly the right spot to be. Right where she was. Alone with her child on Elspeth's Beach. There was no better location on the planet. He was all that she needed, Nikolai, anyway.

As Suzannah mulled this over, as she thought about the fact that beyond desire — and let's face it, he wasn't always so fucking desirable, Nikolai; he wasn't what you might call exactly fucking easy — she required him now for survival. Suzannah reached out and grabbed the kid, pulling him close to her.

"All I need is this child," she said silently, or maybe in a hair breadth's distance away from silence, maybe she said it in a whisper, into the slightly fermented smell of his sweaty head — he'd been working. He'd been working hard in the sand. Like his father, his work was proving far more compelling to him than Suzannah was, Suzannah and her fierce, smothering devotion, for Nikolai wriggled free of her grasp as quickly as he could. Perhaps she'd hugged him a bit too hard.

She could have lived alone in this world of two, far from the mayhem and pain, far from the death and the destruction; but here on her beach, no longer Elspeth's Beach — Elspeth was dead, thank God, she was dead, Suzannah couldn't stand her, Elspeth was so obviously in love with Gerhard and he so obviously couldn't care less about using her affections to his advantage *philanthropically*—here on their beach, now Suzannah's and Nikolai's, when Suzannah squinted under the visor of her saluting hand, there was that surfer. Zippered sleek as a seal in his wetsuit, riding the crests in and out on his funky purple board; it was attached by a leash to his wrist, a rubber umbilical cord. Once, the guy waved to her. Did she care? It was private property—how could anyone claim ownership of the beach? Why would anyone want to?—but she didn't give a shit. It wasn't hers to guard. Go ahead and surf, she thought. Surf if that's what you were born for. You might as well enjoy yourself. Who knows what the future will bring, anyway?

As if on cue, the surfer, who had been paddling out farther and farther into the ocean, caught sight of a rising swell, turned, and rapidly began to propel himself and his board toward shore. This wave was a doozy, Suzannah noted, and even Nikolai looked up for a moment—the moment when Suzannah called out, "Look at that!"—to watch the wall of water rise and the surfer race it first and then, just when the wave was about to overtake him, let it curl around him, before taking it on himself. He hopped up onto the board, achieving a kind of balance even Suzannah the ballerina could only dream of, and rode that sucker in. She couldn't help it, but the theme from *Hawaii Five-O* escaped out between her lips, a campy Pavlovian response.

Suzannah had to laugh: today of all days, her references, what comforted her, were the theme songs of the television shows of her youth. As reactions go, this one was pathetic, but oddly funny still, and humming that tune in the sunshine while watching that man surf the wave made her feel closer to happy than just seconds before she would have deemed possible.

"Cowabunga," Suzannah whispered into Nikolai's hair. But he was working, Nikolai, and he did not bother to acknowledge her.

Then the wave began to crash. The board shot out from below the surfer as if he were slipping on a banana peel, sending him up into the air and then, back first, arms and legs akimbo, down into the water where he was buried by foam and spray. Two heart-stopping seconds later and the guy surfaced again, at least his head did, and then his arms, one after the other, as he swam toward shore. All of a sudden the surfer was up and running, the board beneath his arm, out of the surf, through the run-off up onto the sand, right toward her. Like in a TV commercial, Suzannah thought. He was running toward her, like she was his long-lost lover.

For an instant, Suzannah felt like springing to her feet and running toward him, too, running right into his wet, slippery embrace. If she ran up to the surfer and he hugged her, could he pull her into an alternate universe, one where she was a surfer chick and he was her hippie lover and Nikolai was their suntoasted beach baby? Could she enter endless summer? The impulse was strong to rise to her feet, to test this cosmos' psychic membrane and the permeability of another. But she did not.

Instead, Suzannah stayed where she was, and the surfer's run slowed to a jog and then a walk as he trudged up the beach to where Suzannah and Nikolai were sitting. He walked more and more slowly, as if the ocean itself had propelled him up onto shore and now without its push he was losing his momentum. At one point he stopped, to spit out, it seemed, seawater from where it had collected in his lungs.

"Hey," said the surfer. He was about twenty feet away, now, twenty feet and gaining.

"Hello," said Suzannah.

"Is this your beach?" he said. As he came closer she saw that he was a rather handsome young man in his mid to late twenties, with dark hair that clung to his head in wet ringlets, a little bit of silver gilding the curls. His jaw and nose were strong. He pointed up to Elspeth's manse. "Is that your house?" the surfer asked.

"Yes and no," said Suzannah. "I mean we stay there. But it doesn't matter, you know, as far as I'm concerned the beach belongs to everyone." She took a deep breath. "Especially today."

The surfer stopped a few feet away and plugged his board into the sand. He stood where he stood and dripped. He looked at Nikolai.

"Cute kid," said the surfer.

"Thank you," said Suzannah, her body instinctively closing in around Nikolai—to protect him, to hide him?—like a little Venus flytrap, Nikolai pushing past her, roughly unfolding the enveloping petals of her legs and arms, nothing could stop his digging. Suzannah noticed that Nikolai was humming. Sometimes she noticed and sometimes she didn't.

The surfer watched him for a moment, an odd expression on his face. Then he looked up at Suzannah. He smiled at her.

"So you don't care that I was riding your waves?" He said this like he was picking up the thought, the thought that had been hanging in the air awaiting resumption, and he said it kind of flirty, with a big, toothy grin that gave his handsomeness a boyish grace and made it less imposing. He had a broad, flat Long Island accent, which Suzannah had always liked, because it sounded masculine to her—like men who labored, who called their friends their brothers, who drank beer and worked hard and sometimes bent the law a little—like the Bronx brogue she had heard all her life had always sounded. They were different, of course, the inflections, but she found both familiar and somehow comforting.

"No, I don't care," said Suzannah.

The surfer leaned over and shook out his hair, like a dog would shake out its coat, water spraying everywhere. He stood up again and grinned.

"I forgot my towel," he said.

Suzannah instinctively reached back in the sand for one, but she hadn't stopped to bring out a towel either.

"Me, too," said Suzannah.

"What's your excuse?" said the surfer. His eyes were brown and his lashes, still wet, twinkled in the sun like the diamond-tipped kind you could buy at Duane Reade, the false ones. The kind Suzannah and her girlfriends had bought together when she was a kid. The kind that one season, during a performance of a reinterpretation of the *pas de deux* from Balanchine's *Jewels*—where Petipa meets Tchaikovsky as interpreted by Falk-topf, hmmm—Suzannah had worn as Diamond Queen.

"My excuse?" said Suzannah. What was her excuse? "I guess I was too freaked out. I wanted—I needed," she corrected herself, "to see the ocean." Something big and unsullied that even now felt inalterable.

The surfer looked at her in puzzlement, but the grin was still plastered to his face. He unzipped his wetsuit and started to peel down to his waist. There was dark, curly hair on his chest and his belly beneath the fleece was cut. The sun twinkled off the gemlike drops of water that clung to that hair. Had she ever made love to someone so young? She tried to remember. She wasn't sure.

"It's a beautiful day, hunh?" said the surfer.

It was, it was.

"Yes," said Suzannah. "Beautiful."

"I was on my way to work—I live in Port Jeff," he said, "when I saw that sunshine, and the waves . . . and I thought, man, are you just going to be a working stiff all your life? Or, you going to take advantage of hurricane season . . . the warm water, the big clean waves . . ." Here the surfer's voice got a little far away, like he was drifting off to a dreamy place. "A day like today, this is what surfers live for." He said this to Suzannah as if he were telling her a secret, his secret, the secret of his universe. Then he almost sounded a little pissed off. "I thought, what the hell, I'm going to play hooky. I always leave my board in my car, and I'd forgotten to unload my wetsuit over the weekend. So I hung a U-ey," he motioned steering his imaginary car into a steep curve. Then the surfer pointed up toward the bluff. "I'm parked over there. Inside you'll find a pinstriped suit and a pair of wingtips and a briefcase. A fucking Blackberry. I can't believe it, myself, sometimes." He shook his head, and then he laughed. It was a cleansing laugh, like a brief sunshiny rain. Like it was preposterous that he could be old enough and accomplished enough to warrant the wingtips.

A whole torrent of mixed and passionate emotions had just passed through this young man while he was talking to Suzannah for reasons that were inexplicable to either one of them, and now that it was over, he didn't quite know what to do. "Well, I best be getting to the office now. I mean how long can you be at the dentist?" The surfer shrugged his broad shoulders.

"I don't know," said Suzannah.

"You don't know what?" said the surfer.

"How long you can be at the dentist," said Suzannah.

"Right," said the surfer, looking even more puzzled than before. He picked up his board and started to walk away from her, the arms of his wetsuit swinging behind him like twin tails. There were dimples on the bottom two quadrants of his back, above his butt. At the hips, he had the faintest hint of love handles, so nascent, and he so arrogantly handsome, he was probably still in denial over them. He walked about ten feet past Suzannah and Nikolai, her eyes still watching him, before he turned around.

"Why were you freaked out?" he said. "If you don't mind my asking? I mean, you and the kid, you're okay, right?"

Again that intense stare; the open portholes of his eyes.

Suzannah swiveled to look at him.

"By the towers—I was freaked out by the towers," said Suzannah.

Now the guy looked really puzzled. Was it possible he didn't know?

"How long have you been surfing?" Suzannah asked.

"I don't know," said the surfer. "Pretty much all morning. What time is it?" As if to answer himself he looked up at the sky, at the sun. "Is it 12:30? 1:00?"

"They fell at ten o'clock," said Suzannah. "The South Tower. The other one fell at around 10:30."

"What are you talking about?" said the surfer. His face was white beneath the tan.

"The Twin Towers," said Suzannah. "The World Trade Center."

"Lady, are you crazy?" said the surfer. "Did you talk to Donna? Did she put you up to this?"

He looked around, as if Donna were hiding somewhere on the open sand.

"Two airplanes flew into the Twin Towers," said Suzannah. She said it slowly, as she would tell it to a child, simply and without much emotion. "They caught fire and they fell down."

"The airplanes caught on fire?"

Suzannah looked at the surfer's face. It expressed what was going on inside him, which was that he was caught between knowing and not knowing, his face was sorting out his reality, and shock was winning. Frightened, he wasn't nearly as handsome. His teeth were bared and fangy. Terror releases the animal in some of us, Suzannah supposed, as if she were somewhere else, watching a movie maybe, somewhere where she was meant to be observing something. She supposed that if she were standing closer to the surfer that she could smell the sourness of his fear.

Suzannah got to her feet. She edged up the beach sideways, a little bit away from Nikolai, toward the surfer, her head turning from left to right, not knowing which boy to focus on, worried that all this scary stuff might upset her son. But Nikolai wasn't paying attention. Nikolai was digging. He was humming and digging. Hum, hum, hum.

Suzannah walked closer to the surfer. He looked very angry. He looked angry with her. It was a little alarming how angry he looked, so she stopped approaching him.

"Two airplanes flew into the Twin Towers on purpose," said Suzannah. "Both buildings caught fire, and then they fell down."

She kind of hissed this at him, in a whisper, and she instantly felt bad about it. She wasn't handling any of this very well, she thought. She tried to soften her stance.

"They fell down," she said, quietly.

"The Twin Towers? They fell down?" said the surfer.

His surfboard dropped to the ground. After a brief awkward moment, as if someone had pressed the pause button, he started hopping around. "Are you shitting me? The Twin Towers fell down?" It was like his feet were dancing on hot coals. Reflexively, Suzannah reached out a hand to grab his arm, to soothe him.

"It's okay," said Suzannah, when of course it wasn't.

Just then, Nikolai began to scream. At the sound of his screams, Suzannah's hand tightened on the surfer's arm. She whipped about, pulling the surfer off his feet, making him lose his balance. He crashed into her, which hurt—he was heavy, a big man—and she stumbled and fell. Her palms scraped the sand. Nikolai was only about fifteen feet behind her, there was nothing in between them, but it was as if he couldn't see her, as if he were blind. Nikolai was turning wildly around in circles; his screams were earsplitting. He reminded Suzannah of something she couldn't quite identify; he reminded her of one of those pinwheels that shoots sparks as its wings whirl round and round, or the rotating light on top of the ambulance, something else, what was it? Something else that incorporated the flinging out of energy, and spinning, plus sound.

"Nikolai, I'm here, Mommy's here." Suzannah pushed herself up to her feet and began to run toward him, that low center of gravity jog that *is* running through sand. It took her forever, it seemed, to go across such a small segment of beach, she was wiping her stinging hands on her jeans, calling out to him, as she went. "Nikolai!" Already Suzannah had begun castigating herself, but even her own superprotective barometer was a little shocked by the severity of his response. She really wasn't that far away from him. She'd just left Nikolai's immediate circle, his personal space, that's all.

"Nikolai!"

As Suzannah approached, she saw that his face was practically purple from screaming and that it was slick with tears and mucus. In half a second, he had gone from A to Z, from zoned out and humming to complete and total hysteria. Suzannah's little boy stood in one place screaming and screaming, like he was a siren himself, a siren on the beach, alerting the boats, the swimmers, the fish even, all the sea and sand creatures, to a clear and present danger. His screams were so loud that Suzannah wondered, are his fingers being crushed by a closed car door? Which was patently ridiculous because she could see him right before her freaking out in the sand, but she thought the thought just the same, because that was what his cries sounded like. Barry, her eldest brother, had shut a car door on her hand when she was a child and that was what her own voice had sounded like in her own ears, so shrill and yet emanating from somewhere far, far, outside of her.

Is this what the people inside the towers sounded like as the flames climbed up, and the floors came down?

In just ten steps and about five seconds Suzannah was brought back to Nikolai's side—the time itself stretched thinner and longer by her own growing sense of alarm—her arms around him, crushing his body to her, her hands discovering his shoulders, compressing down on his joints, finding his hips, and applying pressure. Nikolai was stiff and noncompliant with fear or anger or whatever it was that made him shout so, and Suzannah kept working on him, trying to quiet him down.

"Sweetie-pie, darling. Mama's here, Mama's here."

She wrestled him to the ground. In a body lock, she stroked his little back. Under the T-shirt there was golden fur. She'd once furtively licked it lightly, twice, maybe three times, while he slept.

"I'm right here, Nikolai."

And she was. She was right there, but the surfer was gone.

It wasn't long after that that Suzannah heard Celine yelling. It took a while for her to recognize the sound, its presence and its origins, because of Nikolai and *his* howling, Celine a treble note to his soprano, the caterwauling at once oddly orchestrated and symphonic.

BY THE TIME Suzannah got herself and Nikolai back up the sandy bluff to the cottage and entered the yellow-and-white tiled kitchen — she'd carried him and she'd dragged him, she'd cajoled him and she'd admonished him; finally she'd slung him over her shoulder and trying her best to balance him (he went rigid when he got like that, he was like a board so he kept sliding downward across her collarbones, which irritated the skin there, the rubbing of his shirt against her bra-strap; she had a little raised mole near her shoulder and now it felt like it was bleeding) — Celine wasn't screaming anymore. She was huddled in the corner of the room, sitting on the Florentine hand-painted tiles, canary yellow with little purple grapes or plums clustered at their middles (maybe they were olives), staring stupidly at the surfer. He was leaning over the center island shouting into the telephone, bellowing really: "I'm not dead! I'm not dead! Donna, I'm not dead! Donna, I'm not dead, Donna! Donna! Donna!" He paused, to take a breath, and then he erupted: "I was surfing, for fuck's sakes! I was surfing!"

He started to laugh. He laughed and laughed and laughed, and then all of a sudden, he was weeping. He was weeping so

violently he was howling, and even Nikolai stopped screaming, staring at the crying surfer with curiosity.

"Are you all right?" Suzannah said to Celine, who nodded
yes, yes, dumbly from her seat in the corner of the kitchen,
a few tears leaking out her eyes. Suzannah wiped the sweat
from her brow, her upper lip that felt dirty, she felt like she
was smearing a dirt mustache across her face; it had been hard
work lugging Nikolai. She could smell her own armpits. Between her legs. She could smell herself.

The surfer was leaning on the center island now, sobbing,
sobbing, open-mouthed, drool dangling from his bottom lip,
one hand practically wrenching the curls from his head, the
phone sagging limply from the other. His position was almost
comical, except it wasn't. A voice kept escaping out of the
holes of the receiver. It sounded frantic.

Gently Suzannah wrested the phone from the surfer's hand.
She spoke into the mouthpiece.

"Hello?" she said. "Hello?"

"Oh my God, he's all right, Danny's all right," a woman
wept into the phone. "I thought he was dead," she said.

"He's not dead," said Suzannah. "He was playing hooky. He
skipped work and he went surfing."

"His office is on the 102nd floor of the South Tower," the
woman whispered into the phone, her Long Island accent a female bookend to the surfer's. She whispered it, Suzannah supposed, so the devil wouldn't hear.

For a split second, Suzannah wondered, was the surfer, this
Danny, was he the one she'd watched take that high dive out
of the burning tower? The one with the tie floating gracefully
behind him? Had he miraculously landed safely? Hopped into
his car and driven out to the beach, just like her? Was he just
like her? An escape artist, running away from true mayhem to
counterfeit perfection, leaving insanity behind?

The thought was ridiculous, ludicrous; Suzannah worried

that she was going crazy. She literally shook it out of her head, a rapid *no* side-to-side motion, the madness exiting out her ears. The man she saw, *her* man, he was dead. Unknowable and untouchable. He had to be.

"Wow," said Suzannah, shaking her head. "The South Tower? You are so lucky!"

"Sandler O'Neil," Donna said on the other end. "Do you think they are all gone?" she said this confidingly, with hope in her delivery, like they were intimates, like they were girlfriends. "Do you think any of them could have made it out?"

"I don't know, sweetie," said Suzannah, a girlfriend right back at her. Was it possible? Surely some of those Sandler O'Neil guys must have had the foresight to clear out when the first tower was hit — although on NPR they said that there had been an announcement over the South Tower PA system telling evacuated workers that it was now safe to return to their offices just minutes before that very same building was attacked. Still there must have been renegades, no? Suzannah thought, with hope. People who thought for themselves? (She was afraid she would not have been one of them.)

After the second plane crashed, was it possible for someone located on the 102nd floor to make it down the stairs to safety? Were the staircases open? Was there enough time to get out? Suzannah remembered Shingshang with a start. Shingshang had been breakfasting in the first tower; he'd have had a good extra twenty minutes on those poor guys in the other one. Did Gerhard ever get ahold of him? Would it make sense, or not make sense — that is, which would be better? kinder? more loving? — to try to put in a call to Patti now and inquire about his safety? North or South, after the planes hit, were at least some of the elevators in the trade center still viable? Were there survivors ready to be rescued from the rubble? Anything was possible. After an earthquake, in Turkey, or some Latin American country, there were always survivors waiting to be dug out. She should donate blood. As soon as she went home, Suzannah would volunteer at a local hospital. She would go to nursing school. Get her M.D. Ideas, they flew in and out through her mind like so many swooping birds. In her head, she heard a voice. Instructing her. *You must change your life.*

Whose voice was it? She wondered. Was it *his?*

"Nina? Do you think Nina could have survived?" asked the woman on the phone.

"I really hope so," said Suzannah. She wanted this Nina alive.

"Oh God," Donna whispered. She whispered it like a prayer. "Please, God, just Nina, I would be satisfied with Nina," she said.

Ten minutes before, Donna probably had been making the same plea to God about her Danny. Wasn't that the way it is with people, thought Suzannah, as soon as we get what we ask for, we ask for something more. She'd been the same way about Nikolai. Please, God, just a child, any child. Then when he was born: Please, God, let this child be all right.

The surfer was pulling himself together now, he was taking great, big, deep cleansing breaths; he looked like he was in labor, Suzannah thought, hunched over like that and panting. He reached for the phone. Suzannah passed it to him.

"Donna," said the surfer. "Baby. I'm coming home."

Tears came to Suzannah's eyes, looking at this great, big, good-looking, shaking man, going home to his baby. She reached out and pulled Nikolai close to her. Her fingers ruffled his hair. He was quiet now, thank God.

On the beach, a half-hour or so before, Suzannah had yearned to belong to a different life, to open another book and walk into its pages. This time she wished simply that she were Donna, Donna of the fervent entrusting whispers, Donna who was lucky, lucky enough that she still believed she could barter with God.

If Suzannah were Donna, then later today it would be Suzannah whose breath would stop and whose heart would leap, it would be Suzannah who was destined to be flooded with joy when Danny walked through her front door.

Suzannah could almost feel the blessed mixture of relief and elation in her body, the weightlessness in her bones when he came home to her, when she saw him, big and strong, his great, broad shoulders taking up the entire width of the door frame, filling the space, joy's white-hot light emanating out from the top of her head, making the world glow. The survivor's high.

It wasn't hers to claim.

Suzannah, Suzannah. She hadn't survived anything.

THE coconut cupcakes at the Barefoot Contessa were oversized and snowy white, covered with a creamy coconut stucco frosting. It was all Gerhard could do not to bury his face in the tray of them. They were laid out to the left of the coffee service at the front of the store, which was pretty enough, the silver creamers beaded with cold sweat, the little wicker baskets for the sugars, the cupcakes sandwiched in by a beautiful, impossible-to-cut strawberry shortcake, with its featherlight sponge cake and its red rubies, the ethereal whipped cream that would have no choice but to go *splurt* if kissed by a knife. Next to the cakes were trays of blondies and brownies, linzer cookies and shortbread hearts, banana crunch muffins, and scones, tons of scones, blueberry and strawberry and maple-oatmeal scones, even cheddar-cheese scones (orange-speckled and flecked with feathers of green dill), but nothing held a candle to the cupcakes. Gerhard felt a specific gratitude for them, for their just being there. He felt a reverence for the full spectrum of the pleasures of life, simple and expansive. Which category did his cupcake fall under? It was a voluptuous, luxurious, homespun delight.

"Take one," he gestured to Martine. "You take one, and I'll take one, and we'll take a third to share with your baby."

Martine smiled at him. A shy, uncertain smile, over the head of that little blue-eyed babe, a smiling, gurgling human cupcake himself. Her eyes were almonds. Brown and wide and vaguely oriental. She was a real beauty, this French girl.

"It will be a small, good thing," said Gerhard. He was borrowing from a short story Suzannah had once forced him to read; inelegant, staccato, and graceless, he'd thought at the time, although she was so proud of her find, this overrated minimalist writer who couldn't seem to eke out one lyrical line, that Gerhard had tolerated her enthusiasm. The author had relied too heavily on the bare bones of narrative, and narrative, inherently representational, was always second best to evocation; Gerhard held this doctrine for most of his career. (Hyperrealism, that was another story. Gerhard adored hyperrealism.) Like today, for instance. Was there a plot on someone's desk somewhere that could possibly compete?

No.

But now, at this instance, when he'd observed the worst of what mankind has to offer and, in the moment, was basking in some of the most intense if trivial pleasures, Gerhard didn't care so much about art, evocative, expressive, or otherwise, or that the famous minimalist writer was simply human and thus of course he was lacking. Gerhard cared about where he was, which was standing before an array of luscious treats in a lovely shop next to a beautiful girl with a handsome baby. He was alive, blessedly alive, and therefore capable of enjoying all of this. Surely amid all the horrors of the day there were miniature moments worth celebrating—his own survival being one of them. "A small, good thing." A perfect cupcake could make anyone anywhere feel better.

He and Martine had been browsing the food shop, piling their cart high with crackers and cheeses, fresh fruit, bagels, and the thirty-five-dollar-a-pound lobster salad. At first, back at the house, there had been a period of discomfort and quietude — after she'd gone to the bathroom and washed her face (Martine's cheeks were fresh and shiny when she emerged; she was still young enough that soap and water pulled the flesh taut), after she'd changed the baby. Gerhard had had the bright idea that she should call someone, which Martine had sparked to. Perhaps if she called someone, Thierry, her husband, would call that same someone, too! (Gerhard had done his best to convince her that there was no reason to fear the worst about Thierry, he had been in the food court, no? The sub-basement. Martine had shrugged her shoulders; how did she know? She'd been in New York three days. He'd gone for coffee, rolls — "In the food court," Gerhard assured her. It would not have been hard to evacuate from there.) So they'd placed two phone calls to Europe — Gerhard had forgotten to have the phone lines turned off, he'd left the cottage in such haste back in July to get back to the city and deal with his crisis — and miraculously Martine had gotten through to her own answering machine in Paris.

"Darling, we are safe," she shouted into the machine in French. "Call us," and Gerhard had told her the number, which she'd fumbled, so they'd dialed again and he'd recited it into the phone himself.

After that, they'd had a hard time placing a transatlantic call — the circuits were busy. Martine wanted to call her mother.

"I should have called her first," she said. "She's probably having heart failure. I am such an idiot."

Gerhard would not let her get away with chastising herself. None of it was her fault. She and the child were safe, that was what mattered.

"Let's go buy some food," he'd said. "You and the baby, you must be hungry."

They were. Celine had opted to stay behind. That is, Gerhard had instructed her thusly — "Suzannah might need you later" — and Celine was more than happy to comply. She could run a bath. Take a walk down to the water. Celine wasn't much for errands on a good day. She was a person who instinctively knew how to heal herself and that was by applying as many layers as she could between herself and the world. Prior to today, this had amounted to designer jeans, expensive makeup, and rich Eurotrash boyfriends. Her languid oversight of Nikolai and his activities, whenever Suzannah could be pried away from him, was an optimal employment situation for her — although independent wealth would have also served Celine just fine.

If he took Martine out of the house, Suzannah would have the privacy Gerhard knew she craved.

At the Barefoot Contessa, opulent and down-to-earth simultaneously, with its lavender ice cream and its farm stand baskets of knobby homegrown vegetables, Martine had been hesitant, tremulous, wavery. At one point, he'd had to grab her elbow; Gerhard was afraid she might tumble into the cracker shelves. He loaded up on prime rib and roasted Brussels sprouts (crispy and salted like French fries) and frozen soup and just about anything else his eyes rested upon, and she followed obediently at his side. Ty Nant water. Gerhard would go to the A & P next, where the water would inarguably be cheaper and come in big plastic jugs with little plastic spigots, but he liked the blue glass bottles at the Barefoot Contessa and so he would have them. At the A & P he'd stock up — after all who knew what could happen to the food supply, even way out here, with the country under attack? It was wise to make sure the pantry was full, with staples, sure, and comfort foods, kid-friendly items, those Go-gurts Suzannah was always stuffing in her bag for Nikolai, the organic string cheeses (*God*). Once his mother died, the refrigerator in his father's home had always been empty — they bought what they needed each day for three bland and predictable meals — Gerhard, a growing boy, had always felt hungry. After the A & P he'd hit the liquor store, too, procure some wine. Gerhard would buy the good stuff; today warranted it.

There were several other patrons in the store, a silver-haired man and his elegant wife, a mom in a short beach sarong, tugging along two small children in polka-dot bikinis who were eating sugar doughnuts they'd bought across the street at Dreesen's, the powdered sugar snowing down on their bare bellies, a couple of gay men clucking worriedly to each other. Gerhard and Martine had stopped at Dreesen's first. It was an old-fashioned deli—big square (square?) hunks of ham and a round log of "Provolone" in the refrigerator case, headcheeses and potato salads. Dreesen's sold the *Post*, the *Daily News*, and the *New York Times*, so Gerhard favored it; he'd stopped in almost daily during the summer. There had been a crowd in Dreesen's, and Gerhard and Martine had made their way inside only to find everyone gathered around the television set. The patrons and the passersby, shopkeepers from around the neighborhood, the girls from Scoop, the old lady from the stationery store two doors down, a couple of guys Gerhard recognized from the pharmacy—the whole little village was huddled together viewing CNN. For the first time that day, Gerhard actually saw tapes of the towers falling. Those two tall, blazing towers collapsing within themselves, straight down into a cloud of dust.

The sight was unbelievable, unbelievable except that he'd obviously heard about it already on the radio, from the eyewitness descriptions, reporters with access to television, those broadcasting on the spot. Gerhard was not caught unaware, he was not taken by surprise, he was prepared to believe what he saw before he saw it. Still, the actual film footage came as a shock.

At first his reaction was visceral: disbelief, dismay, revulsion. Then, as he began to comprehend what was laid out before him, he was able to begin the process, however nascent, of examination and analysis. The demolition of the two buildings was both grander and somehow tidier than Gerhard had imagined it to be. The buildings, those two great big towering behemoths, had buckled and flattened. It was amazing. They emptied into and within themselves. Twin implosions. Folding in, draining down, reduced to a squall of paper, smoke, and dust.

When you live in a city like New York you look up at tall buildings all the time, thought Gerhard, but only a guy like himself, someone who was afraid of heights, ever wondered about how they would eventually come down. During their construction, what had the architects been thinking? What had been their exit plan?

In Dreesen's, Martine had stared open-mouthed at the footage of the people rushing away—from time to time Gerhard had turned to gaze at her. Her eyes never met his, they never left the screen, and her lips never quite touched, though she'd used her pink cat's tongue to wet them. Was she searching for her husband amid the scattering dust-covered crowds? Some of the survivors looked like they'd been powdered, covered in what appeared to be a fine, white chalk on the screen, but it must have been more grimy, Gerhard thought, composed of paper and ash, metal fibers, possibly human skin and meat and bone. He grimaced at the thought. Martine stared as the same footage was shown over and over again, looped five or six times in the twenty or so minutes that she and Gerhard stood there with the rest of East Hampton watching the television monitor. It was almost as if the network were presenting fresh and breaking news each instance—it took a while for the most recent members of this waxing and waning audience to realize that they were gawking at the same repeating news coverage, and that the unimaginable was now familiar. Yet even with this knowledge in hand, Gerhard observed, the images still felt mind-blowing upon each viewing. As if all over New York City people were escaping from the collapse of various buildings, the startling sequences recurring and recurring, the way the mind hiccups, stuck on moments of trauma: people scurrying, great big clouds of dust chasing them down the street. Like the running of the bulls, Gerhard thought (which he had once participated in, in Spain, high on drugs and almost young and eager to obliterate his own limits), the dust clouds pushing the people through a warren of winding lanes that marked downtown Manhattan, billowing out and forcing the people through the city's sieve, its labyrinth.

He and Martine and her baby and the townspeople of East Hampton—they'd all stood in Dreesen's and watched CNN: the collapses, the running; they'd listened to Henry Kissinger phone in from Europe, Gerhard shuddering at the thud of his voice (the old gnomic war criminal had always creeped him out, perhaps because the accent made him sound so much like Gerhard's father); they'd watched as the head of the Taliban in Afghanistan proclaimed the innocence of his government in an Afghani monotone that felt a lot like torture.

It was then that Martine said, "Of course, it was Bin Laden." Meaning that this Bin Laden was the mastermind behind the assault. She said it with so much certainty Gerhard immediately accepted her assertion as fact.

"Who is Bin Laden, remind me again," said Gerhard. He knew the name but could not quite place it. Something he'd watched on *Nightline? 60 Minutes?*

"Bin Laden is a billionaire Islamic extremist who hates America," Martine said.

She was a young French housewife; she knew these things. All of Europe must know this stuff. Gerhard was formerly German; he'd grown complacent, gone soft. Almost American. Out of touch with the realities of the world.

It was then that he'd steered them across the street to the Barefoot Contessa. It was not necessary to watch those towers fall again.

Now, the gray-haired counter lady with the sun-parched tan (the backs of her hands looked like they were made up of teeny-tiny tissue-thin squares of origami, like you actually could see her skin's cellular structure) put all three of their cupcakes in a box, using a little wax-paper hankie to handle them, and passed the white cardboard package along to Martine. Above her wrist and the thin gold chain that encircled it, the flesh of the woman's arm puffed up like risen dough. What did she have on him, five, ten years? She was a walking argument for sunblock.

"Napkins?" said Gerhard.

He couldn't help but note that as the counter lady answered his question, by indicating with her pointer finger across the aisle to where the bronzed teenage cashiers manned their stations, that the middle knuckle of her finger aimed east and the top knuckle pointed west. If that ever happens to me, resolved Gerhard, I will knock both knuckles straight with a hammer. The cashiers were four healthy-looking adolescent white girls with shiny ponytails, polo shirts, and white shorts, little twisted friendship bracelets around their bony wrists — they couldn't be kabbalists, Gerhard thought, this wasn't Brentwood. Each appeared to be occupying a different degree on the spectrum of distress, as the girl on the far end was examining her peeling manicure and the one in the middle had a few tears connecting the dots between her freckles.

The checkout counter was laden with bags of pricey, pretty candies, in a kaleidoscope of pastel colors representing indeterminate flavors (violet, mauve, pearl gray), homemade marshmallows of more conventionally associative shades (chocolate, strawberry, and vanilla), copies of *Martha Stewart Living*, *Food & Wine*, and yes, napkins, beautiful expensive cocktail napkins still in their cellophane sleeves, napkins that were sold at the Metropolitan Museum of Art and Eli Zabar's and museum stores all over the country, Gerhard recognized them and their ilk; and then, next to the registers, piles of cheap prefolded paper napkins, off-white, free for the asking. The kind you might find in a Greek diner.

Gerhard and his entourage walked over to an open register. He instinctively picked one of the two girls in the center as his cashier, the one with the puckered forehead and the worried expression who was neither oblivious to the seismic waves hitting the world nor collapsing from them either. According to Gerhard's thumbnail analysis, she was the most sensible. He unloaded his parcels and foodstuffs onto the counter in front of her. He picked up a small pile of the napkins and placed them on top of the cardboard box that held the cupcakes, which he held safely to the side. The girl behind the register went to work, tallying his other purchases and scanning them into the machine before placing them into an attractive white shopping bag with maroon inscription, the paper so stiff and heavy it seemed the bag could stand up by itself. Gerhard appreciated a bag of this stature. Amenities like this, in his opinion, made the elevated prices of the establishment justifiable.

Gerhard's checkout girl loaded up his wares. One of the other young ladies, the teenager who had been crying, was now whispering into the ear of the fourth, the one girl Gerhard had not bothered to inspect. This kid had an appalled comic book character's expression as she tabulated the groceries of her own customer. Whatever her more morose friend was confiding certainly was affecting her. The kid with the peeling manicure was also busy at work, helping out the gay couple, when a middle-aged woman wearing a chef's apron and clogs sauntered up to the checkout counter and announced, "We've decided to close the store early, you can finish up and go home." At that moment all four pretty young faces lit up like a chorus line. The liveliness they exuded, one after the other, tripped a wire in Gerhard's mind—he could add a small Rockette-like movement to "Good Vibrations" for levity.

His ballet. There was still space in there for a little June Tay-lor Dancers thing. As witticism. But also to make use of Wil-son's repetitions, the value of the replicating motif. What was noticed and reinforced upon each subsequent reiteration. What made each incidence innovative, and the underlying intention, therefore, that much more potent and accessible.

Gerhard contemplated what he'd just witnessed on CNN in Dreesen's. The looping reruns, the inveterate and persistent imagery. Of course, thought Gerhard. Jasper Johns. Jasper Johns and his flags, Jasper Johns and his alphabet. What happens when you fiddle with one ingredient and then repeat the same composition except for utilizing a small but significant change in another, even if — as with the taped segments of the collapse of the towers — the alteration itself was simply the placement of the work in time. The audience's response evolved upon each viewing, narrowing and expanding along with the fluctua-tions of his own reality, his own standing in the world, what he knew to be true, what he did not know or could not fathom, al-tered sometimes only by listening to the voice of someone else in the interim, by how much of what was said the viewer chose to hear, how much he could tolerate, how much he could not.

The first time Gerhard saw the buildings fall, he felt one set of emotions, an overwhelming specific awfulness, his own fear and disbelief a pulsing wound. With each subsequent airing, his revulsion deepened, narrowed, varied — both inuring him and opening him up to new elements of terror. Vary the ca-dence, stance, arrangement; distort or press the images and the commonplace icon, be it flags, letters — two tall towers con-tinue to carry the weight of the familiar but also transmogrify into something unreserved and different, as if conceptually the image itself had just been born.

Gerhard could create a camp, bouncy chorus line of kicks and marches, but for a succession of cycles he would augment the movements of just one of the members of his corps — Daniel, he would use Daniel, Daniel if he'd just stay with him, if Gerhard could keep him from defecting to Pina Bausch — Gerhard would give him a small physical manifestation of Wilson's spiritual pain, just enough to make the audience itch.

While Agnes Martin's geometric integrity had a dazzling, mystical quality that moved him vastly and inexplicably, there were often purposeful imperfections within the work that were there expressly to claim it from the divine. Johns goaded his viewers, challenging the expected, reawakening the lazy eye. When Gerhard was done, *Day at the Beach* would be both lushly beautiful and provocative.

A rush of pleasure filled Gerhard from top to bottom. For the first time in forever he existed as a creative force, far outside of commerce, struggles for control, litigation, competition with this or that. In an effort to calm down, he had to remind himself that art was probably not the point right now, not on this day, this day of all days, *beingness* was, survival, an exaltation in living; and finally an exaltation in living was what *Smile*, and therefore, *Day at the Beach*, was all about. Still it was the test and tangle of the process itself that made Gerhard feel most alive. This is who he was.

At the Barefoot Contessa, the teenage checkout girls sighed their collective sighs of relief, oblivious to the firing synapses in Gerhard's brain, and Gerhard's girl couldn't seem to ring up his purchases fast enough. Her fingers flew across the touch pad. Perhaps she would grow up to be an accountant, he thought. She had aptitude.

"I want to see my mother," said the girl who had been weeping; she said it right into Gerhard's cashier's ear, in a loud stage whisper. "Do you think my mother will be home?"

The baby made a loud gurgling sound. It was time to feed the baby.

"Come," Gerhard said to Martine. "Your little man is hungry." Bags in hand, he swung open the store's screen door and held it there with his foot. This way Martine could exit, balancing the cupcake box in front of her, away from the baby's grasping hands, perched high atop a gray cardboard tray filled with Gerhard's lidded coffee, her iced tea, and a cup of milk for the baby. Martine brushed in front of him, and he turned to follow her, when his T-shirt snagged on a bit of torn screen door in the back.

"Well, I've finally got you where I want you, Gerhard."

The voice was female, deep, and throaty. He started to turn to see who was talking to him, when a tender hand pressed firmly on his spine.

"Stop, you'll tear it," she said.

Gerhard felt the gentle tug of someone unhooking the cloth of his shirt. He turned around.

Leah.

"There, no holes," she said, beaming with satisfaction.

His Leah. Short and raw-boned, a little slip of a thing in her uniform black T-shirt and black jeans, those big, oversized black glasses of hers, her usual Doc Martens, and then the signature wildly messy, bleached white mane, making her look like a cross between Cynthia Ozick and Jackie O on a bad hair day, or an alarmingly cute Albert Einstein. Darling Leah. Gerhard was infinitely glad to see her.

"Leah, Leah," he said. He leaned down to kiss both her cheeks. They'd been friends since their Studio 54 days. He'd met her while standing among the hopeful throngs outside the velvet rope in front of the club when out of the blue this woman he'd never seen before just grabbed his hand and told the doorman, "Hey, Benecke, he's with me." The Red Sea then parted, and suddenly Gerhard was in. Leah had been holding his hand it seemed, off and on, ever since. She'd been a costume person and a stage designer—for years she'd done Gerhard's sets and won awards for doing so, a couple of Drama-logues, a Bessie, and an Izzie—and recently she'd begun a line of home furniture. Very modern, sleek designs that he liked but could not afford.

"You are a sight for sore eyes," said Gerhard.

As he said this, Gerhard began to weep. Not much, just a few tears leaking out, a pair of shaking shoulders. This surprised him. Martine as well, it seemed, because her eyes widened with fear. Not Leah, obviously. Gerhard in tears made her almost unearthly calm. Now she was using that same tender, firm hand to rub his back in little circles.

"A terrible, terrible day," agreed Leah. "A disaster."

"Excuse me," said Gerhard. He set down his bags, pulled a linen handkerchief out of his pants, and coughed into it.

Leah smiled at him, sympathetically, her narrow, bony face scrunched up and still beatific. Gerhard smiled, weakly, back at her.

Behind Leah stood a fashionably scruffy young man. He had one of those beards — stubble really, a little like Gerhard's, only not silver, but blondish red like his hair, which was long and pulled back into a ponytail. He was wearing a green T-shirt and jeans covered with paint and one of his ankles seemed to turn in a little awkwardly, lending him a certain gimpy charm. A house painter or an artist — either way just as well, thought Gerhard, there was something workmanlike about him, sexy in the way that old lesbians like Leah liked to surround themselves with, the kind of trophy boy she was fond of collecting. This *artista* would have been her younger, prize boyfriend if she'd swung in the other direction, and one couldn't help but think that for some peculiar but obvious reasons this handsome young man would have let Leah claim him — she had that much charisma, and she wielded so much art world power — so he remained a trophy nonetheless. The boy must have been in his mid thirties. Leah was at least Gerhard's age, but she was always accumulating younger and older intimates, those that interested her.

"Is Lizbeth here?" Gerhard asked, looking past her. Lizbeth

was Leah's partner. She was the anti-Leah, tall and voluptuous and elegant in a Southern belle sort of way, impeccably dressed, widowed when her dashing and impossibly rich young husband had been killed flying his very own private jet. She was sitting on the board of some design museum or foundation when Leah found her and rebuilt her. They'd been together ever since. Perhaps the young man was the boy from that early marriage? It was a possibility. Lizbeth was famously, flame-throwingly, red-headed (gala or barbecue, she wore her hair like a beacon in long, luxuriant waves like a pageant contestant). Gerhard remembered pictures of the child after the accident from the gossip pages of the *Post*. Lizbeth had kept him under wraps pretty much since those days, a devoted mother. Gerhard would ask after him, to Leah, his stepmom, from time to time, out of a friendly, dutiful sense of correctness, never bothering to pay attention while she answered him.

"She's walking on the beach," said Leah. "It's what saves her, the water, at a time like this." She shook her head at the enormity of the situation. "As if there's ever been a time like this before . . ." And then, reaching for levity: "You know, Gerhard, you're not the only devotee of endless summer." She gave him a little wink.

Leah had sat in the studio with him persistently, early in the process of fermenting *Day at the Beach*, listening to the various bootleg recordings he'd collected of *Smile*, helping him choose the tracks. They'd talked a lot about color. Sheer, shiny blue fabrics that swam. Some slightly dusky turquoise. The wet and the dry elements to the recordings. She'd brought him marzipan peaches from his favorite bakery in Erice. She and Lizbeth had spent six months in Sicily "doing God knows what," Leah said, "eating." They'd been eating in Sicily, then eating in Lizbeth's home in Paris. They'd been eating at Katz's Deli in New York. "Thank God," said Leah, "for Katz's." She looked like an anorexic sometimes, Gerhard thought, but all she did was eat. Indeed, these days, when Gerhard and Leah met for lunch,

133

when Leah was "in town," those rare occurrences, Katz's was the place they met. Pastrami and rye, sour pickles. French fries still in the brown bag, melting the paper with hot grease. Gerhard and Leah, they both loved food. Art and food. Perhaps that was what was there to link them. For most of the summer, Leah and Lizbeth had been eating lobster rolls in Montauk, sitting outdoors on the rocks at Duryea's, overlooking the water — Leah had bragged about this to him during a sympathy call for the loss of his company over the phone. "Maybe you should try the simple life," suggested Leah, Leah who had "married well" and thus was saved from the anxieties of bankruptcy, which plagued him, Leah who lived the least simply of anyone. Well, at least she wasn't like the rest of their old friends, touting the benefits of Brooklyn or urging him to take an academic post somewhere in the Midwest . . . Still, it had seemed a little ridiculous to him when she went on and on: "You and Suzannah should move out here." Although today, with its instant and terrifying hindsight, the offhanded suggestion not to live next to a terrorist target seemed wise and prescient, almost a no-brainer.

Lizbeth now had a house designed by Charlie Gwathmey in Montauk where they spent most of the warm months. She'd sold the old potato barn she'd had oceanside in Sagaponack about five years prior so that Leah, the terminally social Leah, could escape the city scene and preserve herself. Lizbeth wanted her "to rest, sometimes"; she'd whispered this in Gerhard's ear, smelling like Shalimar — she was the kind of girl who would always smell like Shalimar, probably a blend of her own natural perfume and sweet soap — at the last party they'd all attended together, a fundraiser in July, at Alec Baldwin's in Amagansett. "I'd like Leah to rest sometimes," said Lizbeth with her honeyed, Southern drawl. Which was true love, Gerhard thought. When she'd breathed into his ear that way, Gerhard had gotten a hard-on.

"We barely escaped with our lives," said Gerhard.

"No," said Leah, her hand reaching up to cover her mouth. The plain silver band that Lizbeth forced upon her twinkled in the sun. "You were there this morning?"

She turned to the young man. "Larry, Gerhard's loft is practically in the trade center."

"We took off the moment the second plane hit," said Gerhard. And then because he couldn't help the immodesty, he was so proud of himself really, for taking charge, for saving all of them: "I insisted upon it."

She allowed him this. This moment of braggadocio. "Oh my God," said Leah. "Thank God, you did. But you are a genius, Gerhard," she said, smiling at herself and at him, warmly praising them both, which was her gift, he supposed. Warmth was. Most people never possess it. Leah's warmth overflowed in natural abundance. "Everyone knows it now, but I was the first. I discovered him," she said to Larry.

Gerhard had always loved her.

It was true, she'd gone to his fledgling tiny performances at La MaMa, she'd introduced him to theater owners and artists and actors and big donors. She'd been his friend and champion for longer than he'd like to admit to anyone.

They were not as young as they ought to be. Age is a surprise for every generation, Gerhard mused. A shock really. We watch the ones in front of us shrivel and shrink, and still we cannot believe it will ever infect us with its poisons. I never thought it would happen to me, Gerhard thought.

But then again, what indeed did he think would happen?

"Where are you staying?" Leah asked. "We have tons of room. Ed Ruscha just left a few days ago . . ." Her arm extended and her little hand made some lazy circles. "Thank God, they flew directly from here to Nantucket along with Arne and the rest of them. There is no one inhabiting the guest house."

"That is so good of you, Leah, but we're back at Elspeth's," said Gerhard. He smirked a little sheepishly. "I still have the key."

"Of course you do," said Leah. "That is exactly as Elspeth would have wanted it." She was the one who introduced him to Elspeth, so many years ago; the company had been in trouble then, too, it was a little fledgling, underfinanced company — Leah had come to his rescue a thousand times.

"And Suzannah?" asked Leah. She asked this while smiling kindly at Martine. "What a darling baby," said Leah. She held out a finger, and the baby took the dare, grabbing it.

"She's here, of course she's here, she's here with me, and the boy, too," said Gerhard. "At Elspeth's. All at Elspeth's."

"Nikolai," said Leah.

"Nikolai," said Gerhard.

"Martine and I, we were just out buying food," said Gerhard. He thought about explaining why Martine was with him, who she was to him, but he had no idea how to go about it, since he didn't really know the answers himself.

"What's this adorable baby's name?" said Leah.

"Name? Name? I don't know," said Gerhard. "What's the baby's name, Martine?"

"His name is Wylie," said Martine.

Leah looked entranced. "We should have had children, Gerhard," she said, her eyes locked on the baby.

He remembered with a start that one night a long time ago, maybe twenty-five, twenty-eight — God, could it be? — thirty years before, when they were smoking pot on some East Village rooftop, some hot, hazy summer night, some fun, dumb artist's party, and she'd asked him to father her offspring. Gerhard had just convinced the dancer he was sleeping with to abort another mistake — What was that girl's name again? Allegra. A dancer's name, but a gymnast's body. She was too short, all shoulders, no hips, Allegra — and as much as he loved Leah and wanted to please her, Gerhard had graciously declined as she wept in his arms. That was such ancient history, such a sad and naked moment, he'd buried it long ago, until now, the remembrance itself reaching a hand out from the grave of their youthful possibilities and clawing the air. All with a little nudge from Leah —why now on this day of all days? Although he instantly forgave her.

"And your boy," said Gerhard, gesturing with his head toward her companion. "What is his name?"

"Pardon me," said Leah. "Gerhard, this is Larry; Larry, this is Gerhard Falktopf. Larry is a brilliant painter, Gerhard. He's going to show at Pace in the fall. That is if there still is a Pace, if there still is a fall. Larry, Gerhard is a—"

"Genius," said Larry. "You said that before."

The baby began to fuss. One of the checkout girls came up behind them and said, "If you'd excuse us, we want to close up now."

"But we never got to shop," said Leah, not sounding too terribly disappointed and still staring into the baby's eyes, still allowing him to grasp her finger, still cooing at him. "Tut, tut," said Leah. "Such blue eyes."

"But of course," said Gerhard, to the girl, and then to Leah, "we'll share our provisions with you," and they spilled out into the street.

"Coo, coo," said Leah to the baby. "Gerhard loves to eat. He's a famous eater, Gerhard."

The sidewalk was bright with liquid sun. Even this late in the afternoon. There wasn't much hustle on New Town Lane. A little postseason foot traffic, a few cars.

"This baby has the bluest eyes in the world," said Leah, still mesmerized. "They look like yours, Gerhard." Suddenly she broke her gaze and stared frankly at him. "*Gerhard*," said Leah. She said it like she was accusing him.

"What?" said Gerhard, with a shocked and injured sound in his voice.

"I know who you are," said Larry.

"You do?" said Gerhard.

"You are Gerhard Falktopf."

They were all silent for a moment. Martine swayed her hips side to side, unconsciously, rocking the baby, keeping him calm.

To fill the silence, more to get away from them, Gerhard said, "We have so much food now, why don't you guys come by later? Martine and I have some more errands to run first," and then pointedly, "and of course I have to prep Suzannah." He paused to let this sink in. "But I know she would want to be with friends at a time like this. Old friends," he said to Leah.

Leah gazed at him. "Why don't we come around six-ish then? I have a bottle of Wild Turkey," she said, with a sad grin. "We can get soused."

"Soused at six," said Gerhard.

"Soused at six," said Leah. She waved at the baby.

"Bye, bye, baby," said Leah. She turned to Larry. "Maybe Round Swamp Farm is still open," she said. They started walking in the other direction, when she turned once more.

"Martine, Gerhard," Leah called out. She gave a little wave.

"Sweet little baby," said Leah.

GERHARD set them up—their little cupcake picnic—by the playground, near the ball field, next to the A & P parking lot where he'd parked the car. He was under the mistaken impression that with all that grass, emerald green and lush, still August grass, concentrated color, little Wylie would like to crawl. But he was too young; little Wylie was too young to crawl. That much was clear as soon as Martine lifted him out of the baby carrier and plopped him down; he slowly dissolved into a little puddle on the lawn; he couldn't even sit up yet. He just sank down into his soft bones, melted into a fat, wriggly, happy little lump on his back.

"I thought he might like to crawl," said Gerhard, although clearly the endeavor was hopeless.

"Wylie is not yet six months," said Martine. "You have too much ambitions for him," she said. "Perhaps you think he is a genius, like you." She gave Gerhard a Mona Lisa smile.

Gerhard blushed. "You must ignore Leah," he said. "We are old friends and she likes to tease." He felt his cheeks grow hot. When was the last time he blushed? Gerhard never blushed in his life.

Martine passed him his cup of coffee. "I hope it is not too cold," she said, referring to the coffee. And then, as if they were on a first date, "What is it that you do, that makes you such a genius?"

"I am a choreographer," said Gerhard. He took a sip of the coffee. Of course it had cooled. But Gerhard didn't care. He sipped the coffee anyway. "Better than at McDonald's," he said, which was a lie; it wasn't. He looked over the cup, peered out at Martine from under his eyebrows.

"Are you a very famous choreographer?" asked Martine. "Are you world famous?"

She opened up the cardboard box. Lifted out a cupcake.

"Famous?" said Gerhard. He considered this. "I am known," he said. And then, because he could not help himself: "I am respected."

"I am a wife and mother," said Martine. "I am not known. But I am respected." She placed the cupcake down on a napkin in front of him.

"For you," said Martine to Gerhard.

"And for me," she said, placing another one down on another napkin in front of herself.

"And your husband?" asked Gerhard.

"Thierry? Thierry is a student," said Martine. "Environmen-

139

tal studies. We are on our way to California. He is going to do some research at Berkeley. But we stop in New York first. We are both so eager to see this city."

"It is a wonderful city," said Gerhard. "It is the most wonderful city in the world."

Martine moved some hair away from her mouth. There was a breeze, and an errant strand kept flying toward her lips.

"And for you, little Wylie," she cooed as she dipped her fingertip in some of her cupcake's frosting and made a gentle pass across his tiny tongue.

The baby's eyes opened wide with surprise as he tasted the topping and then he began to chortle, the sound like a rooster's crow.

Both Gerhard and Martine began to laugh.

"It is his first sugar," said Martine.

"Then you will always remember this day," said Gerhard, forgetting himself for a moment, who they were and where they'd been, and how they'd come to be here.

Martine's face flickered with pain.

"I am sorry," said Gerhard, hitting his own forehead with the heel of his palm. "I am not thinking. For a moment, here with you, the baby, the day is so beautiful. Cupcakes . . . I relaxed for a moment. Please forgive me."

Tears slipped down Martine's cheeks, but she nodded, yes, yes, yes, of course she forgave him. She even covered his hand with hers.

"Of course," said Martine. "It is you who saved us. You saved me and my child. I will always be grateful to you. I will never ever forget this."

She was a beautiful, grateful woman. Gerhard had saved her. The thought was so large, so heady, it made him want to shout. Instead Gerhard used every ounce of reserve in his body to contain himself.

"None of us will forget this day," said Gerhard, gently. He turned his hand over, the one she was covering with the awning of her own, he turned his palm to meet hers, and then gently interlocked their fingers. He held Martine's hand and squeezed it for emphasis. "We will get past it, I hope, I hope the family of the world, all of us, we will get past it, maybe we can even learn . . . but we won't forget it." Martine was nodding, but the tears kept coming. Gerhard brought her hand to his lips. "None of us," he said. "Except him," he said, pointing to the happy, squirming Wylie. "He is still too pure, too innocent," said Gerhard. And then, trying for levity, "Even now that he has lost his sugar virginity."

"That depends," said Martine.

The tears appeared to dry on her skin.

"On what," said Gerhard.

"On whether or not this is the day he also lost his father," said Martine.

Overhead, there were no clouds. The sky was so clear, Gerhard got dizzy just looking at it. He looked down at the ground. Those thick green blades of grass. Sky and earth. Still here. An ant crawled on the grass. Creatures, still alive and accounted for. Almost as if nothing had changed yet.

How many innocent people had died today? Had Shingshang made it out?

"Do you want to go home?" asked Gerhard. "I mean, back to the cottage? We can see if he called."

If they went home, after they tried Thierry again, Gerhard could call the Shingshang house.

"Yes," said Martine. But she did not move. Her eyes were so brown, they were almost liquid. Like the center of a soft chocolate.

"She thinks that Wylie is yours," said Martine.

"What?" said Gerhard.

"Leah," said Martine. She removed her hand from his. "Your skinny little friend." She put her hand in her lap, a small fist. "She thinks Wylie belongs to you."

"Who cares what she thinks," said Gerhard.

"It is because of his eyes," she said. She said this so angrily, it was almost a hiss.

Yes, the baby's eyes were blue. This had already been established. Blue, blue, blue—who cared?

"Martine, Martine," said Gerhard; he meant it to comfort her.

But her face grew harder and harder, until it scared him.

"Martine?" said Gerhard.

On his back, the baby grabbed his toes, happily.

AT FIRST, Suzannah had prided herself on being clever enough to stop at the Springs General Store to buy bread before heading to the pond. True, it was a rather damp baguette, but still . . . it showed foresight, didn't it? Buying bread? It showed motherly ingenuity. With bread in hand, she and Nikolai could feed the ducks, do something active, helpful, giving, rather than just sitting back and admiring the game birds, the females' dull brown-speckled backs, the males' bright green heads, the graceful way their plump little bodies sailed across the water, defying the rules of physics (it seemed to her), the ducks so fat and sassy, all that weight and still they floated on the surface of the water, every once in a while diving down, their white tails pointing up in the air like ruffled panties.

Suzannah felt good about this decision, the pond thing, and about acting upon it. It was clearly a small matter to feel good about, on this day of all days, but on any day really it was the pintsized achievements that worked for her. Anna Kisselgoff and her reviews be damned, Suzannah was happier to go unobserved; it was when the pajamas she bought for Nikolai fit him, for example, when she could coax him to eat something not on his five-food roster (bagels, pancakes, bananas, string cheese, yogurt—anything white), the sense of victory she felt when he'd let her swoop down for a hug, that made her feel worthy of walking the Earth. The bread in her hand—they'd parked the car at the general store and crossed the road together, Nikolai's diminutive paw in hers, her kid trailing behind her like a baby duckling himself—made her feel good about herself as a mother; she was a woman who took her little boy to a pond to feed ducks on the worst day of his life. She was persevering. She hoped that in years to come this is what Nikolai would remember: in his girlfriend's arms, or, who was kidding whom, on the shrink's couch, or maybe when tucking his own children into bed one night, Suzannah hoped he would tell the story of how when the world was coming to an end, after they had barely escaped the firebomb of lower Manhattan, his mom took him to a pond to feed ducks, and he had felt safe and loved.

So, subsequent to Surfer Danny's righting himself and hopping into his Subaru and heading home to lucky, lucky Donna; subsequent to Celine's march upstairs to smoke a joint and take a nap (Suzannah had a secret stash in her purse; she'd shared it with Celine in order to soothe her), Suzannah and Nikolai had found the keys to the old VW Bug Elspeth kept in the garage for kicking around in, and, basically, they stole it. They stole Elspeth's car because the desire for escape had not yet left her; instinctively Suzannah felt she must carry on with her flight.

She'd loaded Nikolai up, even without the car seat—Gerhard, that fucker, had taken their car, with their car seat, for some stranger's baby to use no doubt, without even telling her, his wife, that he was taking off—and she drove first toward the village of East Hampton and then continued onward. Suzannah had meant to turn off of Route 27 and park when she got to town, but when she saw the Tiffany's outpost in her peripheral vision she'd just continued driving, she had to get away from all that—the cell phones and the Jaguars, the four-dollar ice creams and the money—farther down Pantigo Road into the sleepier, less tony Amagansett, aiming for Montauk and its refreshing honky-tonk, its soaring bluffs and vast ocean beaches, Montauk Point and the end of it all—when the ducks suddenly sprang to mind. Quack, quack, quack, thought Suzannah. I'm going quackers.

Nikolai was humming in the back seat, two seat belts anchoring him into place, when the ducks called out to her. She'd slipped the car over the train tracks then, swinging left past the golf course, and headed toward the Springs General Store. It was a place she'd always liked. A lot of old hippies in beat-up trucks with big black dogs. Some yoga mavens like herself. Some real people, too. Fishermen and schoolteachers and groundskeepers, the Mexicans (who these days did pretty much all the service work in the area, barring a few fresh-faced, sunburned Irish lassies), some playwrights and sculptors. During the summer months, she often drove far out of her way just to get there, because she loved to stop in for a newspaper and a coffee in the mornings, eyeing the homemade muffins still cooling in the tins they were baked in, little bridges of crust where the dough had spilled, now golden and lacy and hard on the raised portions of the pans. It all felt so homey. There were some battered Adirondack chairs on the porch where you could sit and read the *Times*. It felt good to Suzannah to be there, at the general store—the counter lady whispering over Nikolai's head, "Are you and yours all right?" when Suzannah placed their order.

Suzannah actually felt that her answer had mattered to this woman. That the woman cared if Suzannah and her family were safe and sound. What family? Gerhard was off entertaining his new French girlfriend, her father was dead, her mother literally and figuratively unreachable—I should try and call her again, thought Suzannah, I'll try and call her later—her overweight, successful-enough brothers and their aerobicized wives and their ridiculously normal children, all safely ensconced in some suburb somewhere—Shaker Heights! Newton! Montclair! They'd escaped the city as soon as they were able, escaped each other; were any of them in touch? Who cared? Aside from a few biannual phone calls about her mother's guardianship and treatment—which often the wives handled, as if for Suzannah's brothers a discussion regarding their mother's condition was akin to accompanying her to a Pap smear—it had been a very long time since Suzannah considered "the boys" a part of her life anyway.

She appreciated this stranger's concern. The woman couldn't possibly know how alone Suzannah was in the world; and if she had known, she probably would have wept, a woman like that. They'd even exchanged a little hug, before Suzannah exited the store; an extemporaneous, heartfelt, human expression of kindness and concern, their arms awkwardly wrapping around each other's back, hands patting shoulder blades, breasts pressing together over the countertop. When that was done, she and Nikolai had stepped outside, this afternoon's bread firmly encircled in her hand.

But now, squatting on the grass by the pond, the outing was proving to be disappointing. It wasn't the fault of the setting; no, the pond was exquisite. It was surrounded by rushes and sea green lawn, a picture-perfect red barn in the background. Once each summer a blacksmith would set up shop there during the annual Fisherman's Fair, and you could watch the animals get shod, the black iron horseshoe dipped into fire until it too glowed red-hot, before the blacksmith pounded it into shape.

The red horse barn was behind the rushes. A picturesque little bridge cut across the marsh. Although the sun was beginning to lower, the sky was still blue and flawless. It was not the setting that was at fault for bringing her down. It was this: even as they trotted up to the water, Suzannah tearing off a hunk of bread and then shredding the pieces for Nikolai to scatter, she'd noticed that there was something off with the ducks. When Nikolai flung the bread at them they didn't waddle across the lawn toward it. When he dumped a big wad into the water, they didn't skim across the pond's surface and descend upon it, quacking and fighting over it, en masse, like she'd hoped. Instead, they sat where they sat complacently. On closer inspection, Suzannah could see why. The pond was full of bread. Sodden, swollen slices clogging up the water. The ducks were overfed and overindulged. The pond had in places the spongy consistency of an Italian bread soup. It was saturated with the stuff.

Nikolai looked up at his mother in despair—at least she thought that was the look, she couldn't be sure, the sun was hitting her directly in the eyes—maybe it was an expression that was asking for permission, or perhaps his face conveyed nothing at all. Who knew, or at this moment, who had the drive or the energy to care? He began to wing wads of bread at the birds, and she recognized that she should stop him—no, Nikolai, *no*, honey—but Suzannah was too tired to intervene. She sat back on her heels in the grass. It felt as if there were a boot on her chest, driving her into the ground.

At least it is pretty here, she kept reminding herself. *I could be there*, she thought. I am lucky, lucky, lucky, Suzannah kept saying to herself over and over again. I could have been *him*.

You must change your life.

She heard the voice again. Is that what that man was to her, the diver, the falling body? Was he a messenger, a rescuer, a winged angel sent to save her?

Or was he just some Godforsaken systems analyst or futures trader? Was he just some poor guy who'd simply gone in to work this morning, maybe stopping at a kiosk in the lobby for a cup of coffee, clueless to the agonies that awaited him? Isn't that what life ended up being so much of the time: a compendium of the innocent moments *before*, like the carefree snapshot of a day at the beach that sometimes accompanies the story about a murder victim.

She caught sight of her peculiar child. "Careful, Nikolai," she said. "Don't hurt the ducks." Part of being a good mother was preventing her son from doing harm to others.

"That's the Hamptons for you," said a man, and so Suzannah looked up over her knees and under the visor of her hand.

"Even the ducks are spoiled," he said.

He was handsome. His long, sun-gold hair was loose about his shoulders. He was at least a few years younger than she was. He gave her a crooked grin.

"It's such a disappointment," said Suzannah, unaccountably opening up to him.

He nodded at her. He hunkered down a few feet away, pulling up a blade of grass and placing it between his teeth. "That your boy?" he asked, indicating with his head toward Nikolai. He was humming, Nikolai was, and since his bread bombs hadn't gotten a rise out of the birds he was now throwing dirt clods at them.

"I know I shouldn't let him . . . Nikolai! Nikolai!" Suzannah tried to get his attention.

"No mind," said the man. "Boys will be boys."

Boys will be boys. What a relief, thought Suzannah. If that was all this was.

"You're Suzannah, aren't you?" said the man. "What a coincidence," he said, shaking his head. He was sitting down now, not exactly next to her, but not far away either. She noticed some paint splattered on his jeans. So he was local. An artist or a workman. She did not recognize him.

"I am," she said. "Do we know each other?" she asked, politely.

"Used to," he said. "That is, I used to know you." His green eyes crinkled up at the corners. His skin was darkened by the sun, so the green in his eyes was that much more concentrated and potent. "I'm Lawrence from down the hall—5F remember? Remember"—and here his voice went into falsetto, a falsetto and a rough Bronx Jewish accent—"'Lawrence! Lawrence! I said, *now*, Lawrence! I said, *This instant!*'"

Suzannah laughed out loud because the voice was so comical. Lawrence grinned at her laughter. And when she stopped laughing she said, "That's so funny. But I *don't* remember you," and she laughed again.

"You don't remember?" said Lawrence in mock horror. "We lived down the hall, the Shapiros, Fred and Evelyn? I have a big brother, Murray?" Here his voice sounded a little more insulted, more incredulous. "How could you not remember?"

"I remember the Shapiros, Mr. and Mrs. Shapiro," said Suzannah. The woman had worn coffee-colored knee-highs under her housedresses, and the flesh had spilled out over the elastic. "I think I remember Murray, I think I went to Hebrew school with Murray . . ."

Lawrence nodded.

He'd been cute, Murray. Tall and redheaded, but not freckly. So bony his knees were bigger than his head. Murray was cute, but this one was cuter.

"You had a sister, Molly, who was older, right? She used to babysit for us, I think, before she went to college . . ."

"Yup, Molly," said Lawrence. "She's an accountant living in Great Neck now. Two husbands, three kids, Molly."

"I remember Molly, but I don't remember you," said Suzannah.

Lawrence looked down at the ground.

"I'm sorry," said Suzannah.

"That's all right," said Lawrence. "I mean it's disheartening," he said—was he flirting with her? "But I can accept it. You don't remember me, but I remember you, Suzannah," said Lawrence. "You were quite the little ballerina, weren't you?"

"Yes, I guess I was," said Suzannah.

"I used to sneak out onto our terrace and cross over to your parents' terrace and look through the glass doors and watch you dance in your living room."

"You did?" said Suzannah. Her voice came out with a squeal.

"I did." Lawrence laughed. "You were partial to Joni Mitchell."

"I was!" exclaimed Suzannah. "Still am." And then, "God, how embarrassing."

"Don't be embarrassed," said Lawrence. "You were gorgeous, I loved watching you. I had such a crush on you," he said.

"You did?" asked Suzannah. She felt shy and disbelieving when she said this. Imagine, back then, knowing someone had a crush. Back then when she'd felt so valueless and invisible.

"I used to watch you all the time," said Lawrence.

"Oh," said Suzannah, trying to remember what she did. She used to put music on, and her toe shoes, and dance around the house. *Swan Lake.* Once in a while she'd used her mother's shawl for a tutu.

"One time when you were dancing, Barry came in."

Suzannah startled. Her brother Barry was such an asshole.

"He turned off the music and he hit you. He was pissed about something. He punched you in the stomach."

He was always hitting her, Barry. Anything could send him off. If she touched something in his room, if she forgot to set the table—his chore, his chore that he'd bully her into performing. She remembered one time, when she'd played his new album, *Led Zeppelin IV,* she'd borrowed it without his permission, he'd kicked her repeatedly in the stomach. It was a series of kicks that knocked the wind out of her, dropping her to her knees, and later she'd spit up blood. Barry hated her. Her mother's pet, the ballerina; he was glad to make her suffer.

"He really waled on you," said Lawrence. "And you were so skinny . . . I even tried to tell my dad, but he said that's the way brothers and sisters are. He said, 'They fight.' But you didn't fight, I noticed that. He hit you and he hit you, but you didn't fight him back."

It was true. All the times that Barry hit her, Suzannah never hit him back. She never even told on him. She took it. Why did she take it? She wondered this now, for the first time really; it was astonishing to think she'd never wondered about this before.

And yet she knew she took it because on some strange cosmic level she thought that she deserved it. She didn't tell on him, because telling on Barry would break the unspoken covenant between them, saying out loud what he did to her would in some weird way make it true. If she didn't say it, she could pretend it never happened.

"Who are you?" said Suzannah, rising to her feet, shame and outrage spreading throughout her veins like icy water. This stranger had watched her; he'd studied her. He knew far too much about her. It would have been better if he had confessed to seeing her binge and purge, if he had watched her masturbate, seen her steal.

"Lawrence Shapiro, 5F," said Lawrence. He stood up now, too. "I always wondered what happened to you. I mean I know you dance—I've paid money to see you. Your early forays in the living room, they kind of inspired me—and I know you married that guy, that Gerhard Falktopf, but I always wondered what happened to you in your soul. I mean it seemed kind of extreme, the way you just stood there and took it."

No one had ever talked to her like this before. No one had ever looked at her this closely—oh sure, Suzannah was used to being observed, scrutinized really, by Gerhard, the critics, her audiences, but that was physical scrutiny. Even the shrinks, like everyone else on the planet, had focused on Gerhard, Suzannah in context with Gerhard. She'd never commanded *this* kind of attention alone before.

She felt like she might throw up.

"Where is Barry these days?" said Lawrence.

Barry was married and living outside Boston, but Suzannah wasn't going to tell him this. Barry was fine.

"I think he's dead," said Suzannah.

"Really?" said Lawrence, raising his eyebrows.

"He worked in the South Tower," said Suzannah. "I mean I guess he could be alive. I don't know." She was lying. But it felt good to lie. Who was this guy anyway?

"I don't know," said Suzannah, and then with anger, "I don't care."

"If he's dead," said Lawrence, "he's probably the only guy there who deserved to die."

Suzannah couldn't believe he said this. The idea, and Lawrence's willingness to voice it, both sickened her and thrilled her.

Her head was spinning. The sky and the earth were changing places, seesawing right-side up and upside down. "I think I'm going to go now," said Suzannah, like she was narrating her own movements in a play. She wanted to get away from him. "I think I'm going to gather my son and go." At that moment, she realized she'd broken her own cardinal rule. "Nikolai! Nikolai!" She'd stopped paying attention to him.

Suzannah jumped up to her feet. But she did not see her boy. Nikolai was not where he had been standing just seconds before. Once again, panic set in. She turned around in a little circle. No Nikolai. She made her hand into a visor; she scanned the lawn, the rushes, the little bridge. She felt like she was going to pee in her pants. Where was he? How could she have let him out of her sight? Could he have fallen into the inlet?

"He's over there," said Lawrence.

Where? Where? Lawrence pointed in the other direction, near the barn. She'd looked that way before and had not seen him. But now, with Lawrence pointing out the way, the top of Nikolai's head was visible above the rushes, like a shark's fin skimming the surface of the water. Nikolai was fine. He was humming and spinning, spinning and humming, whirling like a dervish around and around and around again, by the water's edge.

"There a name for what he's got?" asked Lawrence. "Your kid?"

"I think maybe it's autism," said Suzannah, the words, like the flood of her relief, spilling out of her mouth, even before she had the time to think them up.

"Really?" said Lawrence, his eyes widening.

"It's a spectrum disease," said Suzannah, astonished at the sound of her own voice taking new and independent life in the summer air. "Sometimes I wonder if he's somewhere on the spectrum." Her own voice, betraying her son, betraying both of them.

"You should take him to a doctor," said Lawrence. "Maybe there's something they could do about that." He got up and stretched his legs.

"You don't have to leave on my account, Suzannah. I didn't mean to upset you."

He started to walk away. Then he turned, "I live out here now. I've got a studio out on Springs Fireplace . . ."

A car horn honked. The red truck pulled out in front of the general store. Lawrence gave the truck a wave.

"Later then," said Lawrence.

♪

THERE was only one person in the church when Suzannah entered the sanctuary. Nikolai was asleep. He'd nodded off in the back seat of Elspeth's Bug on their way back from the pond, and Suzannah had hesitated in the little dirt patch that served as a parking lot, thinking: who's going to harm a little boy in an empty church parking lot on today of all days? The thought of lifting him was too much to bear—he was so heavy, especially when he was asleep—but in the end she'd unbuckled him and slung him over her shoulder. It was a tiny, white stucco church on Old Stone Highway, a little one-roomer with a bright red door. She'd driven by for years, always wondering about its affiliation and congregation but never wondering enough to stop. After that bizarre encounter at the pond, after the lunacy of this day, she'd found herself pulling into the church's tiny drive. If there'd been a synagogue, she'd probably have stopped there, she told herself as she struggled under Nikolai's weight. She would have stopped at a mosque or a Buddhist temple, she was sure of it. But this little white church beckoned to her on her way home. It looked so peaceful.

Suzannah was hoping for a place of respite; she was hoping for privacy. She hadn't expected to find a young girl inside, as there were no other vehicles outside, not even a bicycle or scooter to mark her arrival, but there she was.

In the front pew, the girl kneeled, all alone, quietly praying. She was on the edge of puberty—she must have been about twelve or thirteen—wearing white shorts and a blue-and-white-striped top, and her long, silky brown hair fell in a curtain over her face. She prayed and she prayed and she prayed. She prayed without ceasing. Suzannah stood in the back of the simple wooden chapel—maybe there were twelve, fifteen rows of seats—watching her. Suzannah didn't pray, she didn't know how to anymore, or why she should. She no longer believed in God. She didn't believe in anything. She'd pulled into the church instinctively because she'd needed help. She'd wanted comfort. Instead, she just stood and watched the young girl pray. After a while, she set Nikolai down on a wooden bench and sat beside him while he slept, one hand on his little chest as he breathed in and out, her precious angel. The girl in the front pew kept praying. Suzannah kept watching her. She watched her pray for half an hour. Then she stood up, stretched, and bent deep in her knees before hoisting Nikolai up on her shoulder again. She got up and went out into the world, carrying her little boy on her back. The sun was beginning to go down. Inside, she assumed, the girl kept praying. Somehow Suzannah got Nikolai in the back seat. Somehow she got the seat belt fastened safely around him, and then the other seat belt as well, for good measure. She climbed into the driver's seat, shut the door, put on her own seat belt, locking it into place. Then she pulled out on to the empty road.

She drove and drove, past Marty's Deli and the golf course, over the railroad tracks and left on 27 out to Montauk, and then when she got past the first intense clutch of houses by the ocean—one built right on top of the other—the road forked onto both the new and old Montauk highways. Suzannah took the old road, passing the camping grounds and Guerney's Inn on her right and the condos and motels on her left, up and down over the rolling hills, listening to the call of the gulls, now and then glimpsing the sea, each rising swell giving her hope, hope for some sweet form of obliteration; but when she got to the roundabout in town, instead of continuing on her trajectory straight out to Montauk Point as she had intended, instead of driving to the very edge of Long Island, the end of it all; without thinking about it, she veered left. It was as if she were stuck to this road, hugging its curve as if it were the very curve of the Earth.

Slowly Suzannah followed the traffic circle around back to the highway, no longer retracing her steps, but finding herself now driving on the new 27 leading back through Napeague and past the Clam Bar and the Art Barge, through the little hamlet of Amagansett back into East Hampton, past the Tiffany outlet, the East Hampton Library and the First Presbyterian Church with about a million cars parked outside—so that's where the townspeople were gathering, that's why no one was at her little chapel—but she didn't stop. She passed the pond with the swans. The sky was getting pinker. Pinker, more orange, grayer. Suzannah drove and drove. She drove across the circumference of this picture-perfect, expensive little bubble, home to the rich and the famous, the infinitely lucky. Was it possible that their money and their privilege still could help them escape the horrors of the modern world? Or was no one immune? Not even the benefactors by proxy, the hangers-on, like Gerhard, like her, who could enjoy the luxury without shouldering any of the guilt? Or the locals, who both needed and disdained them? Was it true that no matter the power of one's government or the strength of their army, how wealthy or how smart or how pretty or how accomplished one was, the color of his or her skin, the depths of his or her education, the thread count of his or her sheets, the rarity of his or her wine, how *loved* someone was (for no one was more loved than her Nikolai; it wasn't possible to love someone more than Suzannah loved that child), that anyone was safe? Today had proved otherwise. The human being is nothing. The human being is as easily crushed as a fly.

She drove down Ocean Avenue and into Elspeth's drive. There was a car she didn't recognize parked next to their Mercedes and off to the side, a beat-up old red truck. Gerhard was back. Clearly they had company.

In the church on Old Stone Highway the girl kept praying. She prayed without ceasing. Suzannah could feel it in her bones. Probably it would do her no good. Probably it would do that poor girl no good at all to keep on praying. No amount of prayer had ever helped Suzannah. She unbuckled her seat belt and sat for a while in the car, listening to the sound of Nikolai's breathing, the *hush hush hush*, the tiny oceanic breath, rolling in and out like the tide, before gathering the strength she needed to lift her boy up again and carry him inside.

THEY were all splayed out in front of the TV set in the Florida room when Suzannah entered the house, wild-eyed and hollow, Nikolai dead asleep in her arms, her hair a curly black nimbus surrounding her pale, white face.

Gerhard was sitting on the rattan club chair, clutching a gin and tonic, his fingers numb from the icy sweat of the glass, which he continually rattled, playing the ice cube chimes because doing so helped to settle him. Martine and the baby were busy distracting each other at his feet, sprawled out on the pretty rag rug Elspeth had picked up in Appalachia. (It had once been displayed in the Museum of American Folk Art; Gerhard remembered sharing this info with Suzannah several summers before, when, stoned and horny, he'd wanted them to desecrate it connubially.) Martine had reached her mother in Lyon during the interim, and they'd had a tearful reunion over the phone, which had both calmed and drained her. Now, she used a rather large conch shell as a train and ran it up and down the hills and valleys of chubby little Wylie, tummy to toes, letting the *whirr* of the ocean that was magically trapped inside the shell leak into his ears, much to his delight. The *bébé* chortled with pleasure.

Leah and Lizbeth curled up together on the rattan couch, which was upholstered in white linen, jelly glasses full of a fragrant Bordeaux in their hands. When Gerhard glanced at the two women from time to time, he had the peculiar notion that perhaps they were both menstruating. Maybe it was all that expensive white fabric, the daring angle of those glasses filled with blood-red wine, the whole two-women thing—some animal instinct on his part. Leah's head leaned on Lizbeth's sculptured shoulder, Lizbeth petting Leah's untamed white mane, once in a while soothing her pickled brow. They were such a couple, perfectly balanced in their yin and yang. Celine was there, too. She was kneeling by the glass coffee table in front of the food.

Lizbeth had arrived bearing a platter of fresh figs stuffed with goat cheese surrounded by prosciutto skirts, "like little Buddha ballerinas," she'd said ironically, "perhaps they'll improve our karma . . ." and a tray of chilled grapes individually rolled in blue cheese and coated with chopped walnuts. When Gerhard remarked on the wherewithal she must have possessed to stage such a highly sophisticated presentation under the pressures of the moment, she responded apologetically, "It's ridiculous what one does to comfort oneself. My instinct was to feed my friends as elaborately as possibly." Celine was greedily double-dipping her chips in the bean and avocado mélange Leah and Larry had rustled up at the wildly expensive and inaptly named Round Swamp Farm; for all that bounty Celine was the only one with an appetite, her rather long, lovely head at times annoyingly blocking Gerhard's view of the television. They'd switched from the networks about half an hour before when, channel surfing, Gerhard had caught that pretty Paula Zahn midsentence: "—sense of shock could swiftly turn to outrage. Why weren't we better prepared?" Since he agreed with her—why weren't the Americans better prepared?—he'd decided to throw his lot in with CNN/Time Warner.

"The United States is at war, the question is with whom?" some baldy with a red tie had said—Woolley? Woolsey? The former CIA director. Could be Osama. Could be Iraq. Someone else had speculated the Palestinians. Martine seemed certain it was Bin Laden, and Gerhard trusted her instincts.

Larry was nursing a beer on the sidelines, sitting chest to chair back in a wooden farm chair he'd brought in from the mudroom. (He was annoyingly blue-collar, Gerhard thought; one of those artists who liked to pretend they were part of the herd, when in reality he got to follow his muse, attend fancy openings, and inhale paint fumes for a living.) Except for the baby and Martine, everyone's eyes were glued on the television. If Suzannah hadn't let out a last soulful breath before what seemed like an imminent collapse, Gerhard might not have noticed her, swaying in the doorway, he was so riveted by what he saw on the screen. The footage of the destruction of the South Tower that CNN was currently broadcasting was from a new angle, a bystander's video, and it was incredibly real, as if it really happened—which it did, it really happened, Gerhard kept reminding himself, the buildings were gone now—the collapse itself like a tornado funneling down, the resultant crash whirling huge clouds of smoke up and outward in the shape of a brain. An exploding, mushrooming brain. Billowing brain matter.

When Gerhard heard that little gasp and looked up and saw his beautiful wife, vacant and exhausted, her body practically unoccupied—she was as hollowed out and splendid as a Roman ruin—he was on his feet at once and by her side.

"Suzannah, darling," said Gerhard. "You will wreck your back!"

Her handsome, strong, supple back, so pliable still that even at thirty-six she could rise from a supine position on the floor on her stomach, bending both ends of her body toward one another and kiss the crown of her head with the arches of her feet. The tectonic plates of her shoulder blades were like two wings. Her spine was raised and knotted like a string of cascading pearls. The only other spinal column Gerhard had ever seen like that was in a movie, and it belonged to Grace Kelly. It was with no small amount of pride that he noted Suzannah's backbone was the more beautiful.

Gerhard told Suzannah, time and time again, the child was too big, too heavy to lug around. He'd warned her that the boy would be her ruin. Yet there she was in the doorway, letting him destroy her.

Gerhard was on his feet in an instant, rushing to her side, but Larry somehow seemed to get there first. Was that a look of recognition on his wife's face when the young man approached her, or was it fear?

"I'll take him," said Larry. When he lifted the kid off her shoulder, she stood and swayed for a minute. Like a sapling bending in the breeze. Her arms reaching out for the child, always the child.

"I'm a friend of Leah's," said Larry, explaining himself gently to Suzannah. "I won't hurt him."

"Suzie," said Gerhard, and she involuntarily leaned into him it seemed—maybe she was falling over. "Are you all right? Where have you been? We have been so worried about you . . ."

Suzannah's eyes seemed to flutter up into the back of her head for an instant—he could see only the whites—before they trained down on the tableau in front of her.

"Leah?" she said, helplessly.

"Sweetie-pie," said Leah, rising to her feet and rushing toward the doorway. "You look like you might faint." She turned to Lizbeth: "Lizzie, can you get something cold for Suzannah to drink?"

Lizbeth said, "Of course," and started off toward the kitchen. She called out over her shoulder: "Her head should be lower than her knees . . ."

Leah went about the business of bending Suzannah. She leaned her against the wall, Suzannah's knees collapsing, and slid her down to the floor. Once seated, Suzannah's knees flopped wide, her feet meeting like the open pages of a book in front of her, in cobbler's pose. Leah bent Suzannah's head over her legs so that she resembled a closed clamshell. Leah stroked the back of Suzannah's neck for her. "There, there," said Leah.

"Nikolai," said Suzannah, through the muffle of her hair.

"He's fine, darling," said Leah, and then to Larry: "Larry, why don't you get Celine to show you where the baby's bed is? Celine, could you please help Larry?"

"Sure," said Celine, from within the Florida room, still kneeling in front of the coffee table, her mouth full of chips. A few little pieces sprayed out when she spoke, and she covered her lips with her hands, stifling a small giggle. Then she, too, walked toward the entranceway.

Suzannah lifted her head; her face was now red, Gerhard noted, red and shiny with cold sweat.

"He'll be scared if he wakes up there," said Suzannah.

This was probably true, thought Gerhard. The amount of time and energy Suzannah brought to acclimating the kid to a new environment was more than he himself would expend on just about anything other than work or sex. In July, when they'd come out here, she'd brought the kid's dirty linens from his city bed so that this mattress and pillow would smell the same as that one when they tucked him in the first night. She'd arranged his stuffed animals around the border of the bed frame exactly as she'd had them at home, using a little chart she'd made as a reference, because if she made a mistake, Nikolai would notice. She'd brought out his smallest bookshelf, loaded into the back of the SUV with all the rest of his equipment (his cars, his trains, his portable train table) so that there was hardly any room for Gerhard's CDs; she re-shelved it with all the same books in the same order as they had been laid out in Manhattan, and read to Nikolai from them for hours it seemed, before the child drifted off to dreamland. She'd even burned some sage . . . Suzannah was always burning some sage these days, ridding their lives of evil spirits. Evidently, it hadn't worked.

Still, Nikolai didn't look like he was waking up anytime soon. He looked like he was in a coma. His head lolled around Larry's neck, his mouth agape, his eyes were oddly somehow open. Nothing was going to rouse him. He was completely done in. He'd slept in the bed here at Elspeth's a good portion of the summer, anyway. If it were up to Gerhard, he'd take a flyer on this one. Perhaps the whole trick with this kid was that Suzannah coddled him too much. For a moment his mind flickered on the time before, the sweet time before Nikolai's birth, before he arrived like a quadriplegic, penniless alien, who spoke a shrieking language no one on Earth could decipher and took over their lives forever.

"Leave him here, please," she begged.

His wife was begging Larry, Larry the pretentious painter — pretentious in that he pretended to no pretense, which Gerhard found most offensive of all.

Larry looked from Suzannah to Gerhard, caught between husband and wife, not sure what to do with his increasingly heavy charge.

"Gerhard, please!" Suzannah's voice was on the brink of panic.

"Set him on the couch," said Gerhard.

Larry moved obediently from the threshold, into the Florida room and toward the couch.

"Celine, help the man," said Gerhard.

Celine scrambled up on her coltish legs and hovered around Larry, as she was ordered.

"Here, Suzannah," said Lizbeth. She was back with a clean cloth filled with ice chips and some lemonade.

"Drink some of this and you'll see God," said Leah. "If I

know Martha Stewart here, she squeezed this elixir herself."

Suzannah obediently looked up. She took a sip from the glass Leah was holding. Then she took the glass. Lizbeth handed Leah the cloth. "For her neck, Lee-lee," said Lizbeth. "I'll get her feet."

Leah pressed the cloth to the back of Suzannah's neck, while Lizbeth pulled off her flip-flops and started to rub those celebrated arches.

"I always wanted to massage a dancer's foot," said Lizbeth.

"Why?" said Suzannah, breathing heavily between hefty sips. "They are so beat-up and ugly."

"They are historical documents attesting to pain and beauty," said Lizbeth.

On the floor that way, rubbing, sipping, breathing, the three of them looked like a Lamaze class, thought Gerhard. He almost felt left out.

"Have you eaten anything lately, Suzannah?" asked Leah.

Gerhard thought he hadn't seen Suzannah eat anything at all, all day, except for that Diet Coke in Queens, and her break-of-day cup of coffee — could that have been just this morning? This very morning when she'd put out a bowl of fresh raspberries for him, the two soft-boiled duck eggs in the little silver eggcups. Was any part of this same day attached to that one? The world had changed. He had changed. He'd been so angry then, what had he been so angry about? Those problems seemed dwarfed now by these vast, unimaginable ones, and in light of the new problems, the former seemed so surmountable and so fixable. And yet surrounded by his family and friends in this big, gracious house, flush with the awesome gratitude and relief of survival, was Gerhard in some strange sense actually more content? Clearly he was more appreciative.

Suzannah had not eaten, as far as Gerhard knew, not even one morsel, but then again, it had been hours since they'd been together—which kind of puzzled Gerhard when he thought about it, that they'd been separated most of the time.

"I don't know," said Suzannah. She looked up, completely bewildered. "I can't remember."

"It's been a long, hard day," said Leah. "It's easy to forget everything . . . Except how lucky we all are to be safe, here in this beautiful place together." She gestured around Elspeth's house. "How privileged we are."

Suzannah looked up at her, a butterfly in a jar, wings thrashing against the glass. "Nikolai," said Suzannah. She whipped her head around. It was as if it suddenly occurred to her, in the wake of counting her blessings, that her child was missing, that he'd been kidnapped.

"Ssshh, lovey, he's in the Florida room," said Leah.

"I'll make you a little tray," said Lizbeth. "Leah, why don't you help Suzannah to the couch. She'll be more comfortable there, next to her baby." She patted Suzannah on the shoulder. She was a mother, too.

Suzannah looked up at her gratefully. At last, the look said, someone understands.

Gerhard extended a hand to his wife. Suzannah took it. "I'll help her," said Gerhard to everyone and to nobody. He pulled her up to her feet. Then he and Leah slowly walked Suzannah into the Florida room; she was still so wobbly, he kept reeling her in by the elbow. Larry had deposited the boy on the couch and was sitting beside him on the floor, one hand resting securely on Nikolai's abdomen so the kid wouldn't roll and fall off. Martine picked up her baby (they were blocking the path to the sofa) and scooted them both out of the way so that Suzannah and her entourage could get around them.

"I'm so sorry, Suzannah," said Martine. What was she apologizing for? Gerhard wondered. She'd done nothing wrong.

Once around the coffee table, Suzannah sank into the couch, next to the boy.

"Please leave us alone," she said to Larry. "Please." Again, her voice was begging him. "Go away. For God's sake, just go away."

To Gerhard, she seemed borderline hysterical.

Larry moved backwards on his heels, in a crouch, as if he'd been hit. He stayed there a moment before he rose to his feet, once Suzannah's long, thin hand held Nikolai safely in place.

"I should have told you earlier," said Larry, looking intently down at Suzannah. "That was wrong of me."

How large Suzannah's eyes were. How vulnerable.

"Told her what?" said Leah.

"I wasn't going to come here, tonight, but Leah . . . you know how persuasive Leah can be," Larry said this with a little smile. He said this as if he and Suzannah were the only people in the room. As if Leah, who was standing right next to him, was out of earshot. Gerhard found the intimacy of his tone maddening.

"She didn't think I should be alone." Larry kept right on talking to Suzannah, only Suzannah. "She didn't think you or Gerhard would mind . . ."

What was the poseur talking about?

Larry was wearing a torn blue workshirt now over his torn green T-shirt—Gerhard guessed this was his way of dressing up.

Larry ignored them all, he was so focused on Suzannah, and she on him; it seemed to Gerhard that their irises were connected by two ribbons of molten light.

"I was just so moved to see you," said Larry. "After all that time . . ." He stopped there. With a calculated simplicity, Gerhard thought, Larry said, "You have always moved me, Suzannah."

A sharp anger rose through Gerhard's chest into his throat. It was a specific sensation, like knee pain, only not located in the knee obviously, closer to the heart, the lungs, a pointed, skinny pain that for all its narrowness did not lack complexity;

it felt like a cord of nerves, the fraying of ligaments, torn cartilage.

Just then, Lizbeth came in carrying a little sandwich and a bowl of cut-up fruit. She'd located the lobster salad.

"Larry knows Suzannah?" asked Lizbeth.

"Apparently," said Leah. There was irritation in her voice. The woman was a saint, but she hated to be ignored.

"How?" said Gerhard.

He felt uncomfortably possessive when he said this. How in the world did this young idiot know his wife?

"We were neighbors growing up in the Bronx," said Larry. He said it to the crowd, but he was staring at her. "I worshipped her from afar," he said. "For years, I worshipped her."

"You did?" said Gerhard.

"She didn't know I existed," said Larry, a little bitterly. "In the social order of our neighborhood she was untouchable, somewhere up in the constellations. I was just a little dweeb down on the ground."

Up in the constellations? Suzannah had never presented herself to Gerhard this way. She'd seen herself as shy and scared and removed, removed from the world by the fact that even as a child she was already working; she was dancing. Perhaps this was what Larry the artist was getting at, in his romanticized, cryptic fashion.

"Apparently, she knows you exist now," said Gerhard, puffing up a bit. He did not like it when someone seemed to know more about his wife than he did.

"Gerhard," said Suzannah. She said it weakly, but with a little bit of surprise at the proprietary quality of his response. He noted her noting it, wondering if it pleased her. Wondering why he wasn't eager to give her that very tiny little pleasure.

"We ran into each other at the pond earlier today," said Larry. "Otherwise, it's been about twenty years. Except of course when I'd seen you on the stage, Suzannah."

He turned to Leah. Finally.

"She is magnificent."

"This we know," said Leah. She shook her head at Gerhard, rolling her eyes just a little, as if to say *sorry, buddy, I had no idea about any of this . . .*

"You were at the pond?" Gerhard queried Suzannah. All of a sudden he felt like the aggrieved party. "What pond?"

Jeff Greenfield, the pudgy, bespectacled news commentator, was on the television. Gerhard had always respected Jeff Greenfield. "We are going to wake up tomorrow in a different country," said Jeff Greenfield.

"I suppose he's right," said Leah.

"Who's right?" said Gerhard.

"CNN," said Leah. "Jeff Greenfield."

All eyes turned to the television. Jeff Greenfield looked haggard and a little rocked, as rocked as a news commentator was genetically programmed to look, on the big wide screen.

"Oh, why can't we go back to the way it was?" said Leah.

Why indeed? Hadn't he felt that way once himself, as a child, when he lost his mother? Such a futile, damning emotion. The desire to go back, it got him nowhere. So he'd purposefully excised it from his personality. From then on, Gerhard studiously trained his ambitions forward, hurling himself body and soul at the future. He admired Leah in this moment, envied her, too, just a bit, the purity of her response. It was something to aspire to, in a way.

"Our luck has changed," Jeff Greenfield said.

"Do you think that's true?" Celine asked. She was back on her knees by the dip. She sounded like a child when she asked this. Needy and shrill and frightened. Her fear alarmed him. Gerhard wasn't up for it at the moment. He'd had about all the feminine hysteria he could take for one day. Irrespective of his desire, the young woman began to sob quite loudly.

Lizbeth put a motherly hand on Celine's shoulder.

"Ssshh," said Lizbeth.

Please shut that girl up, thought Gerhard.

Lizbeth kneeled down next to Celine and began to play with her hair, twisting all the tiny plaits into one thick braid, as if she'd heard him.

Across from them, Leah's gaunt, shining face . . . it was lit from within.

"All the benefits of an open society," said Leah. "Travel and exchange and trust . . ." Her voice cracked.

"They've been living like this in Israel for years," said Larry. "We were spoiled."

"We were fortunate!" said Leah. She said it with such conviction Gerhard was instantly forced to believe her.

They were fortunate. He was fortunate.

"No one should live like this," said Leah.

In this, too, he realized she was right.

Below Jeff Greenfield, a little strip of text ran across the bottom of the screen the way that neon ticker tape moves around that building in Times Square. It read: "More than 150,000 people visit the WTC on an average day . . ."

"Oh God," cried Celine. "Does that mean 150,000 people died today?"

There was silence in the room.

"That's not counting the people on the airplanes," said Celine, her voice rising to a squeal. "The people at the Pentagon!"

"Ssshh," said Lizbeth. "Ssshh. We can't possibly know that yet." She began to gently massage Celine's shoulders.

What about Shingshang? thought Gerhard. Where was Shingshang? Did he make it home? Gerhard stood up with a start. He'd had better luck with the landline in the kitchen than with his cell phone. He'd try calling him now.

Suzannah sat up as he passed and then almost immediately leaned back again against the pillows.

"Suzannah?" said Gerhard, stopping in his tracks. Is she that weak? Gerhard thought. Is something wrong with her?

"She needs to eat," said Leah to Gerhard. "Eat something," said Leah, patting Suzannah's knee.

Obediently Suzannah picked up the sandwich. She put it down. Gerhard sat on his heels next to her.

"Eat something, Suzannah," Gerhard implored her. Her skin was white as parchment.

But Suzannah was looking at Leah.

"150,000 people? Leah," she said. "Leah."

"I know, honey, it's too awful to contemplate."

Martine began to sob. Long, despondent moans came out of her mouth. Gerhard was reminded of some cows he'd once heard bellowing in a field. Lowing, they called it.

The room was filled with crying, anxious, swooning, complicated, demanding women. His room. His room in East Hampton. In a mansion by the sea. Once, he was a motherless young German thug. Unskilled and uneducated, with empty pockets. Gerhard Falktopf. How did he get here?

How did he get here?

"Martine," he said. He stood up and rushed to her side, leaving Suzannah and tripping over Leah as he did so.

"So sorry, Leah," said Gerhard.

And then over his shoulder: "Suzannah, honey, eat your sandwich."

When he reached Martine, he knelt down and firmly grasped her elbows to console her. "Martine, Martine," said Gerhard.

"Thierry," she cried. "Oh, Thierry, Thierry."

She was crying and keening, with the baby in her lap, making sounds unlike any Gerhard had heard her produce before, and certainly he'd heard her cry enough today.

These were sounds that came from some dark chasm deep inside her; they echoed and reverberated on their passage from her body through her throat. She reminded Gerhard of the mourning women he'd seen at the funeral pyres when he'd toured India, the rocking and the wailing, the intense physical manifestation of their grief as the bodies of their loved ones were reduced to ash and smoke.

"Martine, Martine," he said. "I am sure he will be all right."

Now all eyes were on Gerhard, Gerhard who was embracing and comforting this French woman. Gerhard who found himself patting her back, using his fingers to comb her hair. He could see them staring at him—Leah, Lizbeth, Suzannah, Celine, and that idiot Larry—when he looked up.

The governor of Pennsylvania, Tom Ridge, was on CNN. He was at the crash site of the plane that went down. He was a big man with a thick neck, a former wrestler maybe. He looked completely stricken, out of his depth, his eyes as blank as a page. He was asking for prayers and for blood. Blood and prayers. Neither of these things was going to do the victims of that wreck any good. The man was a fool.

"Look at that," said Gerhard.

The ticker tape under the governor read: "Got a lead, go to ifccfbi.gov."

For some strange reason this struck Gerhard as funny.

"Got a lead?" he said, still patting Martine's hair.

Leah started to laugh. Thank God for Leah. She had a sense of humor! She wanted to help him out, he was sure of it. Why he felt himself in so much trouble, he wasn't sure.

The newscaster Aaron Brown came on the screen to confer with Jeff Greenfield.

"Karen Hughes says, 'The government is running despite it all,'" said Aaron Brown.

Now Lizbeth and Celine joined in the laughter.

"Well, that's certainly reassuring," said Lizbeth.

"Where's Bush," said Leah. She turned and yelled it at the screen. "Where's the president?"

Just then Aaron Brown announced, "In just a few minutes we will be hearing from the president from the Oval Office."

"Hey, Leah, you've got a direct line there!" said Gerhard. "The president heard you! I always knew this little woman could move mountains!"

Their laughter, even laughter this bitter, like rainwater, cleansed the air. Larry let out a single bark.

Only Suzannah stayed solemn.

Just then the phone rang.

Martine looked up at Gerhard, her brown eyes suddenly full of hope. Radiant, really.

"Your mother?" said Gerhard. "Maybe it is him! Quick." They both scrambled to their feet, Wylie spilling out of her lap.

"Wylie!" said Martine.

The baby began to shriek.

"Go, go," Gerhard shooed Martine away from the baby toward the kitchen.

Riinng! went the telephone.

There was just a moment's hesitation before Martine leaped over Wylie as she ran into the other room.

The baby screamed and screamed. Gerhard picked up the screaming baby.

"Don't cry, boo-boo," said Gerhard, and he kissed the baby's silky head, the little triangle where the bones still seemed soft.

The baby continued crying, but they were gentler cries, less shrill.

With Wylie in his arms, Gerhard followed Martine into the kitchen, stopping in the doorway.

"I'll be back in a minute," he said to Suzannah, with his mouth on the baby's crown. The child's hair was so silky, the strands slid and got caught on the dry patches of skin on Gerhard's lips. Wylie's scalp smelled spicy and sweet, peppery like honeysuckle. Gerhard inhaled him like a small bouquet; he could practically taste the scent. "I'll be back," said Gerhard.

⌒℘

THE FOOD came up from her diaphragm with a sharp little kick, and then a warm rush, like a waterfall, through her esophagus and out of her mouth. Suzannah was no stranger to vomiting—she was a dancer; dancers vomit. There is no other way to stay as thin as necessity dictated, especially after a certain age, although if she were honest about it, and why the fuck not be honest about it with herself at least, Suzannah had been vomiting most of her life—and her body seemed to know what to do automatically, just lean forward and out it came. She coughed and sputtered as the hot acids of her stomach juices burned her mouth and nose, and her eyes watered. She hadn't eaten that much really; after the first couple of cascades of solids, mostly it was bile.

"There, there," said Leah. She was holding Suzannah's hair in a ponytail away from her mouth, as Suzannah leaned over the bowl. "I guess you ate too fast."

That was true. After Gerhard had followed that French woman into the kitchen, Suzannah had eaten the sandwich that Lizbeth had made for her in seconds flat, and then with her hunger unleashed like a dam had gone down, she'd gone after the chips, the dip, and those grapes, which were her undoing. The rot of blue cheese, that spoiled, inky vein, awful. It grossed her out now just to think about it, and another wave of food and lemonade and half her stomach lining, it seemed, came up and out of her again.

"Take it easy, sweetie," said Leah.

"Oh God, Leah," said Suzannah. "I'm so sorry. This is so vile."

She wiped the drool away from her mouth with the back of her hand; there were little brown streaks of vomit in the jelly of the drool, which was disgusting, even to her. She began to cry then, out of shame, or embarrassment. Fear was it? Loss. Being ruined.

They were in the small bathroom off the kitchen, the one

with the yellow-flocked wallpaper and the framed antique herbal prints. Basil. Lemon verbena. Dill.

"This?" said Leah. "This is vile?" She turned on the pedestal sink for Suzannah. The cold water. She motioned her toward it. "Are you kidding? The world is vile. The world is ghastly. This is nothing, Suzannah."

Suzannah moved toward the sink, immersed her drooly hand in the rush of cold water, picked up a bar of opaque olive-oil soap, soaped her hands, and then took her soapy palms to her face and washed that, too. The water, it felt so good! The soap smelled so clean. Suzannah washed the back of her neck.

"This is just what happens to a good person in an awful world on a too-empty stomach. This is nothing," said Leah.

Suzannah rinsed her mouth. She made her hand into a cup and once again, that cold tap water. There was a little iron in the water, so it tasted like blood a bit, like a penny on her tongue, and it smelled a tinge like dirt.

She thought about the people in the buildings. How hot it must have been inside. How much they must have wanted to splash their necks with fresh water. She thought, I would have gone into the bathroom and turned on the sink! She thought of *him.* What had he done in the minutes before, that tiny bridge of time between the plane's impact and his jump, between all of his life and the astonishing, desperate feat he took to end it? Was there any time to contemplate his actions? Had there been a choice, even for just a second, of his doing anything else but?

It must have been the heat that led him to explode out of the fire and away into the relief of the cool, fresh air. There must have been no other choice for this man, this stranger that Suzannah now felt so inexplicably close to, closer to than anyone she actually knew really, anyone who still lived and breathed and populated this green Earth.

"God," said Suzannah.

"Yes," said Leah. "God."

And then, "Where is he?"

They both burst out laughing.

Suzannah looked up. "Do you think Nikolai . . ."

"Nikolai is fine," said Leah, cutting her off. "I had Celine take him upstairs to his room . . ."

"His room? He . . ." started Suzannah.

"He's going to sleep through the night, sweetie," said Leah, firmly. "He looks totally exhausted."

At this Suzannah nodded. Maybe Leah was right.

Leah flushed the toilet with her foot.

"You done there?" she said.

Suzannah nodded yes. She sat down on the rim of the sink. The enamel was cool against her wrists.

"Leah, we've known each other a long time," said Suzannah.

Leah's angular face broke into a smile.

"I remember when Gerhard brought you home," said Leah. "We were the only family he had," she said. "You were too young and too lovely for him," she said, "and because you were both these things, and because someone had actually succeeded in taming him—"

"Taming Gerhard?" interrupted Suzannah.

"Whatever you want to call it," said Leah. "He worshipped you. You worshipped him. Whatever," said Leah. "Because you were too young and too lovely and because he worshipped you, we knew, Lizzie and I, that you were the one to save him."

"Who is that woman?" said Suzannah.

"Martine?" said Leah.

Suzannah nodded.

"I don't know," said Leah.

"He said he found her on the floor of the bank," said Suzannah.

Now it was Leah's turn to nod.

"But the baby's eyes," said Suzannah. "They are so blue. I have never seen eyes that blue except for Gerhard's."

Leah had seen it, too. This was clear to Suzannah. From the way Leah's face froze around her smile. It felt like a stream of frigid water traveled down Suzannah's spine, infiltrating her bowel.

"And the way he kissed that boy—he never does that with Nikolai," said Suzannah. "He never kisses Nikolai, Leah."

"Suzie," said Leah. She was the only other person on the planet besides Gerhard who called her this. "Don't borrow troub—"

There was a knock at the door.

"Suzannah? Suzannah? Leah, is she all right in there?"

It was Larry.

"Make him go away," hissed Suzannah.

Leah made a calming motion with her hands a little like she was halting traffic.

"Larry, she's fine, we're fine, we just require a bit of privacy," sang out Leah.

"She's had a tough day," said Larry. "I shouldn't have . . ."

"Lar," said Leah, warningly.

There was a pause outside. A silence. Then,

"All right, I get it," said Larry.

They could hear his workboots walking away. Workboots on Elspeth's pickled floors.

"Who is that freak?" said Suzannah.

"I am sorry I brought him along, I apologize," said Leah. "I had no idea you knew each other—"

Suzannah interrupted her: "I didn't know him, he knew me!"

Leah raised her eyebrows. "Okay, okay," Leah said, trying to calm Suzannah but plainly also a tad exasperated. It had been a long day, of course, for her, too. "Apparently he had some schoolboy crush on you," said Leah.

There was a pause. Leah gathering her patience. And then: "But who wouldn't have? If I were around back then, I would have been the one having the schoolboy crush on you."

175

She was trying for levity. Leah smiled at Suzannah, who could feel herself returning the favor in spite of it all. She had such a good heart, Leah.

"Larry Shapiro is a major talent. He's showing at Pace, he's sold a couple of pieces to San Francisco MOMA, he'll probably be in the Biennial. He's really, really good, Suzannah."

Leah dug into the left back pocket of her jeans and pulled out a fairly rumpled postcard. It was an announcement of Larry's show, an invitation to an opening, a reproduction of one of his paintings. She passed the card on to Suzannah, who studied it. There amid the cracks and creases in the light cardboard was a startlingly beautiful representational image—nobody painted like this anymore—old-fashioned in its faithfulness, a still life composed of human beings, realism. Realism without irony or stance. Realism without judgment. This slice of life, it spoke for itself in all its complexity. A man in boxers. A woman in a slip. (Do women wear slips these days? wondered Suzannah; she herself hardly bothered with undergarments at all, although here in Larry's painting, as always, the slip was sexy and somehow indicated a lack of money, a lower social class, which was sexier still, why?) The man and the woman lay asleep side by side on a rumpled double bed, curled up next to one another but not touching. Behind them, in a Hopper-esque beam of light, stood a little boy. There was something menacing about the child, even in his innocence, as he hovered over what Suzannah took to be his parents.

Suzannah handed the card back to Leah. She did not want to look at it any longer.

"Sounds to me like he sees you as something like a muse . . . I don't know, maybe it's kind of flattering," said Leah.

Suzannah shook her head. That was one role in this human theater that she'd had her fill of.

"I admit he's a little gruff, but I like him," said Leah. "Lizzie likes him. We've been playing with him all summer," she said.

"Met him one morning walking on Gerard Beach. The bay. Hunting for shells. Neither of us could sleep. It was so early, even before the general store opened. He had a thermos of coffee that he shared . . ."

"I don't like him," said Suzannah, feeling like a child.

"Mea culpa," said Leah. She walked toward the bathroom door. "I shouldn't have brought him. Lizzie and I will go soon and we'll make sure he goes with us." Leah's fingers surrounded the brass doorknob. She pushed the door open.

"Don't go," said Suzannah, involuntarily, in a small voice.

Larry was out there, and Gerhard, too.

But Leah was already down the hall.

⌥

EVERYONE was hugging and crying in the Florida room when Suzannah righted herself enough to reenter civilization. Even Larry had a shit-eating grin on his face as they surrounded Martine with their relief and their joy. They were all so hungry, Suzannah thought, for a good thing to think about! So eager for a silver lining in all of this. Lizbeth and Leah danced around Martine as if she were a Maypole and not a total stranger.

Apparently Thierry had been found. He hadn't been at the trade center after all. He'd wandered up to Tribeca, where the guidebook said the best bakeries were, foraging for their breakfast. By the time he'd run back to the hotel, against the tide of humanity, he could not locate Martine and Wylie. They had in all likelihood begun their own mad dash uptown. The young lovers probably crossed paths in their haste, each tearing away at the pavement, searching for shelter, searching for one another. Then the next airplane hit the South Tower and it all became about saving himself. He'd run toward the water, where he'd met a young American couple that had stolen a canoe from a shed, and the three of them paddled across the river to New Jersey. That's where he was now, in New Jersey, in a motel room that he and the couple, all refugees, had taken together. He was safe. He'd been worried sick about Martine. Worried sick about Wylie! He'd been trying to call France all day and then suddenly, out of nowhere, an outside line. He'd used his brains, Thierry. He'd called her mother. From her, he'd gotten their number at the beach.

Thierry was safe. Martine kept shaking her head from side to side. She could not believe her good luck.

"Let's break out the champagne," said Gerhard.

"Great idea," said Leah.

"I'll go get it," said Lizbeth. "Gerhard, do you have any on ice?"

"There should be some in the second fridge," said Gerhard.

Martine stared from one to the other, her cheeks flushed pink, her mouth parted in a smile. Her hands rose to press those cheeks, as if to reassure herself that the smile was hers! That this was *her* happiness. Suzannah gazed at Martine in wonderment—she's so pretty! thought Suzannah, she is so radiant!—before a painful stab of jealousy hit her in the heart.

"You've all been so nice. Everybody has been so nice to me!" cried Martine.

"We have to help each other. The whole world has to come together at a time like this," said Leah. Transformed by tragedy into a person even larger than she was.

"Thierry said everyone on the streets was so kind. He said he tripped as the building fell down, he said he was sure he would go flat . . . be crushed, but a stranger stopped to help him, a stranger risked his own life, he put himself in danger just to pick up my husband! Before the dust cloud could catch them! And the lady and man with the canoe, they are paying for the room, I have Thierry's credit cards! And the owner of the restaurant, he gave them all free food! Thierry said people who had never seen each other's face before were hugging and crying on the street corners!"

Martine was flushed with excitement; she could barely contain herself. She clapped her hands together like a little girl.

"It's true," said Leah. "Even on TV they talk about how the city has rallied, everyone volunteering to help, volunteering their homes and their hearts and their blood. There could have been looting, you know. There could have been riots in the streets."

"It's the greatest city in the world," said Gerhard.

There was absolutely no edge in his voice when he said this.

My God, thought Suzannah, am I the only one in this house who does not glow?

Of course he loved New York. Suzannah knew he did; everyone who knew him knew how much he loved the city. But still! It was the way he said it. He said it like he meant it. He did not sound like Gerhard sounded at all; he did not sound like he'd ever sounded before.

"The rest of the world will follow our example!" said Gerhard.

Suzannah watched this whole scene from the protection of the hallway, a little in awe, a little removed, like she was watching some mythical family reunion on television. Some meaning-of-Christmas special. It was a pleasing scene to watch— all this family-of-man business, all the goodhearted rallying of strangers—but it didn't really have anything to do with her.

She turned away from them and toward the staircase, anxious, of course, to check on Nikolai. But then there was a voice in her ear, and earlier even still, at first, a millisecond before, his hot breath.

"Please, Suzannah, it is late and we need to talk. I need to talk to you before I go," said Larry. His fingers were tight around her elbow.

In the Florida room the champagne was flowing. Leah had come back in with two bottles, Celine was passing out glasses, and Gerhard was waltzing around with Wylie in his arms. Martine kept clapping her hands in delight, watching Gerhard and the baby dance.

They were all only about ten feet away from Suzannah, but it didn't matter, they could have been across the country. They could have been in China. The distance was the distance between being outside and inside a burning building. They were as far away as the stars.

She was alone with Larry in the hall, and his fingers were tight on her arm. She could imagine the bruises that would rise in the morning, faint purple shadows to remind her that this was not a dream, that this evening indeed took place.

"Come," Larry said. "Walk me out to my truck. I don't want to interrupt all that," he said, gesturing with his chin toward the exhausted merriment in the Florida room. "I'll give Leah a buzz tomorrow."

There were two choices available then to Suzannah. To join the party in the Florida room or to go outside with Larry. She allowed him to steer her back through the kitchen and out the mudroom toward the garage. She would check on Nikolai later, when she was alone.

Outside the night was blue-black and cool. The crickets chirped a thousand notes and the stars looked like tears in the sky, little rents in the fabric of the firmament, as if the protective skin that surrounded life on Earth and kept it from infinite nothingness were wearing away. This loveliest of days had given birth to a beautiful night, velvety and soft, enrobing Suzannah in a salty mist that lifted itself off the ocean and settled around her shoulders like a shawl. The crescent moon was rising above the treetops. Larry's fingers relaxed around Suzannah's elbow and for a moment, maybe because she was so tired and so lightheaded, she almost felt as if she were a young girl out on a date.

Of course, she had never been a young girl out on a date — she'd been a dancer, and then there was Gerhard. That was her entire romantic history. Every other encounter she'd had with a man other than her husband, one way or another, had been choreographed by him. Suzannah did not know what it felt like to be a young lover out at night with someone equally inexperienced and excited and new, but she could imagine it. In her imaginings, the evenings felt like this one did; that is, only in this isolated, silent moment, before Larry opened his mouth and broke the spell, revealing to both of them who he was.

First he coughed. Then he stretched his arms high into the sky and gave out a little vocal something or other, a release that was a cross between a grunt and a cry. He undid his ponytail and shook his mane free and once again his hair was loose around his head.

Is he trying to seduce me? Suzannah thought. She felt like she was on acid.

"Look," said Larry. "I'm sorry I brought up that thing with Barry. It was a million years ago and none of my business. I'm not going to share it with anyone."

He was taking the direct approach.

Okay, thought Suzannah. I can take anything straightforward. I can handle this. Anything I don't have to parse.

"He might not even be dead," said Larry.

Which startled her. Was this his attempt at delicacy? For a moment she'd forgotten about her lie, Barry and the South Tower. Why on Earth had she ever said it?

Because part of you wishes it were true.

She was going mad. She was hearing voices. She'd eaten nothing all day and her child was defective and her husband kissed another woman's baby and the country was attacked and the night sky was melting like filmstrip on a too-hot projector—what little had been left to protect her was being burned through by the endless white heat of encroaching oblivion. Suzannah was tired, so tired, she could barely continue recording any of this; she could no longer take it in.

He swan-dived out of the blazing building and into her head.

Suzannah stared at Larry with an open mouth.

"I'd like to see you again," said Larry. "When all of this is over."

Was he a sadist and a stalker? Or was he just some random asshole?

"Are you fucking kidding?" said Suzannah. For the first time in her life, even though she felt entirely speechless, she indeed had something to say.

He was in her head and she was no longer alone.

"Hasn't today taught you anything?" said Larry.

"You could die tomorrow, and you're not happy," he said. "Plenty of people died today who were not happy. You can change your life, Suzannah."

Suzannah leaned over and grabbed a fistful of gravel from the driveway. She pelted him with it.

"Get the fuck out of here," screamed Suzannah. "You freak!"

The look of surprise on Larry's face was fleeting; he tucked it away as soon as it made itself apparent.

She picked up another fistful and sent it flying in Larry's direction.

"Get in your goddamned car and get out of here!" She threw more pebbles at him.

Larry ducked and got into the cab of his truck.

He turned on his headlights, he put the truck in reverse, and he slowly rolled the pick-up out of there. He rolled right past where Suzannah was standing. Her breath was rapid; her heart about to explode.

"I want to see you again," said Larry. The driver's window was open.

"Go fuck yourself," said Suzannah. "Psychotic fucking asshole."

They were falling together forever down the black hole in-
side her head.

She turned and walked back into the cottage.

∽

SHE came in like the wind, like a whirling storm, whipping
through and destroying the house. If he were to choreograph
her entrance it would have included about a thousand *fou-
ettés*, before she stretched her thin torso long and high, hands
reaching up to the sky, then retreating into a contraction with
fists drawn to the gut, fists beating the gut, a manifestation
of her grief and agony. She came in like a hurricane, her hair
wild with heat lightning, the skin on her face bleached white,
the veins on her arms standing up on top of the muscle, veins
coursing at high voltage — she was so vascular, he'd never quite
noticed this before, it was as if her entire anatomy were held
together solely by her circulatory wiring, which was now alive
with electricity and appeared to be pushing up and out of her
thin frame. She looked completely insane.

"Suzannah," said Gerhard.

His arms were around Martine, Martine and her baby. They
were dancing. Leah and Lizbeth were smushed together on
the wicker club chair, Leah's legs in Lizbeth's lap. Celine was
asleep on the couch. *Snnnsh, snnnsh* was the sound of her soft
breath pushing through the plush pink-velvet interior of her
nose, a sweet little piggy snore.

Suzannah stared at him, crazy-eyed, the deranged, rail-
thin, storming woman that was his wife, before she began to
scream.

She was on tiptoe, in *relevé*. He noticed this.

Her hands were by her sides in two fists.

She was a coyote howling at the moon.

"Oh my God, Suzannah," said Leah, jumping to her feet.

183

"What happened?" said Lizbeth.

She turned from Leah to Suzannah to Leah again. "Leah, what's happening?"

Suzannah kept on screaming.

Celine woke with a cry. She, too, commenced screaming. Martine's baby began to shriek.

"Did he *do* anything to you, Suzannah?" asked Leah, frantically looking around, as if it were possible to part the weeds of the cacophony. "Larry? Larry? What did he do?"

She started to move toward Suzannah but then something, some invisible electrified fence, sent Leah back. Lizbeth put her arm protectively around her.

Suzannah just stood where she stood, screaming.

Gerhard excused himself from Martine. It was such a formal gesture. He watched himself make it.

He said, "Excuse me, Martine, something has happened to my wife."

He walked over to Suzannah.

"Darling," he said. "What happened?"

Suzannah didn't answer him. She kept on screaming. She was screaming and screaming and screaming.

He said, "Sweetheart, please, I can't understand you when you make a noise like that, I can't understand you right now. Calm down, so I can understand you."

It was the same tack Suzannah took sometimes with Nikolai. For a moment, Gerhard considered her other strategies. When reason clearly was not working and all hell was breaking loose, she cupped her hands and pressed them down hard on Nikolai's shoulders and elbows and feet. There were times when she would bury the thrashing, hollering hellion up to the neck with large sofa pillows and lean her weight down on him, the theory being—someone had told her—that a calibrated heaviness on his bones and joints would somehow miraculously calm him. She'd even brushed Nikolai with a mushroom brush, its soft bristles up and down his legs, his back, his arms, in an effort to shut him up by "balancing his sensory system," releasing his inner demons — the babysitter before Celine had called them evil spirits — his goddamned tension . . . what did Nikolai have to be so fucking tense about? He was a child.

Suzannah was like a lightning rod at the moment, all that energy coursing through her was simply far too overwhelming; he found the awful screaming physically repellent.

Still, he sucked it up.

He said, "That sound, Suzannah. For God's sake."

He hissed at her: "Get ahold of yourself."

Then he slapped her.

It was such a loud slap. Gerhard's hand cut the air with a sizzle. The impact of palm to jawbone cracked the sound of her shrieks in half. He could hear it over the screams that started at her toes and stretched halfway up and out of her mouth, and then he heard the slap's echo in the resulting silence.

The guests left at that point. The party was clearly over. Leah and Lizbeth. They probably mumbled some reassuring farewells, apologies for overstaying their welcome, excuses for psychotic Suzannah ("She's just tired, poor baby." "She hasn't eaten all day." "It's been an impossible time for all of us!"). Offers of succor and support darted around him like hummingbirds. ("Gerhard, we're just a phone call away.") Then they fled the nuthouse and went back to their own private Sapphic idyll by the sea. At some point Celine must have melted upstairs into her room. She'd seen Suzannah go nuts before, although never this nuts! No, Gerhard himself had never seen Suzannah so wacked out. God knows where Martine and the baby went off to. There were hundreds of beds in that old house; it felt like that sometimes, hundreds of beds and thousands of rooms. Martine had proven herself extremely resourceful up to this point. He could not worry about her now.

He was alone with his silent, shaking wife. No color in her face. She was as thin and pale as a bone.

It took a while for him to speak. He'd never hit a woman before, not like that, in anger, an anger coupled by annoyance and fear. His palm still stung. He'd hit Suzannah so hard! There was a red welt now on one cheek, he could see it. It was in the shape of an autumn leaf, rising above the porcelain surface of her skin. Twice that night she'd entered the house in a dramatic, unseemly fashion. He felt oddly embarrassed by her behavior. If she hadn't looked so scarily pathetic, if the day hadn't proven itself so unimaginably difficult, if he himself were not changing so rapidly and completely under the pressures and exaltations of all he'd risked and accomplished in the last twelve hours, he would have cut the scene short with pure outrage. A scathing, clarifying remark. He would have directed her out of her performance.

Gerhard couldn't quite keep up with who he was at this point.

Force. It was a last resort, but he took it, Gerhard told himself, for the greater good. There were children in the house. A traumatized young mother. Guests. He'd hit her for her own sake. Suzannah had been hysterical.

Now they were both alone in the entrance hall, facing one another, quietly.

Let me be the first to break the silence, thought Gerhard. To do so will be like an offering. So he spoke.

"Would you like a glass of water, Suzie?" Gerhard asked her.

Suzannah nodded.

He turned, and she followed him. In this manner, a man and his shadow, they made their way into the kitchen. He could feel her trailing along behind him, a slender specter, an apparition, echoing his motions, riding his footsteps, reading his thoughts.

In the kitchen, Gerhard went straight for the freezer and broke open a tray of ice, the old-fashioned metal type — Elspeth's of course, from the year when — the stainless steel tongue so cold it stuck to the skin on his fingers as he lifted the lever. He poured the contents into a wooden ice bucket on the granite counter, refilled the tray with water at the double sink, and placed it back into the SubZero. He walked over to the painted-wood cabinets and pulled out a rather large tumbler, and he dropped three cubes inside where they cracked a little when hitting the glass. He reached across the counter to an open blue bottle of Ty Nant water and he filled up the glass. He turned around and offered it to Suzannah.

When she took the glass from him, he noticed that her hands were shaking. It broke Gerhard's heart to see her hands like that. Like an elderly woman's. He thought of his mother. Is this what her hands would have looked like if she had lived long enough to grow old?

"Oh, Suzie," he said, and reached out both of his strong hands to steady hers. Her hands were so cold.

Suzannah looked up at him through her wild, messy hair. The slap mark was still evident on her cheek; it would probably bruise bluish and yellow over night. How he regretted that slap!

With his right forefinger he reached out to trace the outline of his palm print. She winced when his finger touched her flesh.

So it hurt, too. He felt a wave of remorse.

"I am so sorry, Suzie," said Gerhard. "Please forgive me."

Suzannah's big brown eyes widened. They were the biggest part of her. So sad and frightened. He was getting used to them looking this way.

"Let's put some ice on it," he said, turning back toward the ice bucket.

He picked up a clean tea towel and unfolded it. He took the

tongs and used them to pick up three more cubes of ice. Gerhard laid the ice cubes in the center of the towel. He folded the towel back up again, into a neat little square. He turned around to offer the ice pack to his wife.

"Forgive me, darling," said Gerhard. Repeating himself for emphasis.

In the interim, Suzannah's eyes had narrowed. A new storm had gathered.

"For what, Gerhard? What should I forgive you for? For smacking me?"

Suzannah's voice was cold, but her face was red-hot with anger.

"Yes," said Gerhard. He was sorry for hitting her. "No," he said. He didn't exactly regret his actions. "You were hysterical," said Gerhard.

"Then I guess I should thank you," said Suzannah. "I guess I should thank you for stanching my hysteria by punching me in the face. Thank you, Gerhard. Thank you. You are, and always have been, the perfect husband."

There was so much venom in her voice; it stunned him. Her cheeks were beet red now and her eyes were boiling. She'd gone from zero to 80 miles an hour in a nanosecond.

"You needed to get ahold of yourself," said Gerhard. He felt himself backing away from her, the way he might move away from a crazy person on the subway. "You need to find a way to control yourself."

Suzannah put her glass down on the kitchen table.

"Besides, I didn't punch you . . . I slapped . . . I . . . You, you were screaming in the hallway," said Gerhard.

He took a couple of steps backward and leaned against the sink.

The counter was wet there, and he could feel the dampness seeping through the back of his pants.

"You abandoned me," seethed Suzannah. "You abandoned

your wife, and you abandoned your son. Of course I was screaming. There was no other way to get your attention."

"Abandoned . . . ?" said Gerhard. Her attack made him furious. "Suzannah, what is wrong with you? I risked my life, I
shepherded you out of harm's way, I saved us all from danger
. . ." He'd been so good, he thought. So good!

Suzannah started to laugh. "Ha, ha, ha," said Suzannah.
She threw her head back when she did this, and Gerhard could
see the cords in her throat playing like the strings in an open
piano.

"Risked your life?" said Suzannah, her head now wobbly
but correctly placed back upright on the long stem of her neck.
"Who are you kidding? You were never in harm's way." She
spit this out. Her right hand circled in the air for emphasis.
"We could have stayed in the city and ordered in Chinese food
and curled up in front of the TV and watched the unfolding
tragedies of the day like everybody else. Just like you and your
ridiculous friends did out here."

Surely she didn't believe herself, thought Gerhard. Suzannah had spent the day being terrified. Justifiably. He'd spent
the day protecting her.

"Be serious, Suzie," said Gerhard. "All of downtown is in
chaos. They have imposed some kind of martial law . . . The
ash and smoke alone, it would have driven us away."

As he said this, he thought about their windows. Had he
closed them? Had he closed the windows before they fled? All
that soot . . . his piano, his books, the Agnes Martin—had he
closed them?

"We could have stayed at home and helped out our neighbors, Gerhard," said Suzannah. "Like everyone else did." She
spit out the words as if they were discrete little pellets. "All
those heroes, the cops, the firemen. We could have given blood!
We could have been part of the city, we could have helped
somebody!"

Suzannah combed her dancing fingers through her curls, making her black mane stand up on end.

"Face facts, Gerhard. You ran away. Pure and simple. You ran away. You got scared and you ran."

She seemed proud of herself when she said this. Like she'd finally nailed it.

"You always do."

Her certainty infuriated him.

"That is ridiculous," said Gerhard. "We were attacked. I was protecting my family. Only an idiot would have stayed put there, in that hell, that inferno. Don't you think the others wish that they were out here, that they had the choices that we had?"

He stepped away from the sink now. The back of his pants below the pockets was soaking. He reached for another tea towel and corkscrewed at the waist in order to blot them.

"Like you were protecting your family." Suzannah was incredulous. "You didn't even know where we were all day. When we got out of the car, you didn't even follow us out to the beach."

So that's what she'd wanted? She'd wanted him to chase after her? He'd had the car to unpack, Martine to assist, Celine, those frightened French girls to comfort, a house to air and open up. She'd wanted him to forget all those duties and run after her? He'd thought she'd wanted to be alone. Alone with her precious boy. He'd been giving her her space. She should have stuck around and helped him out.

"All you cared about was protecting your lover!" said Suzannah.

"What?" said Gerhard. He untwisted his body counterclockwise, in order to face her. "What are you talking about?"

He instantly thought of Yuki. How he'd failed her.

No, thought Gerhard, I did not protect my lover. I chose you, you screaming banshee. What am I, insane?

"I was protecting my family," said Gerhard, haughtily.

"It was a perfect excuse for you, Gerhard," said Suzannah. "A perfect excuse to run away from all your problems. Your embarrassments. Your lost and losing company." Her voice was acid. It cut him to the marrow. "How convenient for you, a plane hits the World Trade Center and now you can take your lover and run away from it all."

"You are a psychotic woman," said Gerhard. "Do you hear yourself? Do you hear what you sound like?"

"I've got eyes in my head," shouted Suzannah. "I've seen that baby's eyes!"

"Eyes, eyes? What are you talking about?"

"They're blue. They're blue."

"What are you talking about, Suzannah?" Gerhard lifted his hands helplessly in front of him, one of them still clutching the tea towel. A little flag of surrender.

"You said," said Suzannah, in a short, clipped staccato, as if she were spelling the words out for him, "you said you found them on the floor of a bank."

"What? Martine? Wylie? Are you talking about Wylie?" Her inference was beginning to dawn upon him.

"He's got your eyes, Gerhard."

She was one hundred percent, completely crazy.

First Leah, now she too thought that Wylie was his son.

"Suzannah, you are out of your mind," said Gerhard. "You belong in a mental hospital. I never saw that woman or child before this day in my life. I was trying to help out someone in need. I was trying to do good for once. Isn't that what you always want from me? I would think that my good deeds, that this, would please you!"

"You care more about strangers than your own family," said Suzannah. Suddenly the storm that was her argument swirled in another direction; it veered off course.

"That's not true," said Gerhard.

"You spent the whole day with them," said Suzannah. "You didn't even bother telling us you were going out." The storm amassed in strength, spiraling in upon itself like a funnel cloud.

"We went to get food, Suzie. I was trying to comfort her."

"What about trying to comfort me?" said Suzannah, the tornado.

"You didn't need comforting, you *had* your husband."

"*She* had my husband!" Suzannah the tornado shouted this at him.

"That's ridiculous," said Gerhard, "Suzannah . . ."

Suzannah bared her teeth, her lips disappeared, the whites of her eyes stretched wide. "Today was Nikolai's first day of school. You made him miss his first day of school. How will he ever forgive you?" Again, the twister shifting course.

Gerhard couldn't believe his ears.

"There was no school today, Suzannah. No school. No mayoral election, no . . . what did you say? No takeout Chinese food. Get it?" Here he paused to take a breath. "Wake up, Suzannah. The world changed today! Our world. It's gone now. Our world is gone."

"His first day of school!" Suzannah started to weep. "How can I ever forgive myself for letting you do this to him."

Gerhard shook his head. There was no getting through to her.

All of a sudden, she slammed the chair in front of her into the table and strode out of the kitchen. She headed into the mudroom. Was her intention to leave the house?

"Suzannah!" Gerhard was hot on her heels, the screen door slamming in his face as she exited the cottage.

"You selfish bitch," he seethed between clenched teeth. He pressed the door open, took the two steps down to the flagstone side yard, quickening his steps after her, out into the cool, damp, dark night air. "You come back here." He reached out and grabbed Suzannah by her elbow and swung her around.

The light from the kitchen surrounded them in a small, square prison of fluorescent illumination. The light was so yellow, the skin on Suzannah's face looked like ancient parchment.

"You gonna hit me again, Gerhard?" taunted Suzannah, and for the first time in forever, Gerhard could hear the Bronx in her voice. Her upper lip curled like a fighter. "Maybe you can break my nose this time." She sneered at him.

"Cut the shit, Suzannah," said Gerhard.

"You know you want to, Gerhard, you know you want to hit me." It was like something out of *West Side Story*. She was practically begging him. It took all the power he could muster to restrain himself.

"You little bitch . . ." Again, the ugly words twisted out between clenched teeth, just like the condensation rising from his warm breath in the cool September night air. Gerhard's warm living breath.

"You call me a bitch," said Suzannah, her voice wavering again, for clearly this stung, "but I'm not the one who fathered some brat with one of my many girlfriends and then chose him over our very own son."

"You insist upon being ridiculous," said Gerhard. "I have never been this angry with you!"

"So hit me, Gerhard," said Suzannah. "You know you want to."

But he didn't want to hit her any longer. He wanted to place his hands around her long, white, corded throat and choke the life out of her. It took all he had left inside himself not to do so. Gerhard took a deep breath.

"Wylie is not my son," he said. "I never saw Martine before today in my life. I was trying to do good. How can you be so selfish? You who have everything, when so many have lost so much!"

"I wanted to have my husband," said Suzannah.

"You have me," said Gerhard. "You had me."

"Right," said Suzannah. "I had you all day when you were off with Martine and that blue-eyed brat."

The argument was exhausting. Never-ending and exhausting. She made his ears bleed.

"His name is Wylie," said Gerhard.

"I saw you kiss his head," said Suzannah.

"I kissed his head," said Gerhard. "So what?"

"You never kiss Nikolai," said Suzannah. "You never do, Gerhard. You never kiss Nikolai."

Gerhard stopped and stared at her.

"So what if he is completely demented," said Suzannah. "I fucking kiss him. He's demented and I still kiss him. I kiss him, I kiss him, I kiss him."

"Go to hell," said Gerhard.

He turned and walked back into the house.

⌒ℱ

UPSTAIRS, the boy was sleeping. The little boy that Gerhard and that half-crazed wolverine had brought into the world through their improbable, exotic coupling. They had brought him into the world in good faith, thought Gerhard. They had brought him into the world to delight and be delighted, to charm and to be charming. He was destined to be physically beautiful, between Suzannah's genes and his own—Gerhard thought without ego for once, he was just being honest, for they were a strikingly handsome couple—he was destined to be smart, adept, agile, graceful. He was destined to be a prince among men. Nikolai.

The Jew and the German. Were they wrong after all to mix their unholy blood?

Gerhard went into the kitchen. He fixed himself a drink. A vodka tonic, this time, with lime. As he sliced the fruit carefully he noted that his own hands were shaking. She'd infected him, his wife, with her poison.

"He's demented and I still kiss him," Suzannah had said.

The boy was gorgeous. His head was an angel's head of bouncy blond curls. His hands and his feet were perfect. His arch high, his toenails miniature moons. At birth, the skin on his back was so soft it almost hurt to touch it; the thrill in stroking the baby's back, it was enough to bring a man to his knees . . . When Gerhard had stroked Nikolai's tiny, furry back — for Nikolai had been born with that baby down, that lanugo — the aloof, overly controlled Gerhard had almost died of pleasure.

"He's demented and I still kiss him."

Gerhard took a deep sip of his drink. The metallic cold of the vodka and ice bounced off the zip of the lime. It woke up his mouth. A shudder ran up and down his spine, and he used his shoulders to shrug it out of the rest of his body.

His son.

Slowly, Gerhard and his drink walked out of the kitchen and into the center hall, and then he climbed up the stairs.

NIKOLAI.

He was fast asleep on his summer bed, outside the covers, still in clothes, the way that idiot-girl Celine had left him. The window to his room was shut — an atticlike chamber with sloping ceilings and dormer casements so simple and cozy that Suzannah had thought all this closeness would make Nikolai feel safe — and the air inside felt stale. So the first thing his father, Gerhard, did upon entering the room and encountering his child tossed like a sack of groceries that way across the bedclothes was to put his drink down on the hardwood floor by the headboard and open the window. Gerhard opened the window so that thick, healing, salty sea air would enter the room and bathe his child, and so that he himself could breathe. Then he walked over to the bed and looked at his son.

The tie-dyed T-shirt was hiked up around Nikolai's belly. His belly itself was glowing in the silvery light that came from the rising moon perhaps, that and the floodlights that illuminated the back deck that hung over the dunes, facing the sea. Nikolai's lips were parted and a little bubble of spit blew in and out between them. His eyes were half-open in that way of his, making him look more tragic than he was, like some Victorian painting of a dead child. Gerhard balked at his own thought — children had died today, children on airplanes, perhaps children in the towers; what had their parents done to try to comfort them in those last agonizing moments? — shredding the reference to bits and casting its remains out and away from his mind.

He leaned over and undid the Velcro of Nikolai's sneakers. He carefully pulled down each little sock — there were soccer balls on the socks; Suzannah had picked them up at the Gap, as if the kid were old enough to play soccer, Gerhard thought, although undeniably the socks were cute, which made them even more not Gerhard's style. The skin of Nikolai's feet was damp and wrinkled under the socks, and Gerhard gently massaged each foot so that the skin would relax and breathe. Then he gently unbuckled the pants and checked the boy's pull-up, which was full to bursting. Anger welled in Gerhard's throat. When all was said and done, Celine needed to be fired — how dare she put the child to bed that way. The pull-up was as swollen as a small beach ball and its edges were yellow with escaping urine; it was close to springing a leak, and Gerhard had seen what happens to pull-ups when they absorb too much liquid — the tiny, soft crystals inside burst out of the paper-linen casing and get on everything: clothes, furniture, rugs. They were almost impossible to clean up. Their ubiquity alone would be enough to make Nikolai go crazy.

Upon finding the pull-up in such a state, Gerhard's first thought was to fire Celine, his second to rouse her. Who can I get to do this for me? thought Gerhard. The boy needed to be changed. Just as quickly, he found himself searching the room for Nikolai's black bag, where he knew Suzannah kept the diapers and ointments. He found it in the corner of the room perched on the rocking chair. Inside was a pull-up, some wipes, a blue hospital chub, which he'd seen Suzannah use as an instant changing table, and so Gerhard brought all this gear over to Nikolai's single bed. Gerhard leaned forward and unsnapped and pulled down the boy's little faux jams, jams that he'd seen Suzannah lay out with so much care the night before.

It was just last night. Gerhard realized this now, it was just twenty-four hours ago, after his return from shopping at the Fairway Uptown in Harlem, while he'd been fuming, fuming about his company, about *Day at the Beach*, fuming about all the injustices that had rained down one after the other like an unwelcome and wanton deluge on his undeserving head, when Gerhard had taken a small breather from all that self-absorption to note the sweet, silly amount of care with which Suzannah had laid out the boy's outfit for his first day of school.

She could have just wrestled the shorts and top from the mayhem of the kid's drawers in the morning, but no, she'd carefully folded them and laid them out on his toy chest the night before. It was as if she were acting out the role of a good mother, playing dress-up—and her joy in the act of it had almost melted Gerhard's hard heart for the half-second he'd bothered to acknowledge it.

Twenty-four hours ago his heart was hard. Now looking down at the boy, his bare legs, the pull-up torn off and cast aside into the plastic baggie Suzannah kept in the black bag for solely this purpose, the boy's shirt scrunched up above his belly, his small bellybutton protruding impudently, like a street urchin's nose, in the sliver of silvery moonlight that fell across his bed, Gerhard's heart was a puddle.

"He's demented and I still kiss him," Suzannah had said.

Nikolai's penis was soft and pink in that light. It nestled like a baby bird in the tiny bed of his scrotum. They'd fought some over his circumcision. At first Gerhard had been opposed. He'd shuddered at the violence of the act. He'd quite righteously proclaimed to Suzannah that a boy "should look like his father" —although Gerhard realized now that he was almost never naked in the child's presence, that this was among the many intimacies they'd lacked. In hindsight, Gerhard had to admit that his position on the circumcision was more than just a refusal to give a nod toward Suzannah's lapsed faith—they had had some brief, teenagery talks about how this child was no religion and all religions, family of man and all that, late at night in bed, when they were still happy and hopeful, Gerhard's hand on the rise of Suzannah's pregnant belly—but rather he'd opposed the procedure because he secretly felt that they would be taking out a neon sign forever marking his child as one of them. It had meant so much to her, Suzannah said, she'd even forgo the ceremony. (Gerhard still, after all these years, couldn't quite get a handle on the consistently inconsistent stake and hold she had on her Judaism.) She'd do it in the hospital, she said—which was where the surgery was performed, the child altered and returned to Suzannah's private room, squalling a bit and bandaged but no worse for wear it seemed at the time. "In this country most boys are," Suzannah said with real authority, although how did she know this? Gerhard thought now. Had she read this somewhere? He'd acceded to her wishes.

Now Gerhard took a wipe and carefully cleansed his child's genitals, under the testicles and around the small, tense buttonhole of his anus, and then Gerhard used a fresh wipe for the kid's inner thighs, still braceleted with swells of baby fat, swabbing his high, round butt and down his legs toward the knees. Gerhard did not want Nikolai to get a rash, and Nikolai had been lying in pee probably for most of the evening.

Gerhard delved back into the black bag and this time took out a tube of zinc oxide, squeezing a white ribbon onto his forefinger and with it painted a barrier between his child's tender skin and the acid of his urine. He stepped back to admire his handiwork and with his foot knocked into the cocktail he'd set down by the bedside; the liquid splashed a little and the ice cubes chimed, but he did not break or overturn the glass, so he did not bother with it. Instead, Gerhard carefully slipped the boy's legs, one by one, through the elasticized legs of the clean pull-up. He accomplished all this tending without waking the child up, and just that small achievement alone made him feel oddly successful, enough to earn a moment of calm.

Asleep the boy looked like an angel. Awake he was imperfect. More than imperfect, Gerhard's son had more than the run-of-the-mill imperfections that make us all human. His problems were greater than most — there was no denying this now. His deficiencies were handicapping, if not crippling.

He needed help, Nikolai. He might need it all his life. He might never be like the rest of them, Gerhard thought, like the rest of us.

He needed help.

Gerhard gently tugged down the child's T-shirt. He carefully folded the kid up, knees to chest, in his arms, and lifted him up off the bedcovers. With one free-ish hand, he pulled down the spread and turned down the top sheet and blanket. Then he slid his child underneath the sheets, the way one might slide a note to a lover into an envelope, a lover who has left and moved on. He slid the child under the sheets with care and great feeling, with some bitterness and sad longing. There was a small amount of senseless optimism in his gesture and infinite, fruitless hope.

Then Gerhard pulled the bedclothes gently up under Nikolai's chin. He ran his fingers through Nikolai's curls, the curls Nikolai had gotten honestly; he had inherited them from Suzannah, his mother. Gerhard's golden boy. Gerhard leaned over and kissed the sleeping child on the lips, tasting his lamby breath.

<p>

AT FIRST, after Gerhard had left her furious and alone in her fury, out in the side yard, after he slammed the door on her and their argument, and hence, Suzannah thought, on her and their marriage, she considered heading out to the beach. It was her primary instinct. The marriage was over. She could lie on the sand, under the stars. She could rip off her clothes and dive into the cool, black, billowing waves. She could keep her clothes on, fill her pockets with sand and stones and walk slowly out into the water until it enveloped her like the mother she no longer had and drew her out of this world and away from her pain — to be away from pain, Suzannah thirsted for this, not for peace, which at the moment seemed unreachable, but solely for a moment where anguish ceased. She was almost too tired to drown.

These were her options. But the beach was dark and the air was cold and it suddenly seemed much too far away to get to the water. It was a shorter distance from where she stood to the driveway anyway. She could muster the energy to walk around the outside of the house and get into her car. She could turn on her car and drive away, drive to a bar, get drunk, and pick up a man. Drive to a ferry and get off the island and land in New London. She could hit the highway and drive and drive into another life, another skin, become a waitress or a shop clerk in some small anonymous town, a school librarian, the local ballet teacher; she could get a small apartment and a small salary and live a blessedly small life, leaving Gerhard, Gerhard and his greatness, shedding her human history behind her . . . But the country was at war. And she had been driving all day and she'd gotten nowhere. Upstairs lay Nikolai, her child, her boy. She could not drive away from him.

The car keys were in the house. Her money was in her pocketbook; the pocketbook was on the floor of the front seat of the car. She'd dropped it there when she'd turned her attentions to the back seat, to Nikolai, to unlocking him, to hoisting him over her shoulder. Her shoulder still hurt where she'd hung him like a dead weight, a carpet. She rubbed it now. She was hungry and tired. Her boy was asleep upstairs. He needed that sleep. He needed her.

When the fires are out, Nikolai and I will go back. We'll leave Gerhard and we'll go back.

I am defeated, thought Suzannah. I have lost.

We are defeated, he said to her as they fell, hand in hand now, in tandem. We are defeated and we are lost.

With this thought in hand, as if *he* were holding her hand, she made her way back into the house.

༄

GERHARD was sitting at the kitchen table. His fingers were dialing the phone, automatically punching in the numbers, employing that old muscle memory, the numbers he knew by heart. The phone was answered on half a ring.

"Hello," she said, breathlessly.

"Patti?" said Gerhard.

"Dave? Dave? Is that you? Dave, is that you?"

The voice was so full of hopeless hope it was almost too horrible to listen to.

Gerhard felt his stomach sink and a strong urge to just hang up the phone overtook him.

"Dave? Dave? Dave?" The name itself became a plea, a cry for help.

Plainly, Shingshang had not been found.

"It's Gerhard Falktopf, Patti," said Gerhard.

"Oh God, Gerhard, tell me he's with you!" said Patti Shing-shang.

"No," said Gerhard. "The last time I spoke with him they were evacuating."

"You spoke to him? What are you talking about?" And then to someone in the room next to her, far far away from Gerhard, Gerhard in his kitchen in the Hamptons: "Pammy, Pammy, would you shut up?"

The little girl was crying, he could hear her.

"Would someone please shut her up?" Patti screamed into the receiver. Gerhard could hear adult voices murmuring in the background.

"What are you talking about, is he alive?" Patti asked him.

"He was at Windows, he was meeting someone for break-fast," said Gerhard. "He said a bomb had exploded. He said they were going to lead him down."

"Oh God," said Patti. "I didn't even know he was at Win-dows until 2:00. I thought he was at the office. I didn't know he had a breakfast. Gina called, asking if he'd come home. His breakfast was with John Slatoff. John was caught in traffic. He was late. He's alive. He's home with his wife and baby . . ." At this her voice broke off into a sob.

"He said he was being evacuated?" she said.

"Yes," said Gerhard.

Patti put her hand over the receiver; Gerhard could hear this. He could hear her talking to the adults in the background. "It's Gerhard Falktopf," she said. "One of Davey's clients. He talked to him this morning, at Windows, when he was having break-fast. He thought it was a bomb, Davey. He said he was going to be evacuated."

"Was he evacuated, Gerhard?" Patti asked him as if he knew.

"I don't know," said Gerhard.

"If he were evacuated, he's probably in the hospital," said Patti. "He's in the hospital, that's why he hasn't come home."

"Yes," said Gerhard. "I don't know. Maybe, yes," he said.

"My brother and my father are visiting all the hospitals right now," said Patti. "As we speak. They are visiting them as we speak."

"That is good," said Gerhard.

"We've hung up his picture, we Xeroxed the one at the black tie last year, the one for your company . . ." Here her hand went over the receiver again. "The picture of Dave, it's at a function for Gerhard's company," she said to her invisible audience. "We hung it up all over town. In case someone's seen him. In case he has amnesia. Oh God . . ." Patti Shingshang broke down. For far too long all Gerhard could hear was sobbing.

"Patti?" said Gerhard. "Patti? You must be strong. For the children, Patti . . ." but then someone in the background hung up the receiver.

Gerhard listened to the dial tone for a while. Then he hung up the phone and placed his head in his hands.

He began to sob, really sob, not just a tear or two falling down a cheek, but tears in torrents. It had been a long, long time since Gerhard wept like this; he was rusty at it. He did not cry when the company was taken from him. He did not cry when the woman he dated before Suzannah left him, and she had been the love of his life at the time. He did not cry when he left Germany and his father so very far behind him that if he'd bothered to turn his head and look back, there would have been nothing left to see on the smooth and empty horizon. He did not cry when his mother died when he was still a boy, a baby really.

The last time Gerhard Falktopf full-out cried was when he was a child in school, age five or six or so, and some kid had called him a "poof," a faggot. What the circumstances were, he no longer knew. He just remembered that then the tears had flowed and flowed and his mother had still been there to comfort him. She'd taken him into her arms and he'd cried into the softness of her breasts. She had smelled so nicely of soap. Now his chest heaved, and his nose ran, and the tears fell and fell. He took his hands away from his eyes—he needed a tissue—and looked up and across the room to where there used to be a permanent tissue box on the counter, and instead he saw his wife, Suzannah. She was in the kitchen now; she'd entered as stealthily as a cat, and she was watching him weep.

"Gerhard?" said Suzannah.

She was curious. Of course she was. To see him in a state like this.

"What's wrong?" asked Suzannah.

What's wrong indeed, thought Gerhard. What was right? Was anything right left for them to cling to?

"It's Shingshang."

There was some mucus caught in his throat. Thick and stretchy as bubble gum. He coughed a little then, trying to clear it out.

When he looked up, Suzannah was handing him a glass of water. She'd filled it from the tap. She'd probably unearthed it from the sink. Someone else had drunk from it. It didn't matter. A glass of water was what he needed. He took a sip and then wiped his nose and eyes on the back of his hand.

"Don't you have a handkerchief in your pocket?" asked Suzannah.

Yes, of course. They were married. She knew this and she reminded him. He reached into his pocket, stretching out his right leg first in order to get access to it, and pulled the wrinkled hankie out. He blew, a long, loud trumpet. When he looked up, he almost thought he saw Suzannah smile at the sound.

"Shingshang?" she said.

"He must be dead," said Gerhard. "I just called Patti on the phone. He's not come home. He must be dead, Suzannah."

"You don't know that," said Suzannah.

"No," said Gerhard.

"He could be in the hospital, are they checking all the hospitals?" asked Suzannah.

"Yes," said Gerhard. "And they've made signs."

"Signs?" said Suzannah.

"In case he has amnesia," said Gerhard.

"Oh," said Suzannah.

"He must be dead," said Gerhard. "How could anyone get out of that building in time? How could he have navigated around those fires?"

There was silence for a moment.

"He must be dead," said Gerhard.

"Yes," said Suzannah.

"He must be dead."

℘

UPSTAIRS in their room, they sat on opposite sides of the bed and took off their pants, Gerhard his khakis, Suzannah wriggling out of her jeans. They both kept their shirts on, and Gerhard pulled back the bedclothes and Suzannah got in first; she swung her legs off the floor and folded them under the sheets. She turned her back to him and curled her spine like a shrimp on the fire, slowly getting smaller and more furled, until she was in a fetal position. Gerhard got in after her, beheld her back for just a moment, then bent his body to spoon around her, his knees behind her knees, his thighs zippered to hers, his pelvis snuggled up into her butt, his arms around her waist, his mouth inside her neck. It isn't possible to know who fell asleep first. They were both exhausted.

And so they slept.

℘

GERHARD woke to several beams of radiant pink light. Outside, the sky was streaked with more pinks and oranges glowing in the pearl-gray dark. It was a riot of rosy colors out his window and stripes of all this orchestrated illumination shone into his room, hitting his bed, and the empty pillow next to him, where his wife had recently slept—that is, if he had not dreamed that Suzannah had spent last night in his arms. She was gone now.

Her jeans were missing from the floor, her shoes out from under the bed. He was alone in their room as the sun rose. He sat up. He folded his legs under him and knelt on top of the bedclothes to get a better view out the window. Experience told him that he'd have to crane his neck east up the beach to see the actual sun and not the blushing multihued aura the sun presented, the corona of vivid drama that heralded her arrival and that she flamboyantly left in her wake. Before he sought that rising fireball in the sky, Gerhard first looked out to sea—and that is when he saw Suzannah walking slowly in the sand. She was heading for the water. Up so early. She was heading out there alone.

Gerhard leaned over the edge of the bed and picked up his khakis. He swung his legs, one after the other, over the side and into the open pants. He pulled them up past his hips with a little hop, then zipped and snapped them. He ran his hand through his hair. He needed to brush his teeth. His tongue stretched around the inside of his mouth; it tasted old. There were probably some toothpaste and guest toothbrushes downstairs in the pantry, Gerhard thought. He'd brush his teeth and go outside after her. He looked out the window again. Suzannah was walking through the sand, and it looked like she had a mug of coffee in her hand. She brought it to her mouth and took a sip, and then she turned around and faced the house.

Does she know that I am watching her? thought Gerhard.

Can she feel me?

It was then that he saw Nikolai, following behind his mother like a little wagon. Nikolai, back in his first-day-of-school outfit, trudging across the sand. How many mornings had they woken up this early, the two of them, alone, together? What was the texture and tenor of the secret life they shared?

Barefoot, Gerhard made his way down the stairs. The rest of the house was quiet. Celine, Martine, and the baby, they were all still blissfully sleeping. He could almost hear them breathing. In French, Gerhard thought. All these French folks in his home. Well the Americans and the French, they had a certain something between them, didn't they? Not like the Germans. In this, too, he was the odd man out.

He entered the pantry. True to form, on the metallic wire shelving, in the "housewares department" as Suzannah referred to Elspeth's bomb shelter approach to toiletries, amid the stacks of guest soaps and shampoos, individual packets of Alka Seltzer and aspirin, rows of toilet paper and paper towels and what looked like eleven packages of tampons ("She hasn't menstruated in twenty years," Suzannah had loved to scoff) was a pile of toothbrushes and toothpaste tubes. Gerhard chose a red brush from the pile, a travel-sized tube of Crest, and went back into the kitchen.

There was a pot of coffee burning on the counter. Coffee grounds dotted the granite surface. He turned off the machine, brushed a few of the grounds into the sink with the side of his hand, and then turned on the water. He brushed his teeth in the kitchen sink. When he was done he placed the damp toothbrush in a coffee mug alongside the toothpaste and poured a cup of the still steaming coffee. He took it black, as was his way, and after one hot, bitter sip, he walked back into the Florida room and turned on the television. Nothing had changed overnight. Nothing but everything. On the TV screen, above the dark circle of the city there was a hole in the skyline, a hole filled with pink, smoky light, glowing like a comet had hit the Earth. It was a shot of the remains of the towers at daybreak. The light was like a Magritte—it emanated from the ground instead of the sky, as if the Earth itself were giving birth to daylight surrounded by the shrouded hulks of buildings still immersed in darkness. It was a hell of a sight. Gerhard left the television on and walked back into the kitchen, through the mudroom and out the door to the side yard, the flagstones cold and wet with dew beneath the bare soles of his feet.

Gerhard turned left and traversed the grassy terraced backyard. In the dusky morning the lawn spread wide like a blue-green infinity pool, the yard married the water until it dropped away at the edge of the dune. There he began his descent down the wooden stairs to the beach. Each step was wedged somehow into the dune itself and so sand and wood met his flesh in seemingly equal quantities, rough and damp and scratchy. At first Suzannah had had her back to him—she was kneeling down and fixing the child's shoe—but when she stood, she started; seeing him come down the steps that way, seeing him coming straight toward her. Gerhard stopped to give her a second to prepare herself for their reunion and gave her a little wave. He had no energy for the battles of the day before, that was for sure. Today was a brand new day.

She did not wave in return, Suzannah. She did not turn her back to him again, either. Instead she stood where she stood, waiting for him to find her in the sand.

Now on his hands and knees, Nikolai began to dig with his little fingers. Even before Gerhard was near enough to actually hear him, he could perceive the sound of his son's humming in his head. It took on a life of its own. So as he approached the boy and his mother, the anticipated noise in Gerhard's head and the noise the child actually was making melded into one single buzzing note.

"Good morning," said Gerhard.

Nikolai kept digging. Suzannah said nothing. She looked tired. The sleep was still in her eyes. She would not hold his glance. She raised the mug again and drank her bitter brew.

"Thank you for making the coffee," said Gerhard, lifting up his own mug in solidarity. "I needed it this morning."

Suzannah nodded at him. "You're welcome, Gerhard," said Suzannah, unanimated and affectless, like words sitting flatly on a page.

"Hey there, Nikolai," said Gerhard. "Hey there, boy. Won't you say good morning to your father?"

Nikolai didn't even bother looking up at him.

"He's digging," said Suzannah.

"Yes," said Gerhard. "I can see that. I can see that you are digging, Nikolai."

He walked over to be closer to him.

"Good morning, Nikolai," Gerhard said.

The boy kept humming. Gerhard put his hand on the child's head, his fingers luxuriating in the thick mass of curls.

"Hi, Nikolai," said Gerhard. The boy didn't look up and he didn't stop humming. Gerhard took his hand off Nikolai's head after holding it there for just an extra second. He walked back to Suzannah.

"Some sunrise," said Gerhard.

"It was beautiful," said Suzannah.

"Yes," said Gerhard. "The beauty woke me up."

They looked at one another with the awkward intimacy of lovers that have been fighting, Gerhard thought. As if they knew each other all too well and suddenly not at all. As if they no longer had the right to the private, secret selves they had so heedlessly revealed the night before. As if they no longer had the right.

"Let's sit," said Gerhard. "My legs are tired."

Suzannah obeyed him, mindlessly folding her legs beneath her in one graceful, descending movement, the action so lyri-

209

cal and natural she was probably unaware that she had made it at all.

Gerhard slowly sat down next to her. His knees were not what they once were and he was careful with them.

"Yesterday," said Gerhard. "Yesterday was truly awful."

"Yes," said Suzannah.

She looked out to sea. She sipped her coffee. If it was anything like his, the liquid was now cooler than the air.

"I know how to end it now," said Gerhard. *"Day at the Beach."*

"That's nice, Gerhard," said Suzannah. She said it dully. Was it without irony? She said it like a robot.

Gerhard stole a glance in his wife's direction. She was still lovely to look at. The wind was gently playing with her tangled curls. She gave him her profile, her strong chin, her long, elegant nose. She was all he had, she and the boy. Shingshang was not so lucky.

"I'm going to end it with a duet," said Gerhard.

"A duet?" said Suzannah. She took another sip. She stared straight ahead of her. "A duet?"

A seagull screeched against the morning air, arcing across the sky.

"That's corny, Gerhard," said Suzannah.

"I know it's corny," said Gerhard.

He moved in closer to her. He put his right arm around her shoulders. She stiffened at first, and then she surrendered. She let his arm hang there like a weight.

"Do you know what I learned yesterday?" asked Gerhard.

"That people are despicable," said Suzannah. "That the world is a terrible, terrible place?"

"That art doesn't matter," said Gerhard.

The waves came and went. That was the way it was with the ocean. Each day, all day, each night, all night, in and out with the tide. Every single time they broke, they broke differently. There was comfort in both their predictability and in their uniqueness. His life was like so many others. It carried exactly the same weight as all the rest in the eyes of God. Yet no one else was living the same life as Gerhard. No one else was ever, ever going to live his life.

It was his.

"Come on, Gerhard," said Suzannah. She turned to face him now. "Art doesn't matter?"

"Well, maybe it matters a little," said Gerhard, with a twinkle in his eye, but Suzannah didn't respond to this.

"It's people that matter," said Gerhard. "People are the only thing that matter."

She shook her head at him. Had she left herself or had she left only him? Her eyes were empty. Would she always have such empty eyes? Gerhard wondered. Or would she reinhabit herself over time? He wanted to help her to do so. He wanted to support her and nurture her. Night after night, he would take her in his arms.

Ten feet away from the Falktopfs, their little boy dug and dug. He dug his way toward China. He hummed and hummed as he dug and dug, this child, this mirror, the fractured inheritor of their fractured world.

"You'll see," said Gerhard. "Yesterday was awful. But it was a wake-up call. Already people are rallying around one another, already so many people have put the safety of others before their own . . . The courage they have shown! The society has enlarged itself, our hearts have grown."

Tears came to Gerhard's eyes. He was so moved by the bravery, the bravery he had seen on the news the night before, the bravery he knew would come today and the day after and the day after. He wanted so badly to be part of it. Tears slipped easily down his cheeks. They were tears of recognition. Recognition of mankind's inherent generosity. Gratitude for his own good luck.

"It was a wake-up call. Now we know what we are made of and we are better for it. The world will come together. The world will heal itself of this shocking, brutal performance. The world will rise to the occasion. You'll see, Suzannah. Don't scoff."

Suzannah said nothing. She did not look like she believed him. She did not look like she believed in anything.

"You'll see," said Gerhard. Gerhard pulled her closer. Her head found its way to his shoulder. Like a puppet, relaxed of its central string.

The sky was blue now. The pinks, the oranges, they'd faded and were gone. All that ephemeral, fleeting beauty. Life was so short. This was their time.

"You'll see," said Gerhard. "We will be better, Suzannah." He leaned over and kissed her on the forehead. He felt her flinch. Her cheek indeed was bruised. He brushed the hair away from her face and kissed her again tenderly where he'd harmed her. But she did not respond to him. He would be patient. He would give her the time she needed.

"You'll see," said Gerhard. "You and me, we will be better."

A new age was dawning. For Gerhard Falktopf, and for his family, for the whole world around them.

He had never felt this alive before. He had never been this free. For the first time in forever, they actually had a chance.

He held his wife in his arms. He infused her with his strength. He believed himself.

He believed himself, that day at the beach.

Acknowledgments

A Day at the Beach is wholly a work of fiction, but because it takes place on one of the most terrible days in recent history I wanted it to be *true* in its details. With that in mind, for their help in my research I want to thank the Museum of Television and Radio, *The Today Show*, CNN, the *New York Times*, the *New York Daily News*, and the *East Hampton Star*—specifically, the reporter Susan Rosenbaum, who sat with me for so long one engrossing summer afternoon that neither of us noticed that most of the Eastern Seaboard had been plunged into blackout.

In the dance department, Laura Kang was instrumental in finding information on choreography and ownership—in particular in the written work of Joan Acocella, Jennifer Dunning, Joseph Carman, and Janice Berman. Francine Prose's *Lives of the Muses* was enormously helpful in giving me a sense of the relationship between choreographer and muse. In a twist of happy fate, Hilary Easton and her lovely dance company got me back in the studio in the nick of time.

I'd like to thank my husband, Bruce Handy, for handing over his voluminous archives on Brian Wilson, specifically work by Paul Williams, Steven Dunn, Stephen Gaines, and David Leaf, and for getting me hooked on *Smile* in the first place; I'd also like to thank him for reading and responding to countless drafts of my manuscript. In the course of the book, I quote Michael Kimmelman quoting Thomas Struth (but I don't cite it, sorry).

For their early and sustained support, I'd also like to thank the Corporation of Yaddo, Elizabeth Gaffney, Elissa Schapell, Eve Evans, Barclay Palmer, Jennifer Egan, Dani Shapiro, Jill Bialosky, Rob Spillman, the architect Richard Pedranti, who changed forever how I see both the Twin Towers and Ground Zero, and my mother, Gloria Schulman, for graciously allowing me and my family access to her house in Amagansett on the East End of Long Island.

On September 12, 2001, the *New York Times* ran a picture on page 7 of a man falling headfirst from the towers—it was a picture that inspired and haunted me throughout the years of writing this book, but it wasn't until I was finished with an early draft that I realized that the photograph was taken by my downstairs neighbor, Richard Drew.

Finally, this book owes a huge debt to Heidi Pitlor and the excellent Anton Mueller, and a great big shout-out of gratitude to Sloan Harris, for his unswerving grace and patience, and for steadily supplying me with just the right cocktail of handholding and butt-kicking: thank you thank you thank you!